MORE THAN SURVIVAL

BOOK ONE

THE NEW LIFE SERIES

BY Louise Bouck

ISBN 13 978-1-943984-00-8

ISBN 10 1 943984-00-8

Paper Bound Title ID # 5708086

Printed by Create Space

EBook ISBN 13 978-1-943984-10-7

This book is a work of fiction. Any resemblance to actual events or persons living or dead is entirely coincidental.

ACKNOWLEDGEMENTS

It is important to say thank you to all the people who have encouraged me. A special shout out to Mary Koestner, who helped me paint the basement. Not literally but she will know what that means. "Thank you for your prayer support and gentle questions that set my mind on the right track to release the stories in my heart."

A big, thank you, to my husband, Dale Bouck, my editor, who managed to keep my computer running in spite of the monsoons, and thank you for not complaining when meals were late and simple. Thank you, for not expecting a house that looks like the page of a magazine. Well maybe; sometimes, the before page. Thank you to my family members that suffered through reading rough drafts. A big thank you hug to R. J. Dick who was the first to want to read "The Story of Ben Slater" and to Brenda Dick, who read "Sarah" to RJ when he was ill, and thanks to Donna Shaw, who enthusiastically helped me to keep Sarah's feet on the right path.

Thank you to Ray Shaw, for patiently helping me to learn the technology that I needed.

Thank you to the staff at the computer lab for their technical help. What would any of us do without the public libraries and the wonderful people that work there?

DEDICATION

This New Life Series is dedicated to Jesus Christ and to my family, those that have gone before me, those who are with me and those to come, and all my brothers and sisters in Christ.

†

INTRODUCTION

This is book one in "The New Life Series." The Christian fiction in this series is written to offer the reader a wholesome entertainment, starting back in a simpler but not easier time. Their example of spiritual strength and "never quit" attitude is refreshing and inspiring. The adventurers follow the trail to a new land and challenges they never imagined.

In book one "More Than Survival," follow Benjamin Slater as he copes with the wild isolation of the new frontier and the lessons of self-preservation as he experiences the pain of loss and joys of accomplishment. He travels "Life's Many Journeys," in book two and learns to appreciate the "Land's Heritage," in book three.

In Book four, you will find out "The Story of Sarah"

As you read the books, Ben develops into a man of physical and spiritual strength. His problem solving mind is challenged many times.

When Sarah, his sister returns to him, they are finally "Together," in book five. You will find out how her life affected the Indians that took her and how they became "the Blue Stone People" in book six.

A change of scene takes you to the camp of the Sentu and three survivors enter the story, in book seven "Teewahpanyee the Boy, Two Feathers the Man," Willow and Water Bug bring new strength and young blood to an old people. With Willow at his side in book eight he becomes leader of "The People of The Lion". They are chosen by the Lion of Judah to be rescuers, and are rewarded in book nine, by being allowed to discover "The Lion's Den."

In book ten, the land that Ben Slater's father chose has miraculously remained with the family as time has gone by and generations were born.

In a day beyond today, the series skips to the final times after the rapture. A new heroine stands up bravely to the soldiers of the anti-Christ. She finds Ben's Bible, Mary Slater's journals and the gift of faith. Emily spreads the word and struggles to survive the time of tribulation as she finally realizes that this is Just the Beginning for those who believe.

TABLE OF CONTENTS

CHAPTER ONE

THE START OF THE WAGON TRAIN

It was the beginning of a new life. Everyone was excited and enthusiastic. They couldn't wait to get underway. Thirty-one covered wagons were packed and ready. Some were badly overloaded. None of the wagons were outfitted with oxen. The strong beasts were capable but slow. Many people preferred the teams of big horses that would work willingly. Later they would be useful on the new farms.

The wagon master smiled, showing a missing tooth. Dark, sun-creased skin and a well-trimmed gray beard accented his wise brown eyes. As he carefully rode through the hubbub he nodded to folks encouraging them to get up on their wagons. The congested area surrounding the wagons was crowded with people and a dog here and there, trying to avoid the stomp of a horse's foot and nervously wagging and barking at the same time. The air held the sounds of loud voices trying to convey last messages. A baby was crying, frightened by the unusual energy packed environment.

Horses jerked and were hard to handle, eager to be moving. Women held lace edged hankies, dabbing at their eyes as they clung to those they loved.

He knew that necessity would soon cause much of the unneeded belongings to be hesitantly left on the edge of the trail. This was a once in a lifetime thing. Families were saying good-bye to loved ones. Most of them would never see each other again, and they knew it.

For now, he would give them time to deal with their deep emotions. He urged families to climb into their places on their wagons. Last hugs and kisses had been given and tears streamed down the faces of both those leaving and left behind.

Sarah's Grandfather held her tight for one more moment before he handed her up to the waiting arms of his son, Josiah Slater. She breathed deeply memorizing the smell of his pipe and wool sweater mixed with his English after-shave and the dust in the air and the smell of many horses.

Sarah's mother steadied her with a hand as she moved inside the wagon to a spot that had been prepared for her on top of their folded bedding. Her rag doll and a drawing slate with chalk waited to entertain her.

As soon as she saw the slate Sarah remembered her Grandmother's tight hug and the advice she had given, to always learn as much as she could and to memorize the Holy Bible, a little every day. I'll remember her and miss her. I understand why she didn't come. In all this confusion, you can't say much. Our quiet talk in the kitchen was better. She always got up so early. She had bread rising on the cupboard near the stove and coffee made for the grown-ups this morning before we left. We have a wonderful box of her oatmeal cookies in here somewhere. I can smell them. It is strange that I am thinking about all the different scents this morning. A single tear made its way down Sarah's cheek and she rubbed it away. She promised she would take good care of Smudge. My sweet kitty, she couldn't come. Grandmother said she would probably jump out of the back of the wagon and get lost in the prairie. She said she would write us all a letter and tell me how she is doing but we have to write the first time so she can get our new address.

As the wagon master shouted and waved his hat, the first covered wagon pulled out, heading west along last year's barely visible trail. This was the first wagon train of the season; small in comparison to those that would follow. Cheers filled the crisp early morning air and encouraged the pioneers as one by one the wagons took their assigned position. Arms ached from waving but still they continued, until the people left behind were mere dots on the landscape.

The wagon train was well underway before the wagon master rode slowly by each wagon asking if everyone was all right and if they had any questions. His comments were simply intended to reassure the new adventurers.

The mid-morning air smelled sweet when the wheels of the wagons crushed the grass as they rolled along. This was all new to everyone on the trail, with the exception of the trail boss, scout and a few hands that rode along in case of trouble.

All too soon they would be in Indian Territory. If the wagon train was discovered, their guns and knowledge would be needed. Most of the wagons held families. He guessed that less than half the men would be capable of effective defense, if the train came under attack. Two more experienced men had been added the very morning they left.

The fifteenth wagon, held the Slater family. Like many, they had sold all they had to join the wagon train. They were farmers. Josiah Slater loved to work the land and see things grow, but they had owned a few good horses also. Beside their wagon walked a black stallion, named Dart Away. This one special horse he had kept. The four big workhorses that pulled the wagon were healthy and strong. Each had been raised on their farm. They were gentle, obedient creatures, happy to do what was asked of them.

Weeks passed and then a month and still more days, some dry, some hot, some cold and windy, yet always the same. Follow the wagon ahead of you and don't lag behind. Prepare your food and eat it when the train stopped. Make sure your cooking fire was out when you left. Sleep or try to rest, sometimes while the rain poured down and drenched everything and everyone. The sun baked man and beast until delicate skin turned to brown leather, yet they continued to move west.

"Mary, I wonder how much farther he will lead us before he says it is time to choose our land. I have been watching the soil and it is rich and black. We could grow good crops in it. The trail boss keeps reminding everyone that we are in Indian Territory, but really, it is all Indian Territory when you think about it. Until folks like us come along, they are the only ones here. I doubt if they would bother anyone just making a home. It will take us a while to break the sod and prepare it for seed. It is getting late in the planting season. That has to be done so we have food, even before we can build a cabin."

"Yes Josiah, I know. It will all work out."

It was the Slater's strong Christian faith that placed them here rolling along on the plains. They knew that although they had few material possessions, God would provide for them. They believed he had a plan and a purpose for everyone and felt that His plan had brought them here.

Ben rode along with his feet hanging down from the back of the covered wagon. During the winter, he had grown and he noticed that his pant legs were getting too short. The tall spring grasses of the prairie slid under the wagon making a scratching sound and reached for the soles of his bare feet.

He would be sixteen on his next birthday. He thought of himself as nearly grown.

As the breeze whipped his blond hair against his handsome face, Ben hoped that his mother had not noticed how long it had become. She would insist that he allow her to cut it again. His fair skin had burned several times as they traveled and now it was brown. This morning the sun shone full on his face and into his blue eyes causing him to frown. A fly buzzed near and he batted it away.

Along with the sounds of the creaking wagon, Ben could hear his little sister, Sarah, humming inside as she played with the cloth doll, made by their mother, for her birthday. She had turned nine years old and already was sure that she was going to live on a big farm and have many children of her own. She had more room to play inside, since two days before; it had become necessary to remove several heavy items and leave them at the side of the muddy trail to lighten the load.

Mother will miss the oak chest full of linens, but we will build her another chest in the winter, and she and Sarah can fill it with new linens when time allows. The wooden crate with china from her mother had to be put out. Poor mother, she was so sad. She held on to one pillowcase that had been her grandmother's and one plate that she carefully wrapped and tucked away. She has given up so much to come. Father said the dishes we are using on the trail will do for a while and then he will get her some pretty new ones sometime.

He could also hear his father's comment that the soil seemed to be improving as they rolled along. Ben was eager to stop traveling, but young enough to know that he would feel more comfortable if they had neighbors. He hoped his father would stay with the train until the Wagon Master said it was time to choose land.

How beautiful the prairie is in the morning sunshine, Ben thought, and how blessed we are. His father and mother had instilled in him their faith in God. Evenings he heard his father read from his worn Bible, as they stopped along the trail for their meal and rest.

Often other members of the wagon train would come and join them. They would sit on the grass and listen as the words Father, read drifted over the prairie giving encouragement and strength. That was Ben's favorite time of day, when they and a growing group of friends would gather together and learn more about the wonderful God that was with them. He enjoyed the people and the singing, too. Sometimes it was hymns but occasionally someone would sing a pretty ballad or a family favorite and others would join in. There were a couple of men that played a guitar and Ben wished that he had one and knew how to play it.

Ben's mother, Mary, was on the seat up front with his father. She had a sweet voice and sang with the church choir back home. She spoke respectfully to her husband.

"Josiah, it is going to be hot again today. The horses are showing signs of it, already."

"Look at the clouds, Mary. Maybe they will bring rain and cool things off a bit. Some of the horses up ahead of us are lathered with sweat. I feel sorry for them. Their wagons are still so overloaded. It doesn't do much good to toss out a few things when you are still hauling a ton of books. Can you believe it?"

"I talked with his wife. She is very nice. He is a schoolteacher, Josiah. That's why he has a lot of books."

"That family in the fourth wagon has a bag of rocks! They say they want to use them when they build their fireplace, to remind them of home. One rock would do the same job of reminding them and those poor horses are paying the price for their foolishness!"

"I know you are right Josiah, but it is hard to let go of familiar things. No one knows what lies ahead for them.

The air carried a burden of dust stirred by the horse's hooves and wagon wheels. Mary wrapped her cream colored, crocheted shawl over her nose and mouth to filter the air. She felt nauseous and the movement of the wagon was making it worse.

"Mary, our horses are healthy and happy. God made them strong so they can do the work that we can't. I feel that I made a foolish decision when I put the plow out of the wagon. We will wish that we had it when we are ready to plant."

"You did it because it was necessary. The ground was so muddy that our team was straining to move the wagon with every step. The men said we had to put out our heaviest things. You know that God will provide. He always does. We will help our neighbors and they will help us."

If we have neighbors, he thought. He wore a deep frown.

Ben's father was anxious to stop traveling and to find a place that he could call his own. They were farmers and it was the planting season. Their four workhorses were strong and would be needed. Dart Away was the only riding horse they had brought with them, and he was their very best one. He had won several local races. Ben rode him sometimes, but today the beautiful black stallion walked along on a long lead, without a rider.

From time to time, Ben's father glanced at the ground as they plodded along, each time evaluating the quality of the grass and judging the likelihood of the crops it would grow.

"I think crops could be raised in this region. The grass is darker green and the soil is rich looking." To their left Josiah saw a line of trees, far in the distance.

"Look," he told Mary. "There is water over there and the trees are tall and strong. That has to be a river over there to our left. See that line of big trees!" He was getting excited. "Mary, I think I will take Dart Away and check out that river in the morning. We will be stopping soon. I will head out at first light and you and Ben can keep the wagon in line until I get back."

"Josiah, I don't think it is safe for you to ride off alone."

As the sun crept over the horizon, Mary woke Sarah, and Ben. Josiah had been gone a long time. She looked in the direction he had ridden but couldn't see him.

A worried frown creased her brow as she placed her hand on her growing tummy. She felt a wave of nausea as she helped Ben hitch the horses up and then stirred the ashes of their fire again, making sure no live embers remained. She hadn't told her husband or the children about their expected baby. She felt Josiah had enough to be concerned about, trying to find the right land that would be all they hoped for.

The wagons pulled out in an orderly fashion and soon they were on the way again. It had all become routine, as time and weeks had passed. Part of her worries calmed when she saw Josiah finally returning. He was smiling broadly.

When he described the wide river and suggested they pull out of line and discuss what he had seen, Mary's heart lurched with fear. She didn't want to leave the other wagons. The vast, open prairie was intimidating.

After a quick exchange of the reins, Ben's father pulled the wagon out of line and stopped.

"Mary, I think we could do well if we choose a place near that water. What do you think?"

"I admit that I am tired of traveling, but I have to remind you that the wagon master told us last night that we should stay together. This is all Indian territory."

"Let's pray about it," he replied.

She felt that he had already made his mind up. She could see an excitement in his eyes that hadn't been there during the whole journey until now.

"Father God, we thank you for watching over us and guiding us to our new home. Thank You for showing us that the soil is good for planting, and that we can see the trees in the distance that line the water."

"Amen," they all responded. Ben was thrilled to think that they would soon see the land his father had chosen for their new home.

As the wagon train continued on without them, Ben's father slowly turned the horses to the left and the squeaking wagon headed for the distant line of trees, and the river that he had seen there. They would have to go cautiously. A deep hole or rock could easily damage a wagon wheel. They were off the marked trail now.

Sarah crawled over the sacks of seed and boxes of supplies to the back of the wagon near Ben.

"Does this mean that Father has chosen land and that we will stop soon?"

"I think so, Sarah. We will have to wait and see. Father says we will stop."

"But Ben, everyone else is going on without us. I didn't get to say Good Bye to Ellen."

"Don't worry, Sarah, she will understand. Everything is going to be wonderful."

Just then, the leathery, old, wagon train scout rode up on a big bay.

"Got a problem?" he asked. Ben's father reined the team to a stop.

"Gus, I think we are going to stop," said Josiah. "That is a river over there. See that line of trees in the distance?"

"You can do what you want, but this is Indian Territory. It's their hunting grounds. They won't take kindly to you being here. I don't advise it. It's better to settle where there are other folks. I saw you ride out at first light. I figured that was what you were planning. I really wish you would reconsider Mister Slater. You are putting your family in danger." He waited hopefully for an agreeable reply. None came. "Well, we will all miss you folks and the reading of the Bible at night. When you started reading it seemed to melt all of us into one big family. Everyone gets along better on this train than I have ever experienced. I thank you for that."

Mary smiled at Gus and resigned herself to the obvious, that her husband planned to head for the river. As Gus turned his horse, intending to ride away, she reached for her husband's hand and bowed her head, silently asking for protection for her family and the wagon train.

"Heavenly Father," he began. "We look to you for protection and guidance, for us and our friends on the wagon train. I have heard the warning of Gus and the Wagon Master, and yet I feel that it would be foolish of us to ride past all this good earth to stop somewhere less desirable."

"Be very careful!" Gus realized that with that short prayer, Josiah had made it clear that he was leaving the train.

"We will, Gus, and thanks for everything." Josiah touched the front of his dust-covered hat brim.

"Tell all the folks on the train that we hope to see them again sometime," said Mary, trying to sound supportive.

"Sure will, Missus Slater. Good luck to you folks. I know a lot of us will miss the reading at night. It was a good way to end each day. It has been nice having you along. I know that the folks will pray for you." He turned his horse and rode away, returning to report to the Wagon Master.

Ben watched the wagons continue on without them and noticed that they had filled the space in the line, which their wagon had held.

Above, a hawk circled over the prairie as the wagon pitched back and forth uncomfortably over the rough ground. They were off the trail now and there was no one to help them if they damaged a wheel. Josiah worked to keep the wagon at a cautious, slow pace, carefully choosing his route.

As hours passed, they became weary. It's taking a long time to travel the distance to the river, Ben thought. The trees are much farther than they appeared. The horses could smell the water and moved along without coaxing, wanting to get there, so they could drink.

Finally, the wagon was stopped in the shade of the towering trees. It stood close to an amazingly large oak tree. The riverbank slanted down to a clear and inviting patch of blue rippling water, visible between the bushes. They could no longer see the other wagons and a sense of being very alone settled on the little family.

Just as the wagon pulled to a stop, Ben's father joyfully made his announcement!

"We are home! This is the spot I picked this morning!" Ben's father pulled his rifle from under the seat intending to immediately check the area for dangerous animals.

Mixed with their happy cheers came a burst of shouts and pounding of hooves coming up out of the trees! A single gunshot from the wagon, sounded, as flying arrows sent Benjamin jumping from the back of the wagon. He was chased into the trees by one of the Indians on horseback. Ben had a glimpse of his father slumping and falling to the ground between the horses. The team jerked forward in fright, dropping the left wagon wheels into a deep prairie run off, tipping the wagon on its side. Sarah's scream inside the wagon, mingled with the sounds of the attack, as an arrow sliced the flesh of Ben's shoulder, and flew by. Ben's heart was pounding wildly as he ran, recklessly, toward the water. He tripped and rolled down into a thick bank of thorn bushes. His head hit a rock. He was still. The Indian raced by on his horse whooping and shouting as Ben's mind slid into unconsciousness.

When Ben opened his eyes, it was very quiet. Not even a bird twittered in the trees overhead. As he came fully awake, panic set in. I have to help, he thought. He crawled out of the thorn bushes, unaware of the stinging scratches each movement caused. He would feel them later. I must keep low, he thought, as he crawled up to the place where the wagon now lay on its side.

We are going to have a rough time putting the wagon back up and fixing it, he thought. His mind felt fuzzy, as if his head was filled with jelly.

It was then that he remembered seeing his father fall from the wagon. Ben's chest tightened with fear. The total scene before him registered in one horrific flash. He saw them. Both his parents lay in a pool of their own blood on the very ground they had chosen for their home. His mother's shawl was red with blood, pinned to her chest by an arrow. His father lay face down with his arm extended toward her. His left hand still held a fist full of grass, ripped from the ground in pain and anguish as he died. An arrow had pierced his chest and protruded from his back. His blood had pooled around him, shinning as the sun dried it. Neither would worry about anything ever again, but Ben's trials were just beginning.

"Sarah, I have to find Sarah," he said out loud. Ben sobbed as he searched first in the wagon and then the surrounding area for his little sister. He called for her over and over until his voice grew hoarse from yelling her name.

"Sarah, the Indians are gone now. You can come out. It's safe now," he pleaded through tears. "Sarah, oh Sarah, where are you?" Only silence answered. "God, help me find her," he wailed. He continued to search and call loudly; rushing, stumbling through the trees, tripping and landing so hard that it knocked the breath from his chest but she was not there. He did not want to accept what he already knew. She had been taken.

As his legs buckled, he knelt in the grass beside the wagon.

"I don't understand. Why did you let this happen?" He felt angry and frightened all at the same time.

"We just got to the land that Father liked. He saw that the soil was good for planting crops. He didn't even get a chance to step down from the wagon and walk on it with

Mother! Why did you let this happen?" He screamed out in rage between clenched teeth, beating the ground with his fists, and then he just sat there unable to move, not knowing what he should do. He had a concussion, but wasn't even aware yet that he had hit his head or of the slice in his shoulder, caused by an arrow as it passed.

There were columns of smoke in the distance. He noticed. It has to be one of two things. Either the wagons of the train are being burned or it is the Indian's camp. I have to decide what to do in case they come back.

His father and mother had taught him to rely on God for wisdom and strength, and so he forced himself to kneel again in the grass beside the wagon.

Humbly Ben prayed.

"I don't understand why you let this happen, but now, because of it, I am here, all alone. My parents are dead, my sister is gone and I don't know what I am supposed to do! God, I feel so angry and afraid. I have always believed that you would protect us and provide for us! They followed your word in all they did. This is so unfair! Why? I don't understand." Ben wept until he felt he had no more tears. His body trembled as he finally forced the words. "Please show me what to do." He remembered Psalm 91 NIV. His Father had read it often. Ben and Sarah had memorized it along with many other parts of the Bible and he began to recite it.

"Whoever dwells in the shelter of the Most High will rest in the shadow of the Almighty. I will say of the Lord, "He is my refuge and my fortress, my God, in whom I trust." He said the verse over and over until he felt a little stronger and calmer. Ben questioned why God had allowed him to live. "Why did you leave me alive? Why am I here? How can you have a plan like this?"

Ben stood and started to move, slowly at first, like a person with wooden arms and legs. He found the shovel in the wagon and dug deeply between the spreading roots of the tallest oak tree.

"Father chose you as the marker for his land, now you will be the marker for their grave!" The ground was hard and smaller roots crossed in the spot he had chosen. The spade bruised his bare foot as he slammed it down to cut through them and continued to dig until the whole was deep and large enough. He wrapped each of his parents in a blanket and struggled to move his father's heavy body as he placed him respectfully into the grave.

A slow realization came that he had been right with his suspicions. He could see that his mother was pregnant as he gently wrapped the blanket around her slightly rounded tummy and lowered her body beside his father's. She had been sick mornings and avoided breakfast. The smell of coffee had made her sick. She had always liked coffee and said that it was a luxury, until recently she quit drinking it.

When he had finished piling stones over their grave, it seemed to blend into the landscape. There were so many rocks here near the river. He took out his knife and carved a cross on the trunk of the oak tree. Their grave faced the river. He would add names later. Sobs shook his entire body as he prayed fighting the knowledge of his loss. He would have had a new sibling, maybe a little brother.

"Jesus, receive them into your arms." Prayers continued as he figured out a way to keep safe during the night that would soon come.

He was frightened for himself but even more afraid of what had happened to Sarah.

All the time that he was working his thoughts were focused on his sister, praying that God would watch over her. Frustrated and fearful, he called her name, hoping for a reply, but now knowing that none would come. Again he shouted out his anger.

"Why did you let this happen? They trusted you!"

It was already growing dark as he left his parent's grave. When he returned to the wagon, he realized for the first time that it was nearly empty. The raiders had hastily taken all that they could quickly bundle. Many things from the wagon are gone, and the horses, too, he thought. With the horses gone, I haven't got a chance of catching up with the wagon train to get help. He pulled out a quilt that the Indians had left behind, and as he did, Sarah's cloth doll tumbled to the grass. He picked it up and tucked it inside his shirt; never giving a thought to the fact that under other circumstances he would be embarrassed to be holding a doll. It gave him comfort somehow to have it near. "With Your help, I will find Sarah, and give it back," he said.

A slight movement in the grass caught his eye and he noticed his father's Bible lying there. The pages were fluttering in the breeze. He picked it up and it was open to the words in 2 Corinthians 12:9, NIV "My grace is sufficient for you for my power is made perfect in weakness." Tears slowly slid down his face as he brushed dirt from the cover and tucked it, too, into his shirt.

Although his entire body still trembled, he didn't feel quite so alone.

With the quilt wrapped high around his shoulders, Ben waded slowly across the river, making sure that the Bible and doll didn't get wet by holding them in his armpits. He struggled, climbing high into a tall tree and wedged himself into a "y" of the branches. There, hidden by the leaves of an old hickory nut tree, he thought if I am high enough, I will be safe from most of the night prowling animals and if the Indians come back, they won't find me here.

With his face ashen, his body cold and wet, he trembled as he braced himself for the long uncomfortable night. Ben sat vigilantly listening to the night sounds. He heard the hoot of an owl and the flapping of its large wings as it flew swiftly by. The growl of an animal in the underbrush along the river made him strain to see through the blackness.

Later he heard wolf song in the distance. The night was filled with sounds and activity. It all seemed eerie and menacing. He had always had his family near. Now he was totally on his own. In the darkness, on the vast prairie, Ben felt very small and vulnerable. From his anguish his mind sprang to anger. This time it was not directed at God.

"You should have stayed with the wagon train! You had no right to stop here. They had warned everyone to stay together. This is Indian Territory! The scout told you again when you pulled out of line, but you wouldn't listen! Now everyone is dead! You are dead! Mother is dead and the baby is dead. Sarah is gone and I will probably be dead soon. He continued to lash out, venting his grief and fear. How can I survive out here alone? Someone or something will kill me, too! You did it! It's your fault!"

He suddenly realized that he was shouting. Not the best of strategies for someone hiding, he told himself. He was back in control enough to begin to feel guilty for blaming his father. He started to make excuses. Father didn't know that the Indians were there. He thought that being watchful and alert would be enough to protect us. There is a lesson in that for me. I have to keep out of sight and erase any sign that I am here. They think they killed me. I want them to keep thinking that.

"Thank you God, for being here with me, to protect and guard me through this long night. My faith gives me strength. Please forgive me for being angry with you, and my father. It's just that it is impossible for me to understand or see your plan in this." Although exhausted physically and emotionally, many more hours were spent mulling over his circumstances before he finally fell asleep.

The sun was shining brightly into his nest when Ben woke up. The air was warm and the birds were flitting about, chirping. He climbed down, carelessly leaving the quilt high above in the tree. He knelt at the river's edge and took a long drink. There he lifted his eyes and voice to God.

"Father, please help me to get through this day. I know that I have to be grown up and handle this situation like a man or I will not survive the coming winter. This is the worst morning of my life. You are all I have now. My folks are there, with you; my sister is gone, taken by the Indians and I don't know what I am supposed to do. I will be leaning on you, for a lot of help in the coming days. Show me what I am supposed to do. Lord, teach me and watch over me."

I will go back to the wagon and collect anything I can find that will be useful, he thought.

I am glad they left most of Father's tools. They may have noticed the box they are in but some of the open bag of flour spilled on them when the wagon tipped. I guess they thought it was too much of a mess to investigate. I see a sheet and a pillowcase, a few pieces of clothing and a couple pans, the rest of the flour, sugar, coffee, baking powder and salt. I am making a substantial pile. I wonder why Father brought this roll of strong cord. Here is a roll of wire, too. I will take them with me but I don't know what he had planned to do with them.

"At least the Indians didn't take everything," he said. "Thank You, Father.

I need to choose a place to make my camp. I think Father would have built a cabin on the prairie side of the river, but right now I need someplace that won't be easy to spot in case the Indians return." He had already decided without really thinking about it, that he would make his camp on the other side of the river.

"I want to be away from this place where the Indians attacked the wagon." Just a short distance upstream the bluff looks promising, he thought. He crossed and climbed carefully to its very top.

Anything I put up here can be seen for a long way. He looked in the direction of the smoke from the day before. I can't see it now, he thought. As he climbed back down he knew he had to make an effort to create an easier route to the top as soon as time allowed. I can see in every direction from up there, but anything I put up there could also be easily seen. The rocks above make a good windbreak.

"All right," he said, "Now I know why you sent me up there, God. You wanted me to notice how much better it is here. This is where I'll put my camp. The trees cover this area from being seen from up or down river but I will have to create some kind of a shield from straight in. Thank You, God. Please guide me every hour of every day. Without You, I will surely die, too."

How can I get that load from the wagon, across the river, without having to wade back and forth many times? He thought about it for a moment. If I pry boards loose from the wagon and use my father's rope to lash them together, I will have a raft. I can float the tools and the few essentials all over to this side in one trip.

After a couple of hours, Ben had a large pile on the opposite riverbank. I think I should stash this raft in the bushes. I don't want it seen, and I can use it again. Ben made several trips, carrying his belongings to the spot he had chosen, at the base of the bluff.

"If I use the rock of the bluff for the back wall, it will be less work." He started to cut branches and wove them into his walls and roof until it felt strong. I can go back to the wagon and get the canvas cover and use it to shelter the top of the shack so it won't leak.

"As you give me ideas, I'll act on them. I know that you are directing me, God."

Once this canvas is on, I think I need to rest, but it is so white that it would be very easy to spot even from a distance. My clothes have the solution. They are as brown as the riverbank. I can fill one of the cooking pots with mud and smear it on the canvas, he thought. He continued until it was totally coated.

"After that messy project, I better wash the pot and myself." Wading into the river and submerging, Ben washed his hair and then his clothes without taking them off. The cold water was soothing but shocking at the same time.

It wasn't until then that he acknowledged the wound in his shoulder and the pounding headache he had been ignoring. Gently he felt the large lump just above his temple. He had forced himself to work very hard and he hadn't allowed himself to feel anything all day, not the ache in his heart or his own physical discomforts. The cold water made his shoulder ache as it washed away the dried blood. The wound had sealed itself and didn't reopen.

Ben crawled up onto a large rock in the sun to dry off. The warmth of the rock was a comfort as he lay back against it, closing his eyes, trying not to think. He concentrated on the pleasant sound of the willow tree leaves growing near the water. He slept.

When he woke, he automatically reached for his aching shoulder and realized his shirt was nearly dry.

"I slept a long time. I have wasted time. I could have been looking for food or doing something. I have to figure out how to make a fire to cook. Once I tried to twirl a stick as I saw others do along the trail to help Mother, but it just didn't seem to work for me. She was good at it."

I know how to set a snare and I can fish, too, but I don't have a gun to use for hunting. Father's gun and shells are gone. The Indians took them.

"Someday, I'll deal with them. Someday, I will get Sarah back and everything they took! He felt tears of frustration and sorrow, sting his eyes. He brushed them away roughly with the back of his hand. "I don't have time for tears," he said loudly. "Not now." He slid from the big rock and bent low, cupping the water of the river to his mouth. He drank his stomach full and then pulled the things he had salvaged from the wagon into his little hut.

He had eaten mush before the wagons started to move that terrible day, but nothing since. His stomach needed food.

"I wish I hadn't left the quilt up there," he complained, as he climbed to retrieve it. My muscles are sore from building the hut, and climbing up this tree is hard work. It seems taller and the branches seem farther apart. It's late and I am hungry. I don't feel as strong as I did. I have got to find some food tomorrow. He felt the tree sway a bit in the evening breeze. The movement made him dizzy.

After bunching the quilt in one hand while holding on with the other, he tossed the quilt down. It went half way and caught on a branch. The breeze moved it back and forth just enough that as he climbed down, he was able to grab the edge of it. The movement triggered his dizziness again.

"Carefully now," he instructed himself. "Don't tear it." By the time he returned to his camp it was growing dark. Wrapping the quilt around his shoulders he crawled into his little hut and pulled down the corner of canvas he had left as a flap.

"Some door that is! It wouldn't stop anything." He knew that he wouldn't be able to sleep unless he felt safe. He went back out, and cut two thick branches to wedge across the opening of the doorway from the inside; he tossed them in and then cut a third to use as a club, against intruders.

"Just in case," he said with a yawn.

Now that the doorway is blocked, I can rest, he thought, but his sleep was troubled by frightening dreams. Unseen enemies chased him. Over and over he heard the war cries of the Indians as they swept over the wagon. His father's hand gripped the grass as an Indian pulled him down into a black hole. His sister's scream shattered his sleep. He jerked up, looking around at the blackness, feeling the sweat, trickle, down his chest. He thought for an instant that she was really there, just out of sight.

As his fists rubbed his eyes, he realized that they were filled with tears and his heart was pounding wildly. I must force myself to rest, he thought, as he lay on the quilt, listening to each night sound and trying to recognize its possible threat. He needed a drink but was too frightened to go out to the river in the dark.

At daybreak, the need for food and water brought him out of his hut.

"I have to get food, and I don't care what it is." He said, as he splashed water on his face and drank.

As the wagon train traveled along, I watched the women gather roots, berries, and leaves of certain plants. Some of the things they cooked I didn't like but at least they can keep me alive, if I can find some.

"Father, please guide me and keep me safe, as I search for food." I'll take the pillowcase to carry things and my knife. He wandered through the trees and brush near the river, deliberately making a lot of noise, hoping that he would not see any big animals. Before long he was gathering cattail roots and berries.

"These berries are delicious," he said. His hands and mouth were stained red with the juice.

"Thank you, Jesus," he said as he crammed in another handful. He found wild onions and a crabapple tree with withered fruit still clinging to its branches. Each time I find a food source, I need to make a mental note of where it is so I can go back for more, he thought.

He returned to camp to make a fishing pole. Sitting on the grassy bank, he baited the line with a worm, and dropped it into a deep spot by the rocks under the water. Sunshine bounced from the ripples of the water and lulled Ben into relaxing. It is nice here by the willow trees, he thought. Ben could hear a frog croak and mosquitoes whine as they flew near. One lit on his arm and he slapped it, leaving a red smear.

Before long, he had two small fish. With no fire, he knew he would have to do what a bear does; eat the fish raw. He scraped the scales off and gutted the fish with his knife and removed the head and tail. He sat there looking at it for a few seconds; dreading putting the raw fish in his mouth. He thought that it was disgusting.

"Father, I am grateful that I have something to eat," he said softly. Ben raised the first fish to his mouth and ate it in three quick bites. It crunched between his teeth and caused him to gag. I'll put the other fish in a pan of water. It will be for morning. The truth was that he couldn't bring himself to eat another one raw just then.

"Sure wish I could make a fire," he stated out loud. "Somehow, I have to learn."

I need to make some snares. I can use cord from the roll that was in the wagon to fasten them, he thought.

Ben returned to the wagon and found some of the leather reins in the grass where they had been dropped. The rest of the harness must have been used to lead the team away, he thought. Dart Away is gone, too. I wonder if they know what a special horse he is. A heavy stone of pain and sadness settled in his chest as he looked around. Ben turned his back on the scene and hurried back to camp.

"I can't think about that day now. I just can't," he said out loud, as once again he felt angry and betrayed. Ben worked feverishly trying to remove the grief he felt, by activity.

Several small paths made their way through weeds and under bushes, to the edge of the river. That is where I should set the snares, he thought, as he formed loops with pliable branches.

When he returned, he realized that the shack would be far too small, if he had to spend the entire winter in it. He could see no hope of being rescued. He knew that he should make it big enough to have a small fire inside and he had to be able to place the fire away from the walls so that it wouldn't catch the whole place on fire. He started to mentally list the things that he would want inside it. I need room for a bed and the few things from the wagon. I would like it to be a little taller. It makes me duck.

"Father, I don't want to stay here alone. Please, send someone to find me, but if you don't, I need to get ready to live here." He jerked the canvas off and violently tore the front wall apart.

"This needs to be more livable, and it is the last thing that I plan on doing over," he shouted angrily to the trees. It was healthy for him to be able to release some of the anger pent up inside. He had reached the second stage in his grieving process.

As he cut the biggest branches that he could reach, he planned. This space should be wider and much higher.

"I am grateful that I have Father's shovel to make the holes for the upright corner posts. I will probably need uprights in the middle of the walls also."

When evening fell, he had a room that was about twelve by fourteen feet, and it was high enough that he had to reach far above his head to touch the highest point inside. It was strong and felt safe. He felt glad of his decision to redo the hut.

"Tomorrow I will fill holes between the large branches with smaller ones and make a layer of willow bundles and then grass bundles to thatch the roof. A grass and mud mixture, stuffed in the holes of the walls from the outside will stop the wind and make it warm in winter. I want the canvas back on top and tied down tightly. He fell asleep planning.

At daybreak, he put his plan into action and by late afternoon he had finished.

Once again searching for food, he found some hickory nuts under a tree. A few remained from last fall's crop that the squirrels had not carried away. Crack, munch, crack, munch. He ate as many as he could find. Back at camp he gobbled in the second fish without thinking about it and rinsed the pan and used it to finish filling his stomach with water. He felt satisfied.

This time as he crawled inside his hut and wedged the branches in the doorway, Ben had a feeling of ownership. He felt that he had accomplished a major task and that he had completed it satisfactorily. He had used every branch he had cut for the small hut and added many stronger, longer ones where they were needed. It was growing dark as he entered for the night. His recovered items, from the family wagon were in a neat row up off the floor and setting on a branch, used as a shelf near the sidewall. Being back in his hut was a pleasure, but he was very worn out.

"Thank you Father, for helping me today, I have many things to do and learn, in the days ahead. It is a comfort to know that you are here to guide and help me. Thank you for helping me to find some food."

As dawn came, Ben was awake and planning his day. I need a bow and some arrows, so I can hunt, he thought.

"Father thanks to you, I was able to finish my hut yesterday. Please help me today to find the right wood for a bow. I know that it must be strong and able to bend." He crawled out of his doorway determined to find a straight, small tree that he could bend. He walked through the trees and cut several, before he found just the right one. I will save the others. I might be able to make spears with them.

Ben made arrows, copying the ones he had seen at the wagon. He had pulled one from the ground undamaged. Just the thought of it made him shudder. Each time he thought of that scene at the wagon, the pain of sorrow, hit him so hard that it was difficult to breath. He deliberately shifted his thoughts to the task at hand. I can use pine pitch for glue and I will wrap them with some of the cord from the roll. That cord will make a good bowstring too.

"Now, it is time to try this out." At first he couldn't pull the string back far enough, or hold it still. When he released it, the string slapped his wrist, making a red welt.

"I can't give up," he said. He shot his bow over and over, getting tired of retrieving his arrows until he thought to create a target in both directions. He practiced until he could hit whatever he aimed at. His arms grew stronger with each try.

"Of course all of my targets are still," he said. "Can I hit a moving target? I'll soon see," he told himself. "I'll go upriver. I haven't gone that way yet." With the pillowcase tucked in his waist for gathering, just in case he found a food source, he headed out.

There is no easy path, he thought. Thorns on the berry bushes scratched his legs and mosquitoes bit and whined near his face. Flies buzzed near his shoulder and head wound, drawn by the scent of blood. He stuffed berries in his mouth as he went along. Sweat stung his eyes and he was thinking of turning around and heading back to camp when he thought he saw a slight movement ahead in the brush, at the edge of the river. Easing forward slowly, until he froze, with his heart pounding so hard it seemed it could be heard, Ben silently stood looking.

The big deer was nibbling the sweet grass at the edge of the water and standing with its head down.

"I have to do this slowly and carefully. Please help me Father, I know I will only get one chance," he prayed silently.

When the bow was bent to its fullest, he let the arrow fly. "Thunk," and down went the deer. With God's direction, the arrow had pierced the deer's heart. Had anyone been near, they would have heard his whoop echoing through the trees. He jumped up and down near the deer with his arms in the air, shouting, "Thank you, God. Thank you, Jesus!"

After he calmed down a little, he realized that the big deer was far, too heavy, for him to carry or drag. I have to figure out how to take it back to camp, he thought. He hurried back and brought the raft.

Raised on the farm, I helped my father butcher chickens and cows. I know what I need to do, he thought.

After cleaning the deer, he used the raft and floated it back near camp.

"It is so heavy. If I can just drag it and hang it high in a tree for safekeeping, that will give me time to figure out what to do about a fire. I can use the hide to make my bed warmer, but I am too tired to do anything more, right now."

Ben's hands stung from the abrasions the rope had made as he toiled to get the deer up in the tree and wrapped the rope around the trunk fastening it with several knots.

Near the entrance to the hut, Ben stood listening.

"I can hear thunder in the distance and that cold wind is picking up. I think that it will be raining soon. I better gather my things."

In the hut for the night, he sat by the doorway with the Bible in his lap, reading, and thanking God for the deer. He knew that killing that deer was an awesome miracle. With no experience and a rough made bow and arrow, without God's hand, it could not have happened.

The wind grew stronger and threatened to take the canvas off his roof. It flapped and cracked at the edges like a whip. The rain started. First it came lightly but it soon changed to a fierce, cold downpour, with wind so strong that at times it sent the rain flying sideways. Ben was afraid it would wash his hut away. He sat against the sidewall, away from the doorway, bundled in the quilt, shivering, and praying for protection. The sound of thunder growled overhead, as lightening revealed the streaks of rain outside.

"God, have I chosen a bad place for my camp? The rain is coming down so hard. It is pouring down the bluff and some of it is coming in my hut along the back wall. Please watch over me." With each lightening flash, Ben watched the floor of his hut turn into several rivulets that ran out under the front wall. He slid tighter against the sidewall to stay out of the water.

In the night he heard a terrifying sound, a rumbling that he didn't understand. It wasn't thunder, but it seemed to be above him. Then something heavy and hard hit his roof, causing the wall he was leaning against to shudder. He heard and felt more pounding, bumping and thumping, until he was sure that it would cave his roof in.

He sat huddled, and afraid. Whatever it was, on the roof, had stopped moving. It was dreadfully silent.

I can't hear the storm anymore. How odd, he thought. It is so quiet and black.

As he pushed the flap on his door aside, Ben discovered that the branches he had used to stop intruders were now imbedded in a solid wall. His hand searched in the dark for an opening.

"I can't see a thing, but I can tell this is mud and rock. I have got to unblock my doorway! I must stay calm," he instructed himself, groping for anything he could use to dig.

"Please help me, Father!" In the complete blackness, his hand found only an arrow. I'll push it into the mud, he thought, but when his efforts didn't yield a hole, he began to dig hysterically with both hands.

"I'm buried. I don't know if I can ever get out," Ben was panicking.

CHAPTER TWO
A FIRE AND A FRIEND

Ben dug franticly with his hands clawing away the mud until finally when he pulled a rock back, he felt a bit of cold air come in through a small hole. He continued digging until he could reach outside. He could hear the storm and feel the wind driven drops hitting his palm. Peering through the opening he tried to see out but it was very dark. The air coming in was cold. He could easily tell that his hut was warmer than the air outside. He quit digging and stuffed the rock back in the hole to block the cold air.

He was calmer now. I know now, that I can dig out he rationalized. The roof is holding what has landed on it and if no more falls, it should be all right. The rain will probably wash some of it off. I'll finish digging out in the morning, when I can see the daylight in the hole, he thought. I will feel safer if I get nearer the wall, by the door though. He felt the floor and inched as close as he could without sitting in water.

"You helped me again, God. Thank you."

His little hut seemed almost cozy as he curled up in the quilt and waited for morning.

"Father, I think this little hut is holding up a lot of heavy dirt and rocks. Please keep it strong and safe. Be beside me through this night."

Ben had been through so much. As soon as he recognized the explanation for his problem, he was able to trust and rest.

A very tiny beam of sunlight played on the floor of his hut as his natural body rhythm brought him awake. It took only a few minutes of digging before he was able to wiggle out a hole in his doorway. As he looked around he realized that things had drastically changed.

The river is higher and running faster, he thought. It would be harder to get across it right now. My deer is still safe in the tree. It was then that he looked back at his hut. My shack is totally covered. It looks like a mound of dirt. I am not sure if it is safe now that I see how much dirt is on top of it. I need to make a brace for the ceiling. It's a miracle that the hut is still standing with all that weight on it.

"Thank you Jesus, for protecting me during that storm, and for holding my roof up." he said.

Near his doorway, a tree lay that the sliding dirt and rock had uprooted. Several small pine trees lay beside his hut and one clung to the bluff above at a strange angle.

Ben chopped off the branches and the spray of roots on one of the trees and after enlarging his doorway and digging a hole in the center of his floor, he struggled to get the pine tree trunk inside.

"Now, if I can get it upright, in the hole, it will hold the roof up and the hut will be strong and safe." After more pushing, pulling, and chopping, it stood, forced upright, pressed tightly against a cross section of ceiling branches.

Ben puttered around camp wondering if he could get a fire going to dry the deer meat to preserve it. He knew he had to do that soon so it would not spoil.

"It is really going to be hard now after all that rain last night, all the wood around here is wet." Just then he realized he could smell smoke. "Fire, where? There it is! I can see the smoke curling up across the river, far out on the prairie. The lightning last night must have started it. Why didn't the rain put it out?" I wonder if it would be possible to bring back a burning branch. His discovery was so exciting that he almost left camp without his mother's biggest cooking pot to use for carrying the coals.

During the time he had spent struggling to install the tree trunk as a center brace in the hut; the water level had gone down some. Ben stuffed his knife into his pocket, and bravely entered the rushing water. He battled, at first partly walking and partly swimming to cross. It is reaching up to my chest, he thought, as the strong force of the water pushed hard, sweeping him off his feet.

Clinging to the handle of the pan, he continued to stroke and kick, working to keep his head above the brown, roiling water. He was being carried by the current, until he could finally pull himself to the edge. He crawled out onto the grass coughing, and rested to catch his breath.

"That was worse than I thought it would be. At least, I kept the pan." He checked his pocket to see if he still had his knife. He felt it deep in the bottom.

Ben walked out onto the prairie and headed in the direction of the smoke. I can see now that the fire is farther than I imagined. The river had taken him down stream, and saved him an even longer walk. The sun was high overhead before he could finally see the edge of the flames and in the smoke, he could smell cooked meat.

A wild pig lay under a burned bush. The dense grass had burned away.

"Dinner is served," he yelled. His knife cut through the burned skin to find juicy meat hot and ready to eat.

"Thank you, God. You know I need this." He stuffed his mouth and sat down on the fire-warmed ground.

Movement to his right made him aware that other animals were near; hungry ones. I need to be careful. I'm not the only one that needs to eat. He cut off a chunk of meat and put it into the pot and moved away as a large scraggly looking wolf, came snarling and sniffing, to claim the rest of the meat. Ben knew he couldn't carry more than he had already taken so he let the fierce animal start its meal as he went to the fire's edge.

"A thick, burning piece of branch is what I need," he said out loud. He found one. "Now what am I going to do with the meat? I want to put the fire in the pot, to carry it. If I cut a charred branch and make a point on it, I can push it through the meat and swing it over my shoulder like a fishing pole. Finding a branch out here that is still strong won't be easy."

As he searched, he had to watch where he stepped. Some of the root clumps and twigs were still hot enough to burn his feet.

"This one will hold it and not snap," he said, as he whittled the end to a point and shoved it through the meat. He was joyous over his blessing of both cooked meat and fire.

"Thank you, Father," he said, as he rolled a large chunk of burning wood into the pan and added several smaller ones.

The metal handles of the pan soon grew very hot. I need to protect my hands, he thought, looking around. When he couldn't spot anything that would work, he pulled off his shirt and rolled it into a long thick pad.

It was difficult to walk and hold the pot away from his bare chest. He realized that his bare feet were getting tender. He had walked a long way in the harsh stubble of the prairie grass. Ben was used to being barefoot and usually it was something that he didn't even notice.

The river was still higher than it had been before the rain but had gone down more while he had been gone. Ben breathed a sigh of relief when he realized that he had the raft to use.

"I can leave everything on the bank and swim over to get my raft. I am sure that I can take the pot across on that without drowning the fire."

Ben's heart was light as he finally saw his camp come into view. He felt relief that he had made it back and the wood was still smoldering. This was a big victory!

"Once again I have you to thank."

He quickly dug a pit in front of the hut, ringed it with stones, and gently rolled the embers into it. He added dry twigs and needles from deep under the pine trees and pulled small dead branches to add.

"I want to get this fire going and then I will gather lots of branches and put them near so they will dry out from the heat of the flames.

As he thought about how his mother and the other ladies had dried meat, he knew he had to make a drying rack, and place it close to the fire. If I retrieve two of the big wheels from the covered wagon, I can use them for drying racks and not have to make any, he thought.

It was very difficult for him to lift the heavy wheels from their axles and he discovered that once again the raft was needed. Some of the wheel was made of wood but a heavy portion of it was made of iron. They would not float. He finally rolled them up to the fire with a feeling of satisfaction.

Now I can just prop them up and begin to slice the deer meat, he thought, as he fed the fire. Soon the thin slices of deer meat were covering the spokes of the wheels and branches he had strung between them.

"Thank you God, for your provision of fire. The deer meat would have been spoiled soon if I couldn't dry it," he said out loud.

He had most of the meat sliced off the bones when he heard a whimper. The sound came from the trees near the edge of his camp. When he heard it again he walked cautiously closer to investigate. There under a tree lay a big brown and yellow dog with an arrow in his hind leg.

The arrow had been chewed off about two inches from the leg but the dog had not been able to pull it out. I have got to make a friend of this animal before I can help him. The frightened brown eyes watched him as he walked back to his campfire and cut off a large piece of the deer meat, slowly bringing it close enough so that the dog could see and smell it; Ben spoke softly being soothing and reassuring.

"Easy boy, take it easy, I won't hurt you. You poor boy, that leg must be hurting something awful and you look like you could use a meal." Ben slowly placed the meat where the dog could take it without having to get up. The meat quickly disappeared. The tip of the dog's tail did a slight wave back and forth and then his head went down into the leaves and he slept. The fact that the dog has allowed himself to go to sleep so near me means that he is already starting to trust me. That arrow has to come out and the wound will be painful, he thought.

"Please God, help me to help him," Ben prayed. "I want so much, for him to get well and to stay."

"I remember that my mother made some willow bark tea and a poultice of it when I fell and twisted my ankle. It is good for easing pain. It sure helped me. There are lots of willow trees by the water." Ben cut into the bark and peeled away the outer layer so that the inner layer was exposed. I need to get enough of the soft bark to relieve the dog's pain. Ben put some water from the river in a small pan, added the shredded bark, and set it near the fire. I hope I can do this right. I have never done anything like this, he thought. He sharpened his knife and cut a strip of hide from the deer.

"This will have to be the outer bandage," he said out loud, to shore up his own courage. He cut a strip off the bottom of his shirt and added that to the pan. He put another piece of meat between the big front paws of the dog. Ben talked to him again and scratched the dog's ears and then slid his hand over his back to the wounded leg. The dog lay still, watching him unblinkingly. Ben wrapped a thin piece of cloth from his shirt, gently around the stub of the arrow and grasped it with both hands. With one quick, hard jerk, the arrow was out and the dog let out a shrill yelp as he jumped up. Blood was flowing freely from the wound and Ben knew that was a good thing for it would clean out the hole the arrow had left.

"It's all right boy. I didn't want to hurt you but that arrow had to come out. Come on boy, I made you some medicine. Come on don't be afraid. It's all right now. The arrow is out. See?" Ben held the arrow out so the dog could sniff at it. The dog stayed just out of reach.

After the pan was pulled away from the fire, Ben draped the strip of cloth over the edge of the pan to cool. When he turned around, the dog was standing near him on three legs, holding the injured one up. Ben sat down near the fire and added a few more pieces of wood.

"Please make him want to stay, Lord. Don't let him leave now. I want him to stay with me." Ben patted the grass and the dog took a step nearer. With a little coaxing, he was beside Ben in the circle of safety that the fire provided.

"It has cooled enough now," Ben, said, as he placed a patch of the boiled bark on the wound and wrapped the cloth around it. He covered that with the deerskin and tied it on securely with another strip of his shirt. He held the pan near the dog's mouth and stroked his head as the dog drank from it.

"Good boy, you are a good boy," said Ben. "After a while that will help you feel better and sleep."

Ben thought about the aggressive wolf he had seen and knew that the deer meat he had drying and the dog's fresh wound could bring hungry night hunters. He pulled a large stick to his side and with the tip of it he rolled several of the stones that surrounded the fire, closer, where he could reach them if he needed to throw them.

They heard wolf song in the distance and the injured dog moved a little closer wanting protection. He knew that in his weakened condition, he would not be able to defend himself well enough to survive a pack of wolves.

"Jesus, this has been an exciting day. Thank you for helping me with the dog's wound. Thank you for sending him to me. Please let him heal fast and stay. Thank you for the idea of the wheels for drying racks. That made it a lot easier to start the meat drying. I can feel you here helping me. I feel comfort from your presence. You are our protection through this night Lord. I am weak but you are strong."

He heard sounds in the woods that he could not identify. In his imagination he pictured huge bears or a wolf pack creeping closer. Soon he had added far more wood to his fire than he needed and had rigged a pair of branches to support a large chunk of the meat for a meal. He sang loudly far into the night as he finished slicing the deer meat.

A soft wind blew at Ben's face and woke him.

"Hey my friend, we are up just in time to add some wood to this fire." The dog's tail thumped on the grass and Ben thought he looked like he was smiling.

"I hope you are going to live here with me. I want to give you a name. How about the name Stump? That's for the stump of arrow I took out of your leg. Do you like that name, boy? Hey Stump. Good boy, Stump," he said, as he patted the big brown head. "Do you think you would like to stay here with me? We can be friends and help each other. Will you stay and be my friend, Stump?" Thump, thump, thump. I sure hope he stays, thought Ben.

Ben put a leg bone with plenty of meat left on it, by the dog's front paws and offered him some more of the willow bark tea

"You stay here and watch that nobody steals the meat off the racks, while I go dig a cache to keep it in." Stump responded by licking his hand. I wonder what kind of dog he is. He could be a shepherd, but he has a big square head. If he stays, then he will eat and not be so thin. He will look different when he is well.

He chose a spot in the back corner of the hut, for the cache. He removed one rather large rock and then was able to dig down. When he thought the pit was deep and large enough to hold lots of food he brought smooth rocks from the river bank to line it on the bottom and sides. Next he added wood to the fire again and stopped to pat, scratch and stroke Stump.

"Good job boy. Good boy Stump. No meat missing." The dog lifted his sleepy head and yawned, waving his tail slightly before he closed his eyes again.

"Stay here Stump while I look for a stone to use as the top." He walked a long way before he found what he was looking for. He wanted a piece of slate big enough to cover the entire top of his meat cache. When he found one, he realized that it was too heavy to move. Guess I'll have to use smaller slabs, he thought. I'll use some of Father's braided rope to drag the stones into the hut. That will be easier than trying to carry them. The back piece will stay in place and the smaller front one I can lift easily. Each time Ben came near, he checked on Stump and the meat again, adding wood to the fire and talking to his new friend.

As Ben returned to the fire, he found that Stump had moved a bit closer to the hut and away from the fire. The big dog accepted another drink of willow bark tea and then rested his head on his paws, watching Ben. I am glad that he seems a little better, he thought as he rubbed Stump's soft ears.

"I think I should turn all the meat over so that the backside will dry evenly and if I remember correctly, I should rub it with salt," he told Stump.

"I will get it. I think the Indians would have taken it if they knew what was in that sack," he said as he rubbed a small pinch into each piece." With the salt back in the hut where it would stay dry, he held his hands out to Stump and let him lick the salt and meat juices.

As Ben washed his hands in the river again, he glanced in the direction of his snares. "That's a project for tomorrow," he said.

"Tomorrow we will check the snares boy. Do you want to do that with me? Do you think you will be strong enough? You poor boy, you had a rough time didn't you, Stump? Let's pull the quilt around us and we will spend the night outside by the fire again."

Although they heard the sounds of animals in the trees and the wolf song in the distance, none came near the fire. Ben woke to find Stump cuddled close with his head in Ben's lap.

In the morning Ben pegged the deer hide out on the sod. He had seen his mother work a hide into leather on the farm. He tried hard to do what he had seen. He scraped it over and over and finally rubbed grease into it so it wouldn't get hard.

A piece of meat from the rack for their lunches passed the test. It was dry enough to store and had a hint of smoke in the taste. He liked it. The soft breeze had helped to dry it quickly. Ben had sliced the wild pig roast that he had brought back from the prairie fire and it, too, was dry now. Ben packed the meat neatly into the cache and put the lid on tightly.

"We have room for lots more Stump." Then he realized that the dog had followed him back and forth from meat racks to the cache and had managed quite well on his three good legs. "Hey boy, you are getting around really well! Let's go check the snares."

Along the riverbank, most of his snares were disturbed but empty. He reset them as they went along. Only one held a big fat rabbit.

"Look Stump." He held it up to show Stump. "This rabbit's fur is the start of a warm winter hat and a good stew for our supper." He cleaned and skinned it, stretched the fur near the deer hide and started the stew cooking in the big pot.

"I can add some cattail roots and wild onions and let it bubble. Thank you Jesus, for the deer meat and the rabbit cooking, but most of all, Thank you for Stump," he said.

Ben decided to take the raft to the other side of the river. He wasn't sure why he had.

"Just in case," he said to Stump. The dog was nervous on his ferry ride, but had developed a trust beyond the norm. He would always trust Ben. The raft was hidden in the bushes as they headed for the wagon. Fear caused Ben to be careful and he was still learning what he should and should not do to keep his presence as secret as possible. Living in the moment he had been foolish singing loudly by his fire. Making the large fire could have given away his location. When he thought about it, he knew he had to be more cautious in the future.

There are still a variety of useful items in or near the wagon, he thought.

"Here is another pan, a sewing kit, some silverware and the wooden stool that Grandfather made. Here is a wrinkled old squash." Ben told the dog. I'll put the smaller things in the pillowcase. Many household items are broken or gone. "Hey, look. Here is the water keg. It rolled into the bushes. It doesn't seem to be damaged. That will be useful this winter in our hut," he said. "I want to take some of the timber from the wagon, but I didn't bring the hammer back. I think I can pry a couple boards off of the seat without it." He carried everything back to the raft.

"The boards will serve as the top of a table," he said to Stump.

"The water level has dropped since the night of the big storm to a more manageable depth. I wonder where you were during that storm. It must have been awful for you," he said. "Climb on Stump. Let's cross." Ben put his arm around Stump, to help him on and pushed the raft against the bank to stabilize it at the same time. He crossed, pushing the raft carrying Stump and his items without mishap.

After he carried everything to his hut, he brought several big stones inside to support his new tabletop. He smiled to himself as he went to the river to fill the water keg with fresh water. This holds a lot, he thought, as he struggled to carry it up the bank.

"Thank you, Father, for taking care of all my needs," he said as he strained under the barrel's weight.

"We need to go see what other food is out there, boy. We haven't enough for the cold winter months. I don't know how cold it gets here or even how much snow falls in this area."

The only answer Stump offered was the usual wag, of his beautiful long tail. Ben looked at Stump and stroked his head.

"I am glad that you are here my friend. I hope that you will always stay with me," he said.

This time Ben headed into the woods away from the river past the bluff and into the dense shade of the trees. He could hear the sounds of many ducks as he drew near a small lake. Ben gathered his hands full of stones and crept closer to the water's edge. There are so many ducks that they seem to cover the surface of the water, thought Ben. He threw stones fast and hard and at that same moment there was a big splash. The ducks flew up in a noisy blast that startled Ben.

Much to his amazement, Stump had caught a duck in his mouth. He brought it to Ben and returned to the water to bring the two floating ducks that had been hit by flying stones.

"You are an amazing helper! Good boy, Stump, but your bandage is wet and hanging. Let me check it for you." Ben knelt and unwrapped Stump's leg and saw that it had healed over and was doing well. He decided it was better to leave the soggy bandage off. Ben tied the feet of the ducks together with the strip of his shirt from Stump's bandage and carried them over his shoulder, whistling nearly all the way back to camp before he stopped himself.

"I shouldn't do that. It probably carries a long way through the trees. I have so much to learn. I am back just in time to save the fire from going out. That does it," said Ben. "I promise that I won't go to bed tonight until I have learned the technique of starting a fire." He plucked the feathers from the ducks and stuffed them into the pillowcase and readied the duck meat to be dried. Once the meat was drying, Ben and Stump enjoyed the last of the rabbit stew.

"It is amazing. There are so many kinds of food right here. We will not starve this winter, Stump."

"We need to get something to eat for our supper, but we can't go far or our duck meat may be someone else's meal. I can try fishing again. What do you think boy? Do you like fish?"

This time I will be able to cook it, he thought. As they neared the water's edge they heard a big splash. That was followed by Stump diving in. He came up with the biggest frog that Ben had ever seen! Ben laughed at him.

"I like ducks better than frogs, but if you want to eat it you can." Stump dropped the big frog and watched as it jumped back into the river.

After digging some worms, Ben put one on his line and dropped it in the dark area by the roots of the old willow trees. Three wonderful catfish soon lay in the leaves beside Ben when he heard a branch snap behind him and Stump began to growl. Immediately, Stump raced after the intruder barking.

Ben called him back.

"I have been relaxing fishing and I forgot to keep an eye on the drying meat at the campfire." Ben saw a flash of fur enter the trees as he stood up. He ran up the bank to the camp to find several pieces of duck meat gone.

"Guess I need to be more watchful," he said. Then he realized he had left his fish on the riverbank and ran back down to collect them before they disappeared. He built up the fire and gutted the fish and wrapped them in big wet leaves and placed them on the hot stones to bake.

"Tomorrow I need to check the wagon again and see if there is anything else that I can use. And maybe I can pick a lot of the raspberries and dry them. They will be a good treat this winter.

He suddenly remembered that he had promised himself that he would practice twirling a stick to make a fire until he had learned the skill. He felt that having a fire for winter was absolutely necessary to survive. He found a smooth dry stick and a thin flat piece of wood and set them beside the hut. He gathered fluff from milkweed pods and even pulled a clump of loose fur that was hanging on Stumps back and added that to the pile. He made a pile of wood shavings with his knife and gathered small sticks for kindling. Ben had watched the women on the wagon trail do it but he had not been successful when he had tried for his mother. "I might have a problem getting dry wood in the winter. I'll need dry branches piled in the hut for fuel and another pile nearby, under the pine trees where I can get it easily when I need it," he said. "There, I think I have everything gathered that I will need to start a fire. I will do it right after we eat," he promised Stump and himself.

After the fish had baked and he and Stump had eaten, he wrapped the rest of the fish in big clean leaves and placed it against the cold stones in the back of the hut, to keep for the next day.

He acknowledged that he was once again in need of help.

"God, please show me how to start a fire. I failed when I tried before. Please help me." Ben found that making a fire with a twirling stick was the hardest thing he had ever had to learn. Finally when a small ember was glowing, he blew on it adding fluff and to his amazement and joy, a small, yellow flame appeared. He added tiny shavings, then tiny twigs, and then, last, some small branches until he had a second fire going as big as the first. He was so happy that he danced around it and clapped his hands as he sang,

"Praise God, thank you God," over and over. Although Stump didn't understand what the excitement was all about, he decided to join in the fun by following after Ben barking and wagging his tail.

Ben took the duck meat off of the wagon wheel spokes and placed it in the cache with the deer meat. It's still not nearly enough, Ben thought, but it's a good start. He snuggled down with Stump inside the hut, for the night. The main fire was banked, the other slowly died. A very important skill for survival had been learned that day and a wonderful feeling of comfort and confidence washed over him.

When he opened his eyes, he knew that it wasn't quite day. I wonder what woke me, he thought. Stump's low growl answered that question. Ben wrapped his arm around the big dog's neck, shushing him. He could hear soft stirrings in the river. A canoe, with two men in it, was working its way up the middle of the river. Had either person looked his direction, they would have seen his camp. Ben was glad that it was still quite dark out. They were paddling hard upstream and seemed in a hurry. I have to camouflage this camp, he thought. He wasn't sure how he would do it, but the Lord had shielded him from discovery this time.

"Thank you, Lord, for keeping our camp undetected."

"Thank you, that the wind carried the smell of my campfire away from the river and thank you, Father, for Stump. He is a good guard."

When he woke again, the sun was shining and the day was already quite warm. He went down to the river and got a drink and decided he needed a bath. This time he removed his clothes and scrubbed them on the sand and laid them on the big rock to dry. He swam up stream against the current, giving his muscles a good workout, and then allowed the river to carry him back. Stump was lying in the grass not far from Ben's clothes. He wagged a greeting and then went up and stood near the fire waiting for Ben to follow.

As Ben looked up at Stump and the fire he knew that his first chore this day was to create a shield that would hide his fire pit and the opening to his hut. It has to look natural, he thought. Then he noticed all the footprints he and Stump had made. We have to do something different about our route down to the water, too, he thought.

As he pulled his clothes on, he saw what he needed to do. The storm that had brought the rocks and mud down on his hut had also dislodged small pines. They lay at the base of the bluff with their roots partially exposed.

"I have to somehow put those trees and some rocks between the fire pit and the river and then I need to lay rocks and branches to walk on so that we don't leave a trail when we go down to the water's edge," he planned out loud.

Ben got his rope and wrapped it around the partially buried trunk of a small tree and pulled hard. It didn't budge. He pulled again, but this time he had help! Stump had grabbed the rope and was pulling hard. He thought it was a game.

"I am going to use the shovel to loosen it and then together we can do this."

"Good Boy, Pull, Stump. Pull." By pulling and then rolling the tree, they were able to put it in place. The hole he had prepared wasn't large enough but after a bit more work, digging, the tree stood and the dirt was pushed tightly around the base with his foot as he held it upright. Several rocks against the base helped to support it until its roots could grow into their new position. Another small pine was moved into place, along with a third and fourth. He had created a thick clump of trees that obscured the front of his hut completely. Once the planting was done, the big pan was used to dump river water on them.

"I hope they live. I should have thought of it sooner. Good boy!" said Ben, as he hugged Stump's big furry neck. "I couldn't have done it without your help"

"We did it! Now all we have to do is make a path that blends in and doesn't leave footprints."

As he loaded his arms with fallen branches, Stump grabbed a big branch and ran along beside Ben dragging it proudly. When it was time to scatter the branches, Stump thought it was a new game of tug and wouldn't let go of the one he had picked up. Ben laughed and decided to place a few flat stones here and there. It will do, he thought. Now I need to teach Stump to walk on them so he won't leave prints.

"We still have time for that walk to gather food, if we get going," he said. As he prepared what he would need for his foraging, he thanked God for showing him that he needed to camouflage his camp and for providing just what he needed to do the job. He felt that it was far less apt to be detected now.

He ate a piece of the fish and gave the rest to Stump.

With his bow and arrows, knife in his pocket and the pillowcase tucked into his waist, he headed out. He had to shake the feathers out into a pile in the corner of the hut. I want to save those, he thought, they would make our bed soft and warmer when I get enough.

As he walked along in the tall grass, he saw that without thinking about it, he had been walking in an animal trail. I know getting that deer was just a miracle shot, but if I knew where they went, it would help me to plan and give me a better chance.

Ahead on the path, Ben spotted a bit of black and white as he strolled along. In an opening where the weeds parted, he was able to see that he was walking along behind a mother skunk and a parade of three babies. I think I will let them get a long way ahead of me, he thought, as he stopped and watched their progress. They are cute, but I certainly don't want to get that mother upset with me. He waited silently until she disappeared into the brush far ahead.

Skirting the area that sheltered the skunks, his course took him near the berry patch where he gathered the last of the berries. There wasn't as many as he had hoped, because over the last few days the birds and animals had taken a large share.

Next he headed for the crabapple trees and realized that he was learning the area. He thought about the oak trees and knew that the acorns were safe to eat but that they had to be soaked to take out the bitter taste. I can get some of those, later on. I wish that I had better containers to store some of my supplies, he thought, as he looked up to find he was walking under a hickory nut tree full of big nuts wrapped in their dark green casings. "They will be a good treat! I can get those late this fall," he said to Stump. When they arrived at the crabapple trees Ben realized that he would need to wait to get more when this summer's crop was ready.

He headed back to camp on another game trail that curved toward the little duck lake. Once again he and Stump were successful. He was able to down a couple and Stump plunged in and came out with a squawking, flapping gander. The look on Stump's face made Ben laugh until his sides hurt. As the feet of the ducks were tied together, Stump, reached for them and proudly dragged and carried all three back to camp. It was then that Ben realized that he had just laughed out loud for the first time since that terrible day.

"What a wonderful friend and help you are," said Ben praising Stump as he took the birds, while scratching the big furry neck.

The fire was out and Ben moaned when he saw it.

"I know I can restart it, but I am too tired to do it." He cleaned the ducks and saved the feathers. I'll put the ducks in the biggest pan filled with cold river water and place it in the back of the room against the cold stones. That should be all right for tonight. He curled up inside, with Stump, on the quilt and fell asleep thanking God for the food he had found and just talking to Him like the wise old friend that He is.

"This has been quite a day. We were able to camouflage the camp, but Father, I wonder, will I ever feel safe here? And when someone finally finds me, will it be someone I want to see?"

CHAPTER THREE
MEETING A BEAR AND JED

The next morning, Ben woke to a gray, overcast sky. A light mist threatened to turn into a heavy rain. I have got to hurry to gather wood inside, before it all gets soaked, he thought. He tossed the deer hide and the rabbit's skin that he had been working, inside the hut. I need to bring stones inside for a fire pit.

"Father, please direct me as I do this, so that it will be safe. Thank you, Jesus, for this day; and thank you, for showing me another necessary project," he continued to pray as he worked gathering dead branches from the trees near his camp. Ben quickly dug a pit out from the corner of the room and lined and ringed it with rocks from the riverbank. I'm glad that my ceiling is high, he thought. I think in time I will plaster the whole corner area with clay from the riverbank to make it safer. It will need a hole over it to let the smoke out, and it shouldn't let the rain in. A propped up piece of slate on top of the dirt roof, and a few random stones around it and that should still look natural and hopefully the smoke will drift up over the bluff, not down to the river.

By the time he finished, the rain was falling steadily. Little rivers of rain ran down his hair and tickled his back.

He sat with his twirling stick in hand.

"Father this is my second time starting a fire. Please help me." Ben began to work hard at twirling the stick. The small ember dropped and went out. He was sweating from the effort and his arms ached. He peeked out at the heavy sky.

"I have to get this going before nightfall. I want to cook one of the ducks and dry the other two, and it will be cold tonight after this rain," he said. He got back in position, picked up his stick and began again with a steady downward pressure. A small curl of smoke rewarded him.

He blew gently adding a dry leaf and a shaving of wood. A tiny red flame appeared. Soon a steady small fire burned in his new fire pit.

"It is amazing. It is hard to take my eyes off the dancing flames," he said. Ben sensed that he should keep the fire as small as possible.

He put the duck on a skewer of green oak and balanced it above the flames with two up-right branches shaped with a "V" at the top. He steadied it by piling rocks at the base of each for support. As he watched the duck sizzle, he realized he was more tired than he had ever been in his whole life.

Stump's leg was healing well and he had started walking on it a bit now and then but Ben knew that it would be good to rest it.

"Stump I am declaring this day Sunday. That means we can rest and read our Bible and eat our meal and not work anymore today. We can take today to thank the Lord for all He has given us and I specially thank Him for you. I would have been so lonely without you." The big dog raised his head and thumped his tail in reply.

Ben sat on the quilt near the fire with his legs crossed and held the Bible on his lap. As he looked around he realized that in such a short time he had built his hut and learned to hunt and dry meat. He had shelter, a warm fire, and food, water and Stump. He had started with nothing and now he had all this. He felt very grateful.

In the tradition of his father, he read out loud although Stump was the only one there to hear him. He read about Moses and the parting of the red sea in Exodus 14:21-22 NIV "Then Moses stretched out his hand over the sea, and all that night the Lord drove the sea back with a strong east wind and turned it into dry land. The waters were divided, and the Israelites went through the sea on dry ground with a wall of water on their right and on their left." Then Ben turned to the book of Acts 12:6-10 NIV and read about

Peter being in prison for Christ. I wonder why God led me to those verses today.

"I guess you want me to see that it doesn't matter how impossible things seem; you always makes a way. I'm a lot better off than Peter was, chained in prison and guarded and God took off those chains and opened the gates for him."

He continued to read until the duck was fully cooked. It was crispy outside and juicy inside. Ben and Stump ate until they were full and the rich duck meat was gone. Ben had been careful to remove all the bones from Stump's portion.

"They seem like chicken bones to me. On the farm, we never gave chicken bones to our dogs," he explained to Stump. Ben's mind drifted back to the farm and the two dogs that guarded the barn and livestock. I really loved Speckle, but Gramps thought I should leave him there. Sassy was more independent. She liked lying on the porch and she was attached to Grandmother.

Ben added wood to the fire. The meat from the other ducks had been cut into thin strips and laid on the hot rocks near the fire to dry. Ben and Stump curled up next to each other and took a much-needed nap. The fat trimmed from the ducks would be useful for cooking. It slowly rendered in a pan, a safe distance from the fire.

When Ben woke, he felt refreshed and full of energy. He looked at the berries. "I am not sure what to do with the berries to preserve them. I will put them onto the two plates that I salvaged from the wagon. It's sad that the others were broken when the wagon tipped over. Mother was always careful with them. Ben shook off the heavy gray sadness that threatened to creep into his chest.

"I can grease the plates and pour the berries on them to dry." He inspected them, picking out a twig and several leaves and decided that they needed to be spread out more, so he brought in a piece of slate. It was clean, washed by the rain. He coated it with grease, too and spread some of the berries on it.

"I think they will dry better if I mash them down flat with the palm of my hand." He held his hand out to Stump, who was happy to lick the sweet juice from it before Ben washed. The berries were placed near the fire, hoping that once they were dry he would be able to peel them away from the plates and slate.

The rain has stopped, he noted.

"Let's go for a walk Stump." Ben shook out the pillowcase tucking it into his waist. He took his bow and arrows, heading across the branches and rocks to the river. Stump had copied him and had not left a print in the sand. The river doesn't seem higher.

"Bright and hot," was what he said, as he looked around. Stump took off into the trees.

"Where are you going?" he called, as the dog stopped, wagged and then disappeared into the trees.

An idea was forming in Ben's mind, as he headed out toward the lake on the deer path, trying hard not to widen it with his own steps. I need to find a place where I can see the path but not be seen. Ahead is a large tree just to the right of the path with branches low enough that it looks climbable. I think that tree might make a perfect place to watch the path to see what animals use it.

He hooked his bow on a branch as high as he could and pulled himself up, stopping to reach his bow and place it ever higher as he climbed. He propped himself into a screen of leaves to wait and watch. It reminded him of another time when he had climbed and braced himself in a tree. I don't want to think about that now.

He didn't know that he was being watched.

The young man in his tree puzzled the big black bear. The hollow at its base was one of his favorite napping places. The huge old bear had wandered his territory for many years unchallenged. He didn't like it when something new happened and he certainly didn't like someone sitting in his tree.

As the bear tried to decide what to do, Stump came bounding up barking and growling. He had picked up the scent of the bear at the same time he had been sniffing the trail to find Ben. His protective instinct told him to place himself between the animal and Ben. Ben saw the bear at that moment. He hollered!

"Stump, get away! No Stump! Get back," As he scrambled down the tree as fast as he could.

As Ben's feet hit the ground he was already placing an arrow in his bow. The dog was keeping the bear busy, barking, growling and circling.

His bow was strong, but he never intended to use it for a bear. He pulled the arrow back as far as it could go. I don't think I can kill a bear with just my bow, but I have to do something to try to save Stump, he thought as he released it.

"God please help us." The arrow stung as it grazed off the bear's neck, infuriating him. He advanced standing tall, bristling and growling.

The bear swung a mighty paw at Stump and knocked him six feet away. Stump landed on his side and laid still.

"Get away from my friend, you miserable big beast!" Ben shouted defiantly and ran at the bear throwing rocks as hard as he could. One hit the old bear in his eye and he roared and scrubbed his face with his paw. Ben foolishly didn't move away.

"Here is another rock for you, and another, you mean beast!" Ben threw rocks as hard as he could, his adrenalin giving him strength. The bear swung his paws intending to attack Ben next. He was growling and advancing.

"You hurt Stump! Take that!" Ben shouted hurling a large rock. This one struck the bear's temple with a loud cracking sound and the old bear staggered and then crumpled. He was dazed but not dead. Ben seized the moment and used his knife to cut blade-deep, across the muscled throat.

Ben ran to Stump, but before he could do anything, the bear lurched forward toward them on all fours. He stopped just a yard away and collapsed.

"Thank you God," Ben breathed. His heart was pounding and tears were again on Ben's face as he examined Stumps life-threatening claw marks.

"Oh Stump! Your side is soaked with blood, but at least you are breathing." Ben picked him up and carried him back to the river's edge near the hut. He washed the wounds and blood reddened fur and then took him into the hut. The claw marks were deep and still bleeding.

"Father, what can I do to help him? Oh God, please help him!" He said. "I have got to sew the wounds shut or he will bleed to death." He quickly got his mother's sewing kit and with black thread and with prayer and big stitches he closed the wounds. The dog still hadn't moved. His breathing was slow and shallow.

Once again, Ben made willow bark tea for Stump but this time he felt that it was not going to help much. He didn't know that the big leaves that he moistened and placed over the stitches would thicken the blood and help the bleeding to stop. He had used them to wrap his fish and knew they were not harmful. He just was using what was at hand as a bandage. He tore a sleeve from his shirt and cut it into strips with his knife. Dipping them into the willow bark tea, he bound the leaves against the dog's side. He wrapped the rest of his shirt around Stump to help keep the bandage in place.

"Oh please buddy, please Stump, please, don't die! Wake up and let me know that you are going to live."

"Father God, my creator and protector. I really need your help now. Isaiah 53:4 NIV says, "Surely he took up our infirmities and carried our sorrows."

"Please God; heal the stripes on Stumps side. You have already helped me with so much, but I can't do this alone. I don't know how to help Stump this time. His injuries are very serious. Father, help me. Show me what to do for him. You are a mighty and merciful God. You didn't send me a friend to have him die now! You are a healing God. Please heal Stump. Please heal Stump. Please heal Stump." He repeated it over and over.

Ben wept as he built two large fires outside in hopes that fear of fire would protect Stump from predators that could smell his blood. Although he had killed the bear he was going to have to return quickly if he wanted to have the meat and hide. He closed the canvas door on the hut and tied it tight. Stump was still. Ben took his rope and the sheet and headed back to the bear. It was fear and pure adrenaline that had helped him to kill the bear and carry Stump all the way back to camp. Even a man with a rifle would have hesitated to take on a bear of that size.

He heard growls and yips as he came near. Even though the bear had been feared in life and animals gave him respect and a wide space, in death he was now food and it didn't take long for the carnivores to start realizing that the bear was no longer a threat.

Yelling, Ben ran, throwing rocks as hard as he could, and flapping the sheet. He wasn't thinking clearly, or he would have been afraid to charge in and take back his bear, but charge he did.

"That's my bear! Get away from it! Get out of here," he screamed.

With his knife he slit the bear's middle and threw the offal into the bushes. A battle took place as his rivals fought for the meal. Ben knew he wouldn't be able to take the whole bear back and anything he left behind would soon be dragged away by animals. I better skin it first, he thought. Rolling the skin to the middle of the back, Ben struggled to turn the bear over so he could complete the job. I can't believe how heavy he is.

Once rolled, he took the hide to the tree and bit-by-bit; he was able to get it up in a crotch, high enough that it would be out of reach and safe for a while. He began by cutting big hunks of the meat and putting them in a pile in the middle of the sheet. As soon as he had a bone cleaned off, he threw it into the trees as far as he could. He thought that his only chance to keep the meat was to give the animals something to keep them busy. As the pile grew on the sheet, the fact that he had killed a huge bear began to sink in. He was astonished at what he and Stump had done!

"Father, please watch over Stump while I am here, and protect both of us."

He knelt by the head and pried the four biggest fangs from its mouth. He stuffed them into his pocket. He was amazed by the size of the old bear's teeth and the length of his claws.

"Someday, I will show Sarah those teeth and then she will understand how big this guy really was," he said. He tossed the head into the bushes about twenty feet away, and the biggest wolf he had ever seen, grabbed it and ran with the whole thing. He whirled around to see another one snarling. It moved away from his pile with a big chunk of meat in its mouth.

He drew up the corners of the sheet. It was so heavy he couldn't pick it up. This is all I can take back, he thought. They can have the rest. He pulled on it and it slid on the deep grass.

"Well this is not the best way, but it's the only way I can do it," he said, as he pulled and backed up all the way to camp, leaving the rest of the bear to the animals and a trail of blood from the meat that led directly to his camp. His back hurt, his arms ached, but worst of all his heart was crushed with concern, as he untied the flap of the hut.

He was worried about his friend.

"Thank you Father that the two fires have kept Stump safe and I think the security of the hut has been a comfort as he slept."

As Ben entered, Stump lifted his head just a little and whined. Ben stroked his head and checked the bandages. They were still in place and the bleeding was almost stopped.

"You rest now and get better" he said as he backed out of the hut, wiping tears from his eyes before tying the flap open to give Stump fresh air. The staggering pile of bear meat had to be prepared for drying and guarded while it dried.

He built up the fires and put a piece of the bear meat on to roast. He added to his rack space by winding more branches between the wagon wheels and holding them with ties of long grass. I hope that the bear's skin is safe in the tree. It was so heavy I couldn't get it up any further, he thought. After sharpening his knife on a rock he began the task of making thin slices of meat to dry. His racks were nearly full and still he had a lot of meat to slice. The fat was tossed into the big pan near the fire and it was almost full and beginning to melt. He wished now that he had kept the intestines. He could have cleaned them and used them as casings for the fat once it was rendered. He didn't know what he would use to hold it.

Ben gathered several branches from underneath a tree to add to the fires and cut green ones to make another rack, and then went back to cutting thin slices.

As he worked, he kept a prayer on his lips that God would help Stump. He took a piece of the cooked meat and pounded it into a soft pulp and added it to the willow bark tea he had made.

He took it in and looked at Stump. The big dog still lay in the same position that he had been since Ben carried him back that morning. His head was hot and his nose was dry. Ben knew that somehow he had to get Stump to drink. He placed the small pan near the dog's head but he made no effort to drink. Ben took a spoon and dribbled a little liquid inside the dog's lips. His pink tongue lapped at the broth. Ben did it several times and was pleased to see that at least some of the broth was getting inside Stump.

He looked at the bandage and decided to check it. The wounds were hot and showing signs of infection. I don't know what to do. I know that Mother would have made a poultice to draw out the bad stuff, but I don't know which plants to use.

"Oh Stump, I don't know how to help you." He prayed again. "God, show me what to do. Help me." Tears made their way down his dirty face.

As he backed out of the hut, Ben heard someone holler.

"Hello the camp, anyone there?" Ben stepped from the hut and turned toward the river. He stopped short when he saw a man climbing up the riverbank, dressed in leather pants and shirt, with long, dark brown hair hanging down his back and tied with a strip of leather. This man looked like he was part of the land, rugged and very tan.

"Hello, I'm Jedidiah Jones. Just call me Jed," The man said, with a smile, extending his empty right hand. His left hand carried a rifle. Ben took a step back knowing that he was at the man's mercy.

"Hey, I'm not going to hurt you."

"I'm Ben," he said hesitantly. Somehow he had not considered that the smoke from the two large fires would bring a visitor. He had been too involved, dealing with everything to think about it. He was not sure of the man's intentions.

"I could smell your meat cooking and didn't think you would mind if I stopped for a spell and rested. I saw the smoke as soon as I came around the bend. Don't you know there are Indians in these parts? It's not a good idea to advertise that you are here."

Ben noticed Jed's canoe bobbing up and down on the current of the river, where he had tied it to a low willow branch. Ben was suddenly glad that the man was there and in a rush of words he told his whole story up to the point that he had just checked poor Stump and that he was really sick and he didn't know how to help him.

"You mean you and Stump actually killed that bear your drying, without a gun? I have to meet this guy," he said, taking a step toward the hut.

"Is it all right with you if I go in? Maybe I can help him." Ben nodded.

Jed bent low and entered the hut. Even in his weakened condition Stump felt that he was on guard and a low growl came from him as the man entered.

"Why, it's a dog. You didn't say that Stump was a dog! I guess I just figured that it had to be a man to help you kill a bear." Ben came in right behind Jed and spoke softly to Stump,

"Jed is a friend and he is here to help us. It's all right Stump." Ben knelt beside him and stroked his head.

"He is pretty bad off, Jed. He has infection in the wounds from the claws. I don't know what to put on them to draw out the poison."

Jed talked to Stump and scratched his ear a little, so that Stump would know that he meant him no harm. Then he stepped back out of the hut and asked if Ben had seen any tall plants growing nearby that had yellow flowers and big light green leaves.

"I think there are some like you are describing on the trail to the lake," Ben said.

"You stay here and I will go see if I can find some," suggested Jed.

"Thanks," was all that Ben had a chance to say. Jed hurried off in the direction that Ben had pointed.

After just a few minutes he returned with several of the plants, root tubers and all.

"Most herbs that we gather are picked, just the leaves or leaves and stem, but for this one, you need the whole thing," Jed said. He washed them in the river and brought them to the fire.

"I'll need something to cook them in," he said, as he hurried back down to his canoe, and returned with a cooking pouch made of leather. He pounded the entire plant between two rocks and put it in the pouch with enough water to cover it. He hooked it near the fire.

"I want it to heat quickly," he said. He poked several small rocks free from around the fire and using sticks to pick them up, he dropped them in the pouch to hurry the heating process. They were so hot that they sizzled when they touched the water.

"We want that to boil, and cool, and then we can use it," he said. Ben watched closely. He wanted to learn.

Jed sat down on the ground next to the fire and Ben offered him some of the cooked bear meat. Jed took out a handsome hunting knife with a carved, white bone handle and cut off a moderate sized piece.

"Ben, do you have anything to make tea?"

"I made willow bark for Stump, but none for myself." Jed began to describe and name things that Ben could pick and dry to make hot tea for winter. Just then Ben remembered the coffee pot and coffee that he had retrieved from the wagon. He hadn't used them and wasn't very fond of coffee. He brought them out of the hut. Jed smiled a broad smile and took the pot to the river to fill it. He tossed a generous handful of coffee in the pot and set it on a rock near the flames to brew.

The pouch was bubbling now so Jed lifted it away from the fire to cool. Ben was puzzled why the fire had not burned the leather and said so.

"As long as the liquid inside is higher than the flames it keeps the leather moist enough so that it doesn't burn," explained Jed. First the stones were removed and then Jed poured some of the liquid into a small bowl. It was dark and looked strong.

"Now when this cools enough to handle we will add a little to that willow bark tea. The plant will make a good poultice. A new one should be put on every day until the wounds are clean and healed. Give him lots of that tea, as much as he will take, every time you check on him. It wouldn't be a bad idea to add some more pounded meat to that tea, too." Ben felt relief wash over him as he recognized that Jed was the help he had prayed for.

"Thank you, God, for answering my prayer and sending Jed to help." Ben had said his short prayer out loud.

Jed smiled.

"Glad that I was around to help," he said

When they entered the hut again, Stump didn't growl. He raised his head a little and then put it back down. Jed removed the bandage and examined the swollen claw marks. Gently he sponged the whole area with the strong, dark liquid from the pouch and then applied the poultice. He went to his canoe and returned with two soft pieces of leather made from rabbit skins. He placed one on top of the poultice and then wrapped the shirt back around the dog's body and tied it there.

"The stitches were a good idea. How did you know to do that?" he asked.

"I saw a man hurt on the wagon train, and a lady sewed him up like that. I don't know what I am supposed to do with them now, though," answered Ben.

"I think you should probably pull them out as soon as the flesh holds together. The longer you leave them in, the harder it will be to remove them. The best way I know, to do it, is to cut the thread and then grab it with your teeth and jerk it out. It will probably bleed a little, but as long as the gash doesn't open back up it should be all right."

Ben was very grateful that Jed had come along.

"I want to thank you for helping Stump, and you are welcome to stay the night if you want." Jed decided he would. He knew that Ben wanted him there and needed the help.

Ben was awake most of the night giving small spoonfuls of the medicinal tea to Stump and making sure the fires were fed. Early the next morning, when Ben got the medicinal mixture and spooned some into Stump's mouth, his nose felt cooler and he drank some of the tea from the pan. Jed was already sitting by the fire and was drinking coffee when Ben came out.

"Good morning, Jed. I think Stump is a little better this morning."

"I know," said Jed. "I checked him earlier. You were finally sleeping. I have another plant cooking. I want to change his bandage one more time before I leave." Ben didn't want to think of being alone again, but he felt that Jed's medicine had given Stump a good chance at recovery.

Suddenly Ben remembered the bear hide. "Would you stay and watch the camp for a little while? I want to go bring the bear hide back to camp so I can work it before something happens to it. I stashed it high in a tree. I hope the hide is still there and all right I don't want to leave Stump and the drying meat alone."

"Yes, of course, go ahead and I will check Stumps wounds while you are gone," said Jed. He touched one of the slices of bear meat on the rack and it was already getting dry and hard. He wondered where Ben was going to put all of it. Then he noticed the clear rendered fat and made a note to tell Ben that after the injuries on Stump healed, to smear a little bear fat on them. It would help to keep them soft and then Stump wouldn't try to scratch at them.

Jed spent time with Stump as he had promised.

"Stump old boy, how are you this morning?" Jed said, as he entered the hut. "Do you think we should change that poultice for you? I made a new one." Jed continued to talk to Stump as he efficiently changed the bandage. "Now I need you to drink some of this rich beef broth. We want you to get strong again. Good fellow, there you go. Now you can rest again." He scratched Stumps ears and gently stroked his head before he left the hut, tying the flap open.

The grass grew tall not far from the hut. Jed cut an arm full and carried it back to the place near the fire where he had been sitting. I'll weave a watertight basket, big enough to hold the melted bear fat, he thought. I better make a lid for it too, to keep the flies out of it. By the time Ben returned with the hide, Jed had the basket more than half completed.

Ben's face was red and covered with sweat from the effort. He laid the heavy hide down in disgust at the buzzing flies that had plagued him the whole way. He ran toward the river and dove in, clothes and all. He scrubbed at his hair and trousers with sand and then pealed them off down to his soggy underwear and spread them on the big rock to dry. He hurried back to the hut, doing his best to cover his embarrassment. He ducked into the hut and grabbed his mother's long skirt, which he wrapped around himself and sat down by the fire.

"I think you have the right idea," said Jed grinning. He pulled off his leather shirt and pants and he too, dove into the river for a refreshing swim. After a few minutes he returned, with his clothes back on. Ben watched him and listened to his laugh, as he pulled his hair back and tied it. I wish he would stay, thought Ben. I don't want to think about him leaving.

While Jed swam, Ben had checked on Stump. He was sleeping peacefully. Ben had started pegging out the huge bearskin, preparing to scrape and preserve it, when Jed walked over to see it. Jed couldn't believe how big it was.

"That bear was huge! You are lucky that either of you are alive! Look at the length of his claws!"

"I know that you are right. I just don't want to think about it. God helped us or we might not be here. When I look at this hide, I am stunned myself."

Ben scraped and stretched the hide. It had to be free of all tissue, and then he could work some of the rendered fat into it by rubbing hard with a smooth stone.

Jed returned to the unfinished basket. Later Ben glanced over to see Jed just finishing.

"This is for you to store the bear fat. It is waterproof, so it will hold it. I made a flat cover for it. Just keep it as cool as you can," said Jed.

"That's great. Thank you. I was wondering what I was going to put it in. I have only a few pans."

"Do you need me to help you dig a cache for the meat?" asked Jed.

"No thanks, I already have done that. It is in the back of the hut under the slate in the corner."

"You sure have accomplished a lot in a short time."

"Thanks, I plan to put all this in there tonight if it is dry enough, so that I can let the outside fires go out. I only had a small one inside until Stump got hurt. I lit these to keep him safe while I went back for the bear meat. I had to dry all that meat so I kept the second one going. When you leave I want you to take some of the bear meat with you. I can't ever repay you for helping Stump," said Ben.

Just then they heard a thump, thump behind them as Stump's tail wagged against the flap on the doorway. The dog took a few more unsteady steps to the edge of the campsite and then he came back between the two young men and lay down.

"I think he is glad to be out in the air," said Jed. Ben rushed to get him some broth, and Jed reached over and rubbed his ears. Stump was definitely feeling stronger.

"His fever is gone," said Jed, as he touched the dog's cool nose. He stood up and gently stroked Stump's head.

"I really appreciate your offer of the bear meat, Ben. I'll just take enough for a meal. I don't need more than that. Maybe I'll see you late this fall on my way back. I'm going down to the place where this river joins with the Silver and widens. Some people I know live there now and I am going to help them build a house before winter."

"Say, Jed, can you tell me how the winters are in this area?"

"From what I've seen and heard you will be glad to have that bearskin on your bed and you will need some warm clothes. The snow can get pretty deep. Take care Ben, and be careful to keep your fire small. The less smoke the better. Sorry about your folks and all, but you seem like a smart kid. You will be all right," said Jed. He shook Ben's hand and then climbed into his canoe and shoved away from the bank.

"Bye Jed. Thanks for stopping and helping us. We will be watching for you this fall. God bless you for all the help you gave us. Keep safe."

"Thanks Ben and may God watch over you."

Jed maneuvered the canoe into the current with the ease of experience and headed down stream. Ben watched until the canoe was out of sight.

CHAPTER FOUR
HONEY AND WOLVES

Ben turned around to find Stump standing beside him.

"We will miss him. Won't we? Hey boy, are you feeling well enough to be up and moving around? Come on boy, let's go back near the fire and hut. Come on Stump. Ben deliberately walked slowly. Lie down and have a piece of this meat and I will get you a pan of water. I want you to rest. I am going to work on the bear skin some more." Stump wagged his tail and was glad to settle in the grass where Ben had indicated. They spent the night by the fires, keeping them going and guarding the meat.

In the morning, after several trips with as much meat as he could carry, only half of the meat was neatly corded in the cache. It was full.

"I have to dig another one in the other back corner so I can store the rest. I think I want to make it deeper and bigger than the first one," he said to Stump. Each time he dragged the dirt-covered sheet to the woods to empty it; he petted Stump and checked the fires. Finding slate pieces along the bottom of the bluff to fit the top of the new cache, was not difficult now that he knew what size he could handle.

"Next, I need to gather the stones to line it, so that our food stays clean," he said as he headed down the hill to the water. "Stay boy, I'll be back with stones." Ben had to make many trips down near the bank before he had the new cache totally lined. Some of the rocks had been wet and Ben knew that moisture could ruin the meat so he left the cache open and placed several hot rocks from his fire pit in the bottom to dry it. Later with the slate lid pieces in place Ben felt glad that he had finished it. He pulled the sheet with the last load of loose dirt, into the trees and dumped it on the pile. The sheet was worn very thin in the middle and had several small holes from dragging the bear meat and the loads of dirt.

"This has come in handy," he said, as he scrubbed the dirt and stains out of the sheet at the edge of the river and draped it over a bush, deep in the trees and out of sight, where it would dry in the breeze. He sat down beside Stump with a piece of the bear meat to eat and the last cup of coffee in the pot. The coffee was bitter. He added a little water to it and sipped it feeling tired and almost old. As the fires turned to embers and died, he covered the ashes with dirt to hide them. The small fire in his hut was crackling and gave a yellow glow as he and Stump went inside for the night. Ben picked up his Bible. He had not taken time to read since Stump was badly injured. Now his prayers were prayers of thanksgiving and joy as he looked over at his recuperating friend. He read psalms of praise

"Father, I know you sent Jed to help us. Thank you, for answering my prayers and thank You that Stump is getting well now."

"Tomorrow, your stitches come out Stump. It will hurt but I have to do it," said Ben. They lay near each other on top of the quilt and the warm night slipped away.

The morning air was warm with very little breeze. The hut was hot from the banked fire, but it still had to be fed if he wanted to keep it going. Ben added a few pieces of oak, knowing that the hard wood burned slowly.

With the door flap open wide to give air and light, he gathered together everything he would need to remove Stump's stitches. His mother's small sewing scissors lay on the quilt; and nearby set a pan containing a new poultice. Ben had also prepared the broth with willow bark. He pulled over the soft piece of leather Jed had left.

"Well let's get started," he said, as he unwrapped Stumps sore side.

‹header›More Than Survival

"Lord, help me do this as painlessly as possible for Stump."

Stump lay very still on his right side, seeming to realize that it was necessary. The bright red stripes had cooled to brown. He knew that pink skin would soon replace the damaged area around the claw marks. Ben's hand shook as he reached toward the black thread to snip the first stitch with just the tip of his mother's sewing scissors.

"I can do all things through Christ who strengthens me," he murmured, as he snipped one stitch after the other. Ben bent low and felt with his tongue until the first thread was between his teeth. He jerked upward and had the first stitch out. Two bright dots of blood appeared where the stitch had been. He placed his left hand on the dog's head and bent low again. He continued until all the threads lay in a small pile on the corner of the quilt. Both Ben and Stump were sweating from the effort. Stump was panting hard but remained as still as he could, sensing that Ben was helping him.

Although he couldn't help but twitch a little as each stitch was jerked out, Stump didn't try to move away. Quickly Ben washed the area with the liquid and applied the poultice, covering it with the soft leather and then held it on this time with a strip from the old sheet he had washed.

"You were such a brave and good boy, Stump. The job is finished and I am glad that it is over. I know it hurt. Come boy. Let's go outside where it is cooler." Ben gave Stump the bowl of medicated broth and a piece of meat along with a pan of water. He praised and petted Stump as he coaxed him into the shade.

"You were very good in there. You are a very good boy." Ben hurried to the river's edge.

"Now it's my turn," he said as he took a drink of water from the river and splashed his face, hair and bare chest. It felt cold and refreshing against his overheated skin. His old

74

shirt was very ragged and missing a sleeve but he scrubbed it anyway and put it on a bush to dry.

I better get to work on the bearskin, if I want it to be soft for winter, he thought. He felt almost happy inside as he brushed the big fur with a brush made from the stems of cut grass.

For the first time since he had lost his family, he didn't have to fight sadness and anger because his focus was on the fact that Stump was going to live and it was possible that Jed would return in the fall.

His thoughts drifted to his parents and he decided to go back to the big oak tree, where they were buried. Under the cross he carved their names, Josiah and Mary Slater, and the year, 1861. He returned to his camp and worked on the bearskin until the day grew too hot. Stump had moved deeper in the shade of the trees at the edge of the camp and was asleep. Ben headed for the river. He pulled his trousers off and rinsed them before wading in, first floating for a while, letting the cool water carry him. It took strong strokes to bring him back to see Stump shaking the water off his coat. His bandage was loose and hanging in the mud. Ben put his arms around the dog and hugged him.

"Guess you needed a swim, too." The big tail wagged as Ben removed the soggy bandage. The wounds were healing and had a pattern of little red dots down each side.

"I think we should leave this off," he said. He scrubbed the strip of cloth from the sheet and the piece of leather in the river and then laid the cloth on the big rock to dry. He thought he would never get the pieces of leather as soft as they had been when Jed brought them, but he couldn't bring himself to discard anything. He might need them again. He pegged them near the deer and bearskin. Jed had left two very soft pieces of leather and Ben wanted to take care of them. I hope I never need them for bandages for Stump again, he thought.

Earlier when Ben came out of the water he had noticed a rock that had a deep, natural depression in it. I can turn that into a candle, he thought. All I need to do is fill that hallow with bear fat. I can make a wick by twisting several loose threads from the edge of the sheet. A candle will be useful.

After pulling his trousers on, he carried the rock up to the hut. Ben sat down in the cool shade where Stump had been sleeping earlier.

"Here Stump, let's have a piece of this bear meat while we sit here." They enjoyed their meal and before long they both were asleep in the shade.

As he drifted into sleep Ben had been thinking about the warm clothes he would need for winter. He dreamed that he was walking through deep snow in his bare feet. They were so very cold. He woke with a start to find that a cool breeze had come up and it was evening.

"I do need to make foot coverings before winter. I don't have a pair of shoes at all and I am going to need snowshoes, warm trousers, and a shirt and a coat, hat and hand coverings. How will I ever do it all?" he said out loud. Stump was puzzled by the words but he wagged his tail in response.

That evening as he was reading he realized that God would help him. Matthew 6:28-29 NIV "And why do you worry about clothes? See how the lilies of the field grow. They do not labor or spin. Yet I tell you that not even Solomon in all his splendor was dressed like one of these."

"He will fill my need for clothes as He has with other things. I am worrying for nothing. God has provided everything we need. All I have to do is my part. He will do the rest. The lilies of the field are clothed by God, and so will I be," said Ben to Stump. The dog replied with his usual "wag, wag, and a quick little lick, that made Ben laugh."

The next few days were so hot that he and stump made only short walks to the lake or out on the prairie past the bluff. Ben stopped often to rest so that Stump would not get overtired. Ever aware of his surroundings, Ben gathered roots and leaves that he knew were edible. He gathered some of the leaves that Jed had suggested for tea. He killed a rattlesnake with a huge rock and made an interesting stew with the meat. The skin was scraped and hung inside to dry. He wanted to be sure that a bird didn't carry it away.

"That could be a trim on my hat," he told Stump as he hooked it up on the branches that formed the ceiling.

Ben's collection of small hides continued to grow. He wanted thick hide like that of a horse or buffalo for his boots, but couldn't even imagine how he would get that, until one day as he and Stump wandered the prairie; he noticed buzzards circling in the distance.

"We should go see what is getting all the attention," he said.

As they drew near they found a horse had broken its leg in a prairie dog hole and had died there. The meat was sure to be bad but the hide would make a good contribution to his stack of leather.

"Thank you God," he said. "It's sad about the horse dying though. It is easy to skin the topside but I am having a tough time rolling him over to complete the job. If this were a tree I would ask you to help me like you did in camp, Stump. I'll take the hooves to boil for glue, and cut the hair from the mane and tail. I can use it to add strength when I make rope or cord." The pillowcase he had brought was getting heavy as he added the last hoof.

"I think I have all that I can carry, Stump. Let's head back."

When Ben lifted the rolled hide to his shoulder he realized just how heavy it was and just how bad an odor it had.

"Whew! This isn't going to be fun to carry," he said to Stump, as he adjusted the load on his shoulder.

"I'll be happy to put this down when we reach camp. It was a struggle to return to camp. The load was nearly more than he could handle for such a distance.

As he pushed the raft across the river, he prayed.

"Thank you, Father, for this large, strong hide. This is a blessing."

Stump was tired when they got back and after a long drink from the river, he was glad to settle in the shade for a nap.

Ben dropped the hide at the edge of the river. Maybe I can wash some of the stink off of it, he thought. He scrubbed it on both sides with sand and sloshed it back and forth until his exhausted arms could do no more.

"There, that should help some," he said. He staked it out and after a few minutes rest, began to scrape it the same way he had the bear's skin. The stone he had used to rub the fat into the bear skin lay in the grass nearby. He had worked nearly two hours scraping, and now he was able to coat it with the rendered bear grease. He rubbed hard with the stone to work it into the hide. Most of the water had quickly evaporated as the sun hit full on it and the wind blew gently.

"After I clean up the scrapings with the shovel, I'll take a break and get a drink of water. I praise You, Almighty God, maker of heaven and earth and I thank You for the strong hide. I can already picture the boots that I can make from it."

Now that the hide can be left to dry, I need a bath, he thought. Once again he jumped in the river, with his trousers on and scrubbed them with sand and then pealed them off and spread them on the big rock to dry. He swam for a while and enjoyed the leisurely feeling for a few minutes.

"I am bone weary," he said to Stump as he pushed the water from his skin and wrapped the old sheet around his waist. He was amused with himself as he observed that his top half was very brown and the bottom half was white until he looked at his feet. They were darker than his hands or arms. I guess they get the most sun.

Ben had taken time to put a rabbit on to cook and it smelled good. It was then that he realized that the bad smell from the hide was completely gone from his campsite.

"Thank you Jesus, the bad smell has disappeared, from that hide! I know sometimes my feet get a little stinky in the wintertime in shoes, but I didn't want them to smell like that dead horse all the time!" He laughed out loud. It feels good to laugh, he thought, and then he thought of his father and mother and a great sadness came over him again. He felt guilty for laughing.

"You would have liked it here. You picked a good place, Father. I will make it. I will be ready for winter and you will be proud of me," he said softly, accepting his raw emotions, as tears made their way down his face. He was tired and hungry and once again feeling lonely and vulnerable.

Ben put some of the greens he had collected in a pan of water and added coltsfoot leaves for a salty taste without having to use his precious supply of salt. He had seen his mother use it and liked how it tasted. He was glad that he had found a generous supply growing near the lake.

Ben shared the rabbit with Stump and as he looked over at him, he wondered how long it would take for the hair to begin to cover Stump's scars. Ben reached over and put a layer of grease on them. Stump tried to lick it off but Ben told him to leave it on there. After a few tries and Ben's hand gently pushing his muzzle away with a firm, "No," Stump decided that he would leave the grease there for now.

When it grew dark, Ben was eager to try the stone lamp. He had chipped the well inside even deeper. With a burning twig from the fire, he lit the ends of the twisted threads. They quickly burned an inch down until the fire reached the edge of the congealed fat and there it continued to burn, melting a small puddle.

"It works," he said out loud. Ben was delighted.

Stump returned to camp, bringing back his catch and placed it beside Ben. He had provided a meal twice over the past few weeks. This time it was a ptarmigan. Ben praised the dog and hugged him. "Stump you are such a good helper. I will clean this and put it where it will cook very slowly from the heat of the coals during the night. If it is wrapped in wet leaves and then coated with clay it won't dry out. Stump I am learning so many things. This will be ready for our breakfast."

When the fire was banked, he crawled under the quilt and fell asleep. His bed now had the deer hide over soft bundles of grass. It was too hot for the bearskin and he still was working on it anyway. He wanted it to be super soft and as clean as he could make it.

A deep growl from Stump woke Ben in the early light. He lay still listening but didn't hear a thing. Then suddenly he saw the silhouette of a wolf in the glow of the fire. The wolf was only a few feet away in the doorway of the hut! Ben thought that the smell of cooking and the raw horsehide stretched on the ground outside had brought a wolf to investigate. The smell of the human and fire inside, along with Stump's growl kept it from completely entering. Ben reached for his bow and as he did, the end of it hit the empty big pan sitting on the floor. A big "clang" sent the wolf scurrying away. She had never heard such a sound before.

"Well that was a happy accident," said Ben. "I really didn't want to hurt her. She looks a lot like you, Stump." He wondered why she had dared to come to his hut.

"I better bring the hides in and put the branches across the door at night. I have been getting careless about doing that."

When Ben went outside he heard thunder and the sky threatened to dump rain at any minute. He dashed to roll up the horsehide and bearskin and take them in. The rain started falling just as he got inside. He realized then that Stump was gone again. He has been venturing off on his own quite a bit lately, thought Ben. He added wood to the fire and made a cup of mint tea and nibbled at meat. I wonder what I can do today, he thought as he looked out at the gray sky and falling rain.

He glanced at the stick he had made with the marks of the days and saw that it was Sunday again. Ben read from his Bible often, in the evenings by the fire. He had honored the Lord's Day five times; since he had made his calendar stick and this would be the sixth. He had been tempted to count back as far as he could but decided that the day he had declared his first Sunday in the hut was a good place to begin. He began to read in 2 Timothy, 1:7 NIV. "For the spirit God gave us does not make us timid, but gives us power, love, and self-discipline."

"I was certainly afraid last night when I woke up and that wolf was coming in our door. Lord, I can feel your power in the mountains, and woods and in the thunder and rain, and your love sent Stump to me, and Jed to help make him well. And the part about self-discipline, Lord, all I can think of is that I need you to give me wisdom so that I can do what I must to make it through winter. I promise I will continue to do all that I can. Help me Lord and be here with me, Amen." Ben continued to read as the rain fell. Later as he peeked out he discovered puddles and sunshine. That rain was short and sweet, he thought. The clouds were clearing. It was going to be a beautiful Sunday afternoon.

"I will take my bow and arrows, the pillowcase and leather pouch and go for a walk. He had been using the pouch for water since Jed left it, even though it didn't have a way to close it. If he filled it just half full, it was enough for them both to have a drink. Ben headed out knowing that it didn't matter which way he headed. I want to find more greens and roots to dry, and watch for game. I know that Stump can find me when he wants to, he thought.

Ben had baked and eaten the wrinkled squash from the wagon as soon as he had found it. He had taken the raw seeds and pushed them into the moist soil near the lake. I should check on them to see if they are growing, he thought, as he followed the trail and walked under the tree where he and Stump had fought the bear, he couldn't help feeling like someone or something was watching him. He was more alert and watchful, since that encounter, considering what unseen animal might be lurking in the trees or bushes.

"Jesus, I am so glad that you are here with me," he said, and then he softly hummed a song that he had learned years earlier. It made him feel brave as he walked along.

Ducks still dotted the little lake, but not quite as many as there had been. Some had left and he and Stump had taken a total of six.

Before winter they would all be gone. He watched as a string of little ducklings followed their mother into the reeds and disappeared. That must be where she has her nest, he thought. She just took them out for a swimming lesson. They are cute, he thought.

The next thing Ben knew he had been knocked to the ground as Stump's big tongue washed his face.

"Oh Stump! What a greeting! Where have you been and what have you been doing? You are soaking wet and smell almost as bad as that horse did!" The dog bounded back and forth and barked with joyful victory at finding the young man that he loved.

"Let's go up the hill and into the woods and see what is there."

They circled the small lake finding their feet quite muddy by the time they walked into the shade of the woods. They could hear the "chip, chip" of the squirrels above them in the trees. Ben watched the ground for tracks as they pushed their way through the undergrowth. The tangle changed to an inviting clearing with soft green grass.

"Let's sit down." He said, patting the grass. With his back leaning against a tree, Ben studied the trees and bushes to learn what was there. He discovered that an old maple was providing his backrest. This will give good syrup later this fall, he thought, patting its trunk. He heard buzzing, but couldn't quite figure out where it was coming from until he stood up. To the left of the clearing was a gnarled old tree that had fallen recently. A bush lay flattened into the tall grass. It had enjoyed its shelter, until a recent wind had brought the tree crashing down. Bees were coming and going from a wide crack in the trunk. One side of the tree was cracked open and a beautiful amber honey was oozing from it. Ben dipped his finger in it and licked it off.

"Yum," he said. "This is wonderful stuff." He stuck his finger in again and offered it to Stump who really enjoyed the sweet treat.

"We have got to bring back the big pan and get some of this," he said. "That will taste good in the tea this winter."

They walked a little farther, and then Ben turned toward the river, pulling leaves from the tips of raspberry bushes and plants that he recognized as good for tea. He picked the center, curled fronds of the fennel ferns, knowing they were good to eat fresh or dried. Jed had taught him a lot in just a short time. As he walked along he thought of the clothes he wanted to make, and wondered just how he should go about it. Even though it wasn't the last of summer now, he knew that it would be fall sooner than he wanted. I dread winter's cold, snow, and confinement, he thought.

What he didn't realize as he strolled along was that he was beginning to think of the area as his. Each time he walked a trail or climbed a small hill, it became part his, as surely as an animal develops a sense of ownership for its territory.

That night as he sat with Stump by the fire, Ben thought of the discoveries he had made and how much the land offered.

"Father, you have put many food sources here. All I need to do is work hard to discover them. The honey is wonderful. You know how much I like sweets."

Ben stretched out on top of his bed and felt Stump's big head settle on his leg.

"Thank you God, I have had a really good day. Good night Stump." He went to sleep instantly.

The next day the sun rose hot above the plains as he started out with the big pan and his father's small hatchet to claim a share of the honey. He was barely aware of circling the lake, or entering the woods. He was focused on the task at hand. The clearing lay ahead.

"Something has changed," he said. The downed bee tree had been moved and split wide open. Big gashes marked its bark where claws had raked it.

"A bear found this last night after I left," he moaned.

"I should have brought the pan back right away. He ate all of it, I think.

There was still a small section of undisturbed bark left on the upper part of the tree trunk. Ben pried it open and was rewarded by finding an unbroken section of comb, full of golden honey.

"I'll just cut the comb loose with my knife and drop the whole sticky mess in the pan." Licking his fingers, he collected other bits of wax, that clung inside the tree and before he realized it, the pan was more than half full and he hadn't gotten stung. The bees had all moved on.

Then he wondered where the bees were.

"Maybe we will find where they have gone, before all of this is used up," he said to Stump. When he looked around he discovered that Stump was not in sight. I wonder where he goes, Ben thought as he walked back to camp carrying his golden treasure. He put the pan inside and laid his mother's skirt over the top to keep flies out. I need something to store the honey in so that I can still use the pan, he thought.

He decided it would be easier to hollow out a section of tree limb than to try to make a basket the way Jed had. If I did get one made it would probably leak honey all over the place, he thought. That might be a good craft to work on this winter when I am inside and bored. I should collect some grass and put it inside to practice on.

After wandering around a while he found just the big branch that he needed for the honey pot. He chopped it to the right length, and carried it back to the area in front of the hut. There he sat down and started with the chisel and hammer to remove a flat piece to form a cover. The branch rolled back and forth and work was slow.

"I need it to be flat on the bottom so that the honey won't spill and that will also make it easier to work on," he said out loud. He turned it over and chiseled off a flat plain. When it grew late he set his project aside to make a meal.

Ben went fishing and he had two big fish frying when Stump returned looking quite pleased and tired.

A broken stone at the edge of the river gave Ben an idea. He tried to scrape the wood of the honey container with the stone's sharp edge. It made a much smoother surface and was easier to control. After his meal he had hot tea and added a little honey to it. A bit of the wax dropped in the tea and became malleable.

"That's what I will do with the wax," he said. "I'll melt it and coat the inside of the wooden honey box and cover, so that they are smooth and it will help the cover to seal."

One morning when Ben was just waking up, he saw Stump head out of the flap of the hut. I am going to follow as quietly as I can, he thought. Stump was following the trail to the lake. As it turned around some large pines he had disappeared. The trail continued on but Stump wasn't on it. He has to be here somewhere. The bluff blocks him from going very far in that direction, thought Ben. He moved slowly peering under the pines and around large boulders until he saw what looked like a small cave at the base of the bluff. Ben was silent as he approached slowly. He heard movement and whimpers. By crouching, he could glimpse inside. There in the cool shade of the den was Stump and a wolf that looked the same size as the one that had visited his hut. Ben wasn't sure but he thought he saw pups. He backed away so that the mother would not feel that her cubs were being threatened. She had spotted him and was starting to growl.

"So this is where you have been going. Have you been helping provide for this lone wolf and her family, Stump?" He questioned, but he already had the answer. He could see that Stump was an accepted member of the little den. Stump's tail was wagging as he stood in the mouth of the den looking at Ben. Ben headed back up the path to camp. He felt like whistling. He didn't know why he felt so happy but he did.

Stump was gone most of the day, but came back in time to eat a meal with Ben and sleep on the bed with him. Stump somehow had become a friend to the lone female wolf, hunting for her and her cubs. Something must have happened to her mate. That is why he comes back to camp hungry. When he does catch food, he gives it to her, thought Ben.

"I am grateful that Stump still comes back at night and thinks of the hut as his home. Thank you, Father."

CHAPTER FIVE
INDIANS AND GINGER

Awake in the night, as his small fire warmed the hut and crackled softly, Ben considered a trip. I should go farther up on the prairie or maybe down river to the place Jed had mentioned, where another river joins this one. Perhaps, I could follow the trail to find out for sure what happened to the wagon train. There are possible adventures in every direction. It's hard to decide which way to go but I need to expand my territory and range farther from camp to see what is available.

Ben started to plan what he would need to take with him.

"Water won't be easy if I leave the river, but food isn't a problem. I can take dried meat and I can find greens along the way. I will need to take the rope, knife, bow and arrows. Most of the stuff can be packed inside the quilt and tied on my back like a pack with the rope. I'll take a small pan for Stump, the big pan to cook in, pillowcase and the leather pouch. Father's hatchet would come in handy if I need to cut wood. I think I'll take the deer hide, too, in case the weather gets bad. I can use it over us as a small tent. I wish I had a horse to help carry all that."

Ben had gotten in the habit of speaking to God out loud.

"With you along, I know that I will be safe and on the right track," said Ben.

"I would appreciate it, if you would put an angel on guard here while we are gone. I don't want to come back to any surprises." He had mentally put the Bible on the list of things to take. "I don't want to be without that," he said, as he finally drifted off to sleep.

He was eager to be underway, and was out of the hut at daybreak. Dragging his hide and quilt out into the open, he began to collect things to take. Stump knew that something different was happening and bounded around happily, grabbing a corner of the quilt and trying to pull the whole thing.

"No Stump. Don't do that! We aren't playing a game of tug and pull. I am going on a trip and you should come with me. It will be fun. Do you think your wolf friends will be all right for a few days without you? Of course they will. She is probably a very good hunter, too."

Stump barked and trotted back and forth near the growing stack on the quilt. Ben handed Stump a piece of dried bear meat and tucked one in his pocket, as he added some to his pack. He walked to the river and took a long drink and then bent lower and ducked his head in the water and washed his face and flipped his head back so that his soggy, nearly-white blond hair laid dripping on his bare back.

"I'm going to tie my hair back the way Jed had his," he said to Stump. He cut a narrow strip of rabbit fur. Smoothing his hair back, he wrapped the fur around his hair several times and tied it. "There, that is a lot better," he said.

He returned to the quilt folding the sides up and placed it on top of the deer hide. He folded it into a square bundle. Figuring out how to lash it together so that the rope turned the whole thing into a comfortable backpack took several tries. He checked inside the hut and all the rest of his food was secured in the two caches.

"To be extra sure that nothing can get in them I think I should place the stones I use to hold up my table, on top of the slate lids." As he worked, Ben felt a peace and joy in his heart.

"I am so grateful Lord that I have a home, and I can leave and know that it is here for me when I come back," he said, as he placed the last stone where he wanted it.

He rolled up all his hides, even the heavy bearskin, and tied them on the high branches of his ceiling. He didn't want any critters chewing on them while he was gone. The fire was out. I better stir the ashes to be sure, he thought.

"Good it is totally out."

Ben closed the flap and tied it tightly, putting the boards from the wagon seat against the doorway and several stones against the bottom. Stump pranced around excitedly, eager to see what they would do next.

"Finally, we are on our way. Heavenly Father, please bless our journey and keep us safe. Guide us. Thank you for this beautiful day and my hut to welcome us when we come back." They headed out across the river. The raft kept the backpack dry but Stump stayed at his side and preferred to swim across, shaking the cold water off in sprays that sparkled in the early morning light. The river was cold and left Ben shivering as he walked through the dense shade of the big oak and out into the tall shining prairie grass. Some of the grass reached his waist. It was an awesome sight to see it move slowly rippling in the gentle breeze. The sun felt good as it dried him. Before long Ben found he was following a game trail that headed out over the prairie. He whistled as he walked along at a brisk pace, with Stump darting this way and that, investigating under bushes and sniffing everything, disappearing here and reappearing elsewhere.

Far in the distance, down river, a gentle rise appeared. It appeared a darker green. Ben headed that way. Midday grew hot and he stopped to munch a few handfuls of young, wild grain heads that grew in abundance. He sipped water from the leather pouch and offered some to Stump from the small pan.

"I think we will find water ahead, but I don't want to be completely out, so let's use it sparingly. We can rest here for a while. The breeze feels cool here in the shade of the bushes. We will have to find a sheltered place later, to spend the night."

It had appeared to be a dark green hill in the early morning, but proved to be tall trees in many shades of their summer green.

"Stump, can you hear that? I thought we would find water without going back to the river. I can hear bubbling water." Stump ran ahead and plunged into the spring fed pool, paddling in circles. The pool wasn't very large, but it was clear, deep and refreshing. Removing his pack, Ben took the pouch to the rocks where the water bubbled out and cascaded down into the pool. He rinsed it and filled it taking a long cool drink.

Ben lifted his head to listen. Stump left the water and had come to his side giving his low rumbling growl of warning. Something or someone was coming! Ben grabbed his pack in one hand and Stumps fur at his neckline in the other and raced for the cover of a line of bushes.

Just as he managed to get both of them hidden, a young woman came into view at the pool. She was short and appeared strong, with brown skin and loose, long black hair. She filled a large crock with water, as it poured from the rock, and then lifted it onto her shoulder, turned, and walked back the way she had come. She had not been aware of their presence. He was grateful for that.

"Now I realize how foolish I was to just wander in without cautiously checking the area first. What would have happened if we had been discovered? We are on the edge of an Indian camp! How could I be so careless?" He was scolding himself. "Thank you, Father, for protecting us."

He hadn't let go of Stump. He guided him back out of the trees the same way they had entered. He checked left and right to be sure that no one was in sight. Then he walked, just inside the tree line going to his right, away from the spring and the threat of discovery. Thanking God for protecting them as he went, he kept Stump jogging along beside him until both felt more relaxed.

Ben sat down under a tree to rest.

"Could that be the tribe that took Sarah? I have to go back and see if she is there," he said to Stump. I wonder if Stump would stay here with the pack. If he follows me, they would probably spot both of us. If I tie him with the rope he could chew through it and come bounding up at just the worst possible moment, he thought. He sat against the trunk of a tree and waited for the cover of darkness.

"I have to go back there, Stump. I need you to stay here and guard the pack. Do you understand? Guard the pack and don't follow me. Stay here, boy." He patted Stumps head and handed him a piece of dried bear meat so he wouldn't wander off if he got hungry, and poured a little water in the pan for him. He might decide he has to go hunting if he waits here without food, thought Ben. Stump seemed to understand. He lay down next to the pack and began to chew his dried meat.

The night was dark with only a slice of a moon that slid in and out of clouds. Ben tried to be careful and quiet, but he tripped over roots and scratched his feet. Overhead the branches slapped his face or poked his body as he made his way back through the trees. He stopped several times to listen behind him, making sure that Stump was not following.

"Lord, I'm glad that you are with me. This is pretty scary," he said softly.

The trickling, tinkling sound of the falling water ahead gave him direction. He found the pool, circled it and finally, just as he crept slowly down the path that the girl had taken, the partial moon came out from behind the clouds and provided a dim light. Ben could see the campfire and smell food cooking, as he got nearer. Four women were seated on logs and blankets beside a small cooking fire. One woman held a sleeping baby, in her arms. Another child lay on a blanket near her, its black hair shining in the firelight.

These people were short and big boned, not at all like the taller, lean raiders that had attacked the wagon. Four tents stood in the clearing.

A man came out of the largest tent followed by two others. They joined the group at the fire. One said something and everyone laughed. Ben could see that Sarah was not there. He longed to know where she had been taken. Oh Sarah, where are you? He thought.

Ben made his way back to Stump to find him patiently waiting. He hugged him and scratched his ears and lavished him with praise.

"You are such a good dog. You did just what I asked. Good boy, Stump." Ben sat down in the grass beside Stump. He leaned against the same big tree trunk with his arm around Stump and there they slept until at first light they moved out. Although the night had not been restful, it had been filled with adventure. Ben felt good. Stump jumped under a bush and came out with a plump pheasant. He brought it to Ben still squawking. Ben pulled one of the beautiful tail feathers and released it into the sky. "Sorry Stump, you are a good boy and a good hunter. If I was stopping long enough to make a fire, that would be a great meal but I don't want to eat it raw. Stump enjoyed his breakfast of bear jerky and they moved on.

Toward noon the tall prairie grasses gave way to a shorter, bright green grass, covering a soft ground that became quite sticky. There seemed to be no higher ground in this direction. They were walking into a swamp or backwater. He didn't like walking in this wet area and felt that it could actually get dangerous if it became any softer. His feet sank in farther with every step. He was turning around when he heard a soft whinny.

A foal was stuck in the mud! It had thrashed trying to free itself and now the mud was almost to the middle of its chest.

"The mud is getting deeper and more dangerous, just as I thought it might. God, show me how to help the poor little thing!" he said out loud.

He signaled for Stump to stop with his hand.

"Stop, Stay boy, I know this isn't a very good place to wait, but I need to try to save that foal. Stay here Stump. Good boy, Stay." He didn't want him to get stuck, too. Ben looked around for something to use to stabilize a path to the little horse. Several dead trees lay on their sides not far away. The mud sucked at Ben's bare feet as he made his way to the closest one. I need to hook my pack between the branches so I don't have its weight to deal with. If I break off as many branches as I can carry, I can work my way to the foal, by laying the branches down and stepping on them, he thought. Ben had to go back and get more. He continued until he had made a path in front of her.

Going back to the tree, he got his rope from the bundle.

"I hope that the quilt will keep things up out of the mud; I need the deerskin, too," he said in Stumps direction. Stump stood where he had left him with mud up to his knees, tail down. "Good boy Stump. Stay there." Returning to the foal, he laid the hide on top of the branches in front of her, and as he did he placed his hand near her muzzle so she could get his scent.

"See little one, I am just a human. I won't hurt you. I am going to try to get you out of this mess. "Easy there, easy, steady," he breathed softly. "Don't try to move now. Rest a minute while I do something. That's it. Good little one." Ben placed the end of the rope in his right hand and plunged it down into the mud following her body around her stomach. With his left hand he circled over her back and pushed down into the mud searching for his right hand and the end of the rope. He pulled it up forming a loop around her body just behind her front legs. He eased forward until he was in front of the exhausted animal. Even with the help of the many branches he was standing in mud up to his knees. She had struggled against the mud for hours.

Her mother must have finally left with the herd when it became clear to them that her baby was lost to her. I think that horses usually stay away from places like this. Something or someone must have chased them, he thought.

This little foal would soon be easy prey for the next big predator that comes along, he thought.

"Father I want to help this foal to get out of this awful mud. It needs protection." Ben spoke soothingly to the frightened baby as he positioned the rope.

"It will be better soon little baby horse. I know you are tired and frightened. We will help you. Please help me lift this foal out, Lord. It is so afraid and tired. I want to do it right the first time. Help me to lift, Lord." He pulled up and forward, with his arms and the rope until finally her front feet came up far enough to hook on the hide and branches that he had placed on the surface. With the encouragement of something a bit more stable in front of her, she gave one last lunge forward and was rewarded by a large sucking sound as her body pulled free. She slid onto the hide and collapsed onto her belly. She had used the last ounce of her strength. She was spent.

Her eyes were stretched wide open in panic, with ears pulled back against her head; she gave a scream of terror mixed with relief. Her sides heaved as she breathed with labored effort. Ben saw and understood the little foal's distress.

"The worst is over. You are going to be all right. Thank you, Lord." Ben lifted her up in his arms and staggered with her weight and the unsteady footing as he eased forward to safer ground. Step by small step, slowly he balanced each step until he laid her beside Stump and gently pulled the rope off her middle and placed it around her neck and tied it. The other end he tied around Stumps neck, telling him to guard her while he went back for the deer hide. When he turned to look, the foal still lay on her side and Stump was busy licking her face clean. She was comforted by the gentle attention.

The bundle and hide had to be retrieved before returning to her side. She needs food soon or she will die, he thought and I need to get her up on drier ground but I can't carry her all the way. I think I can fashion a travois with the branches of the tree. Soon he had chopped two poles from the branches, and tied the hide between them. He placed her on it and gently secured her and his bundle. This should make it possible to take her. He stepped between the poles and lifted the front of the travois and pulled. Ben pulled harder and finally it slid forward with difficulty, leaving two deep furrows in the mud.

Once it was moving, it wasn't as hard to set a rapid pace pulling in the direction of the river that would lead them home. When he found that the wild grain again surrounded them, he stopped long enough to use his knife to gather a large bundle of the stems with the seed heads attached.

"This is the only thing I can think of that I can use for food for you, little horse." He tucked the bundle of grain into the quilt.

When he reached the shade of the trees at the river's edge, he followed along until he found a place where the water had formed a hollow in the bank and the edge of the river was firm gravel. He pulled the travois down near the water and stopped, setting it down gently. The foal lifted her head as he freed her from the travois. With what seemed like a great effort she tried to stand up but failed. Ben lifted her off the hide and helped her stand at the water's edge. She drank some water and then staggered as she walked slowly to the grass a few feet away and again lay down on her side.

Ben arranged wood and twigs and cut a few shavings that would burn easily in the hollow of the bank. Then he hunted for a stick he could use to start a fire. I need a fire to prepare food for this baby, if she is to live. He twirled the stick but was a long time getting a good ember.

"Come on fire, light!" He commanded. A few minutes later, with a small fire crackling, he gathered more dry wood in a pile nearby.

He pulled the bundle of grain and the small pan from the quilt.

"I think I need to grind the grain heads fine enough so that they will cook into a mash that the foal can accept. It won't be mother's milk but it is all I have," he said to her. It seemed to ease his anxiety, to express his thoughts out loud. He picked up a smooth stone and crushed the grain against the bottom of the pan. After adding water, he set the pan next to the small fire. It would soon be boiling.

Everything he looked at was covered with mud and so was he. Stump had gone swimming and shook hard as he approached.

"Well I see that you are a lot cleaner. Guess I need to do that, too." He spread the quilt out by the fire, untied the hide from the travois and entered the water dragging it behind him. He rinsed the mud from both sides of it and hurried it up onto the gravel.

"I don't want to totally soak it. Even after that dunking it will need to be worked or it will get hard and crack easily," he said. "I am wet and cold now anyway. I may as well clean the mud off of me, too." Ben dunked under the water and washed with the sand, untying his hair and giving it a good scrubbing too. He wrung the excess water from his hair and then scrubbed his trousers and smoothed them over the bank where the heat from the fire would quickly dry them. "The heat feels good," he said shivering, rubbing his hands down his legs, pushing the water off.

"Let's see if we can use the stems of the grass to make a brush. Will you let me gently clean the dry mud from your coat little horse?" He talked to her softly, trying to reassure her. She struggled to stand as he approached, but didn't try to move away. "This mud doesn't feel good. Does it?" He said as he gently brushed. "It probably itches. Look how clean you are getting. There, little girl. Your legs are still muddy, but I have cleaned the rest of you." Ben continued to softly run the brush over her neck and back, trying to give her comfort and win her confidence.

The wild grain mash had cooked down to a paste. He pulled it from the fire and added more water stirring it with a smooth stick.

"As soon as this cools you can try it. What do you think little girl? Will you eat some of this? I sure wish I had some milk for you," he said, as he brought the pan near her muzzle. She didn't know what to do with it but instead sought out his fingers and started to suck on them. She was beginning to trust him.

"Poor little baby girl, you are so hungry." He scooped some of the mash onto his fingers and let her suck again, then lowered his hand into the liquid in the pan. She sucked in a mouth full of the mash and jerked her head up. It surprised her! She reached for his fingers again and after a few tries she was able to suck the mash into her mouth without a problem. "That's a good girl; see that was pretty good wasn't it? I'm going to go pick more grain and get it cooking for you."

After pulling on his damp trousers and pulling his hair back and tying it, Ben went to collect more wild grain. He came back with armloads, stems and all.

"Hello little girl, this is for you. Easy, relax. That's a good girl." His voice was soft as he spoke to her. He talked as he used his knife to strip the immature grain heads from the stems and mashed the grain with the rock again. Soon a new batch of mash was cooking. Her eyes followed his every move.

Stump had been out investigating the area and returned with a rabbit. "You are such a good friend, Stump," he said, as he skinned the rabbit and put it on a green branch to roast over the fire. Stump trotted over to the foal and once again licked her face. She nodded her head up and down and backed up. He looked surprised to see how tall she was now that she was standing.

"It looks like we have a new friend, Stump. What should we call her? Maybe I'll call her Ginger? She is the color of gingerbread now that most of that mud has come off. Ginger. Yes, I like that name. Ginger. Do you like that name little girl? Can we name you Ginger?"

She made a gentle whinny as if to answer. Ben pulled the hide from the gravel onto the grass nearer the fire. He pulled a piece of fat from the dripping rabbit and used a smooth stone to work it into the drying hide.

As it grew dark, they heard a wolf howl in the distance. Ginger was afraid of the fire, but even more afraid of the wolves so she moved closer to the human and dog that had befriended her. Ben fed her again and got her to take a drink from the river. It had been a day that Ben would never forget.

"Father, this has been such a wonderful day. You have given me this beautiful foal. Thank you for helping me to get safely out of the mud and to bring her here where she can gain her strength back. Thank you for Stump, too. He is so special."

After gratefully sharing the cooked rabbit with Stump, the little group settled down for the night. Ben stayed alert while the animals slept. I feel so happy inside to have Ginger and Stump as friends, he thought.

"Thank you again, God, for letting me rescue her. Give me wisdom so that I can care for her properly," he prayed.

That night as the dark surrounded them, Ben realized that the animals were a great comfort to him. Ginger came close and lay in the grass beside the quilt. It isn't possible for me to rest here, thought Ben. I need to be on guard. A cougar could jump on Ginger and I couldn't stop it, or a pack of hungry wolves could come. I've got to stop thinking such things, he said sternly to himself.

"Father, I trust you. You are our protector. Guard us and increase my faith so that it is easier for me to trust." Just as he finished the prayer, an owl swooped down and sailed very near Ben's head. The sound of the air on the big bird's wings was the only warning Ben had. He ducked as it swung up and disappeared into the night. We must be near that owl's nest. I can't wait to get back to the hut," he thought with a bit of fear in his mind.

CHAPTER SIX
MOVING THE WAGON

Ginger had gained trust in her two new companions and accepted the wet greeting she received every time Stump returned to their temporary camp. Late the next afternoon he came bounding up with a pheasant in his mouth and dropped it at Ben's feet.

"Well my good boy, you have been hunting again. Thank you for our supper, Stump," he said as he patted him and scratched the big furry neck.

"While you have been hunting I have been busy, too gathering lots of good greens and grain. I have cooked lots of grain so that we have enough to feed Ginger tomorrow. We will be leaving for home early in the morning." Ben talked to Stump as he prepared the bird and placed it over the fire.

The pheasant was delicious, but only Ben enjoyed the greens he had used to stuff the bird. Stump turned down the portion offered to him. While out gathering grain, Ben had discovered wild spearmint growing. I want to gather a big bundle of this. It can wait a day to hang and dry inside the hut, when we get back, he thought. It will make good tea with my meals this winter.

"I haven't any idea how I will get Ginger back to the hut. I could sure use a bright idea right now, Lord. We have to cross the river. I could go all the way on this side until I get to camp and then put her on the raft, but she would be frightened and I might injure her trying to get her on."

Ben pondered the situation as they started out the next morning. I hope I can find a place that is shallow enough, maybe where it gets wider. I'll have to coax her to wade across. She is not going to like it. He made a note to watch for a place where they could cross safely.

Just as the sun peeked over the horizon, with his bundle on his back and an arm around Ginger's neck, Ben walked slowly toward his home with Ginger and Stump.

After a few minutes Ginger seemed to understand that they were traveling and didn't require Ben's arm around her neck at all. She walked along beside him and kept pace. She had traveled with her mother and the herd, and knew that staying together meant security. She trusted Ben and Stump. They were her herd, her family, now.

The unlikely trio stopped often so that Ginger wouldn't tire. Stump covered more ground than the others because he would go bounding here and there checking every new scent.

"Here is a spot where the river has widened and it runs slower. It is not as deep," he said to Ginger. "This may be the spot I have been looking for." He waded in first to check the bottom. "The feeling of the mud on the bottom will frighten Ginger, he thought. It is a safe place to cross if I can convince her and the other bank has a gentle grade up to green grass. I think this is as good as it is going to get."

He walked up to Ginger and placed his arm around her neck again. He scratched her ears and told her that she must cross the water with him. He let her suck his fingers for a moment for security, and then gently, he urged her into the water.

"Come on little girl. Come on Ginger. It is all right. I am right here and I will help you. Don't be afraid. I will always take care of you. See. You can do it." He could feel her muscles tense and her body tremble, as the cold water splashed against her and her feet sunk into the mud and sand beneath the water. He pulled her forward rather swiftly, talking to her, not allowing her to stop or turn back, and coaxing her to trust him. They scrambled up the other side and into the tall green grass.

She was so joyful that the experience was over that she trotted away and broke into a full run for a short burst. She returned to bunt Ben with her forehead.

"Hey," he laughed, "Are you celebrating? You are a good girl, Ginger. Yes, you are." Just then Stump bounded up next to them and shook a fountain of water over the group barking. He was having fun, too.

Ben scratched his ears and said "Come on, you two, we are nearly home." It took another hour before they rounded the last cluster of trees against the bluff and could see the green mound that was the hut. It was then that Ben noticed that summer had brought a growth of new grass to the top and sides of his hut.

"It looks like any other hill along the bottom of the bluff. That's great camouflage, God. Thank you. The mound looks like a hill that has always been there."

When he walked nearer the door, Ben could see that nothing had been disturbed.

"The stones and boards secure the door, just as I left it. Thank you Lord." He rolled the stones to the side and took down the boards and stepped into the dark hut.

He was waiting for his eyes to adjust to the dark inside when he felt a big push and Ginger walked in with a playful snort.

"Wait a minute girl; I'm not so sure that you should come in here." But where will she stay this winter? She needs a shelter. That is another job that I must complete before winter. I need to build her a barn or some place to stay." The responsibility he had accepted when he rescued her was resting heavily on his shoulders and he was feeling the weight of it.

"How am I going to take care of her and Stump? I don't even know how I am going to take care of myself. Jesus, this is going to take a lot of help from you to get us ready for winter. Please help me to take care of Ginger and Stump as they deserve and help me to gather enough food for all of us."

Ben opened his bundle. The mint is wilted. It doesn't seem like as much, he thought. He hung it on the end of a branch near the fire pit to dry. As he brought a pan out of his bundle, he found a head nudging under his arm searching for his fingers.

"Are you hungry again already?" he asked. He opened the pouch and scooped some of the mash into the pan, adding a little water from the barrel. Ginger followed him outside, knowing that lunch was on the way. He lowered his fingers into the mash and discovered that she was sucking the mash up without encouragement. He pulled his hand out and she continued to eat until the pan was empty. He was pleased that she had learned so quickly, but shocked by the quantity of food she required. I will need to collect tons of grain and grass for the winter, he thought.

"How will I ever get everything done? God, I'm so glad that we are back to the hut safely and I know that you will help me do what needs to be done."

Even as he said it, he was already designing a way to build a shelter for Ginger on the side of his hut. He would build it big enough so he could use part of it for storing her food and hay. He put his things in order in the hut, took the saw and walked into the big trees where he cut load after load of thick branches. By early evening he had a pile as high as the hut and almost as wide.

Ben was tired, hot and very hungry. He put the saw inside, and ran to the river and dove under the surface swimming strong strokes against the current and then let it carry him back. He climbed out and onto the big rock, enjoying the heat radiating from it. If I lay here I will fall asleep. It will soon be sundown. I better take the big pan and get some more grain, he thought. He slid off the rock and forced himself to gather enough grain for Ginger before it became dark.

Tomorrow, I will go out and gather more but for tonight this is enough. The fire took only a few minutes to start.

"I think I am getting better at this," he said to Ginger. Ben started the big pan heating and decided to transfer Ginger's mash to the leather pouch. In the big pan he cut pieces of dried deer meat and roots that he had dug coming back. He added some dandelion leaves, onions and colts foot. Then feeling adventurous he added a few of the wrinkled crabapples. It was nearly dark but he thought that if he hurried he would have time to set the snares before complete nightfall.

Returning to camp was a pleasure. As he neared the clearing, he found that it was covered with little twinkling lights. The ground all around him held little dots of pale light blinking off and on. The little bugs were making their position known.

Above his head, patterns of light appeared and disappeared among the tree branches as the male fireflies danced and courted the females below. Ben stood in awe at the spectacular show.

"This is a peculiar, beautiful, wonderful home, as unique as we are, but I am grateful for it and for you. We will all sleep out here tonight. We can watch the light show," he said to Ginger as he pulled the quilt and hide outside, near her.

Next he decided he would put his table back together, outside, near the fire pit. He brought out a spoon, a bowl and another pan and placed them on the table.

"There," he said, "all the comforts of home." He sat on the hide, relaxing for the first time since he had rescued Ginger. After the trip home and cutting the wood for her shelter, he was so tired that he nearly fell asleep watching the fireflies and waiting for the stew to finish cooking. The mash was done and he had put it off to the side.

It would be good, if I could take care of her and see her without going out into the snow if it is deep. She will need a big doorway for her to come and go and I want one from the hut to her area. He continued to plan as he prepared her food and then scooped the stew into his bowl and some in Stump's pan to cool.

"Lord, it is times when I am resting and eating that I miss my family the most. Mother always made such wonderful meals and took such good care of all of us. If she were here, this stew would taste a lot better; but right now, I would settle for nothing to eat, if I could just hug her. I miss my father so much. Now that I am big enough to work beside him and learn from him, he is gone. I wish I could show them the foal that I rescued. I never would have been able to do it, if you had not instilled in me, to trust my instincts and I learned from you father how to care for the animals, and God, I trust you to help me to raise her. Sarah would love that little horse."

Ben's heart was heavy, as he filled the small pan with mash and after very little coaxing, Ginger ate her meal unassisted. With her tummy full she soon slept on the grass near him. He placed a protective hand on her neck as Stump settled his head on Ben's leg.

"Sarah would have Ginger spoiled in no time. Lord, please give Sarah all she needs and a bit more. Give her love and joy. Thank you for looking after her, Lord. And, thank you for today. Everything went well."

The next morning, after feeding Ginger, Ben began fitting the branches together and fastening them with vines and cord. Ginger's new room was starting to take form.

"This isn't as difficult as it was when I built the hut. I have learned how to put the upright supports into holes and secure them with rocks to start a wall. That makes it a lot easier. I want to make it nearly as large as the main room of the hut so there is plenty of space for storage even when she is full grown," he said. Once again he was talking to God as he worked.

Ginger stayed near all day while Ben worked hard to get the walls and roof up. He thatched the roof with bundles of willow on top of the sturdy pine branches, and then tightly overlapped bundles of grass to cover the willow. The roof had enough slope to encourage the rain to run off.

"Your roof is as strong as the one on the main room, Ginger, and it will be waterproof." She came to him, anticipating a scratch or mash. "You have learned your name already. Haven't you?" He said, as he scratched her ears and hugged her.

Hidden by trees, a large section of the end-wall was left open. That was Ginger's doorway.

The work continued the next day. The rest of the walls were plugged with small branches and then with a clay and grass mixture to keep out the winter wind.

Ben trimmed two thick, long branches into smooth, tall posts and carried them into his hut. He planted them in the floor, forcing them against the ceiling in position to be the sides of his new doorway to Ginger's area. Cutting through the branches of his wall and the growing sod, had to be done carefully, so that the hut wall stayed strong, and everything remained securely in place. Once again he was shoveling dirt and dragging it into the woods until the side wall of his hut was exposed from the other side.

When the doorway was cut open, he was pleased by the amount of light that came in. I think when I can; I will make a window in the main room on the other side.

"My next step will be to cover the entire addition with dirt and sod, so that it will match the rest of our hill, but the prairie is dry. I can't do the sod now, but the dirt and sod that formed this side of the hill can go on top."

"I seem to have ideas that take a lot of work," he commented to Ginger, as he struggled to lift the last load of loose dirt up onto the bluff and poured it down onto the new addition.

It will take a big hide to cover her doorway, he thought. Ginger entered and laid contentedly in her new area with the fresh hay spread for her sleeping spot.

"Hey, you didn't even wait for an invitation. You are a smart girl. Somehow you knew that was for you. Didn't you?" Stump came in beside them, wagging and sniffing at everything and then he went back out.

Ben soon decided that the best place for the shovel was just inside the door to the new addition. It looks like cleaning up is going to be another daily chore for me, he thought. Ben had placed a large leaf covered branch in the new doorway to the main room to discourage Ginger from coming into the main hut. She wanted the security of his closeness now, but Ben knew that she would gain confidence with time. I want so much to be able to protect her and have her safe. Her new room will help with that and give her shelter.

"Father, I will do my best to feed her until she is big enough to graze on the prairie, but how can I keep her from all the dangers?" Ben knew there was only so much that he could do.

"Father, I cannot protect her. Only you can do that. Please watch over all of us and keep us safe here. She is part of our family now. Help her to grow strong, healthy and beautiful."

The days passed quickly. Ginger was growing. Ben went hunting but this time his arrow missed its mark and the deer jumped swiftly away. His daily walks, accompanied by the foal, and sometimes Stump, were gathering trips. He continued to learn the area and what it held. He didn't forget to thank God each time he found a new food source, or discovered another blessing that the area held.

Tomorrow, I need to check the wagon again and see if there is anything else that I can use, thought Ben.

In the early morning, as soon as he had fed Ginger and Stump, Ben took the raft over to the wagon, but when he decided that he wanted to dismantle the whole thing, he had to go back to camp for some tools. It was extremely difficult for him to remove the big bolts that held the wagon together.

"I could be stronger," he said, "or maybe a strong angel could help me, Lord. As I get each board off, I'll take it to the river and float it to the other side near the hut, that way it will give my arms and hands a rest from the bolts." Stump seemed to think the whole thing quite a lark and swam back across the first two times with Ben. After that, he thought it better to watch from the bank with Ginger. It took from early morning until dark but Ben brought every bit of the wagon back to camp, even the big greased logs used for axles.

As he worked steadily all day, he placed the nails and bolts in a neat pile.

"I will probably need some of these for something."

Next to that were other larger metal parts. He wasted nothing. When he took the next heavy board to the camp, he returned with a pan to use for transporting the nail pile and the sheet for the metal fittings. At sundown, nothing of the wagon remained on the other side of the river.

Searching the grass in the area, he made sure that he had found everything.

I am going to pick up every piece of the broken plates and cups, too. They will be pretty, pressed into the clay plaster I plan to put on the wall behind the fire pit, he thought.

"A little artistry won't hurt."

Ben struck his foot on a rusted tin box, hidden in the grass. He had to use his knife to pry it open. Inside were little wax paper pouches his mother had made. Each pack, held a different type of seeds. She had saved and labeled them, planning a garden at their new home. Tears filled his eyes.

"I am holding a treasure that you so carefully prepared. Thank you Mother," he said as he walked under the branches of the big oak tree where he had dug his parent's grave.

"It has been a really hard summer but with God's help, I'm going to make it. I miss you, Mother. I miss you; Father and I promise that one day I will find Sarah. With God's help, I will find her," he said, as his tears slid down his cheeks. "I really miss you," he said as he crossed the river holding the tin box high above the water.

He picked up another board.

"My shoulders are bruised from the weight of the heavy lumber. Jesus, now I know a little of what it felt like when you carried the cross for all of us." Ben carried the boards first on one shoulder and then on the other. It was dark by the time he had the entire pile of wood carried from the riverbank and placed in the hut. The longest ones he had to put in at an angle.

"This doesn't leave much room for walking around and I won't be able to get in that cache until I have used some of this lumber but this way, it is completely out of sight and will stay dry". The greased axles he leaned against a tree out of sight. "I don't want that black grease getting on stuff in the hut," he explained to Ginger as she sniffed the grease and backed up.

A full moon was shining over the trees. Absolutely nothing of the wagon remained on the other side, to mark his location. He was glad that he had done it for that reason, too, but at the moment he was already cutting pieces and making doors in his mind as he ate jerky and drank some hot mint tea with a little willow bark added to ease the discomfort in his shoulders.

"That was really hard work, God. I am very tired, but thank you for helping me to see the provision of lumber you had for me in the wagon. Thank you for the seeds. I will be able to plant a garden next spring."

Stump had curled up on the sleeping pallet, Ben had made from the hide, bearskin and quilt. It wasn't where it had been but it was soft, cozy and inviting.

After her batch of mash, Ginger slept on the hay in her new area. The night was quiet. As soon as Ben covered with the quilt, Stump adjusted his position so that he could lay his head on Ben's leg. I am so used to the weight of Stump's head that I wonder if I could sleep if it wasn't there, he thought. He reached down and gave Stump a scratch behind his ear.

"I love you, boy," he said softly as he drifted into a terrible dream. He had worked so long and hard on the wagon that his mind could not rest peacefully.

He was again sitting on the back of the wagon. He could hear his sister humming and playing with her doll inside. All the events of that horrible day replayed in every detail and he was reliving them. He heard the Indian's horses and shouts, and his father's rifle shot and Sarah's scream. He saw his father and mother lying in the grass, stained with their blood.

Next, he was scrambling through thorn covered bushes, injured and bleeding, as he ran yelling, "Sarah, Sarah," over and over.

Suddenly he woke with a cry, jerking into a sitting position. Stump jumped up and started barking. The glow of the banked fire and Stump brought Ben back to reality. He was covered in sweat but the night air drifting into the hut was cool. He walked to the doorway and opened the flap. A slight breeze stirred the leaves above him. A shimmer of moonlight touched the trees and outlined them against the night sky. Looking up at them and the stars, Ben lifted his mind and broken heart to God.

"Thank you, Lord that you are here with me. Thank you, for the trees, river, stars, Stump, Ginger and the hut." He paused, forcing himself to think what each one meant to him. "Thank you for the fire, the deer and for helping me every day. Thank you for watching over Sarah." The litany of thanksgiving and the cool night air had a soothing affect. He drank some of the left over tea and after a few minutes, he was able to calm his nerves enough to return to bed.

Ben slept peacefully the rest of the night and late into the morning. Ginger was out beyond the trees on the edge of the grass and Stump was off on one of his adventures.

When Ben sat up he felt rested but found that his shoulders were very sore, especially his left one where the arrow had injured it the day of the attack.

"I am hungry. What I need is a good breakfast," he said in the direction of the fire. "I'll make a large batch of mash and have a bowl of it with some honey on top. The rest will be for Ginger." I better stop talking out loud when no one is here or I might turn into one of those crazy people I've heard about, that mumble all day long and never make any sense. He grinned at the mental image of himself as an old man with a cane and beard, mumbling as he walked down a street in a small town, frightening women and children. He made more hot tea, and felt much better after his meal.

"I think I'll try to make the doors for your area, Ginger. The horsehide is large enough to make a good door for your outer entrance but I need to be sure to leave enough to use for my boot soles. The inner door between your area and mine will need to be wood and I want to make it in two parts so that the top can be open and just close the bottom, or close both to secure it from animals when we are gone."

I think the front door should be one solid door with strong leather hinges and a latch inside. I have lots of work to do, he thought. I better get busy.

The nails I saved from the wagon will be useful. Ben held up the hide to the outer opening. "I need a solid board across the top." It took a bit of experimentation since the wall was made of branches and not an even surface. "If I just nail the hide on, Ginger won't be able to push it aside to go in and out." He puzzled over it for a few minutes and then an idea blossomed. I will cut the hide into strips and nail them so that they overlap as they hang down. She likes to bunt me, so maybe it will be easy for her to push it open. I don't like cutting this big piece of leather into strips, it seems wasteful, but it will serve a good purpose. I hope I don't find that I need it for something else."

Once it was finished, Ginger came to exam it, not quite understanding the concept. He lifted it and she went in. She turned around and wanted to come back out but didn't know how to do it. She nudged it and pawed at the ground. She finally got the courage to give it a bunt and it swung out of her way but it promptly came back into position and bopped her on the nose. It was stiff, and heavy enough to work well. She tried again and brushed through. She was pleased and seemed to think that she had a new toy.

"You are a smart girl, Ginger." She gave it a bunt and went back inside. Later Ben noticed that she was out under the trees. So you have figured it out easily, he thought. I am glad.

"Next, I want to do the inside door. I have the scraps from the hide. From the small ones I can cut rectangular pieces for hinges. I'll need several on each half door because the wood from the wagon is so thick and heavy. I will need to square the frame of the doorway first. These planks are difficult to saw. It takes me a lot longer than it would father. I am not as strong."

Talking out loud had become a habit. At first he had talked to God for help and courage. Later when he found Stump he started talking to him, too, but Stump felt no responsibility to remain within the range of hearing. Like now when Ben was explaining how he would build the doors. Stump was nowhere to be seen.

"For the doors, if I attach two across with one going up and down in the middle it should work. I want the top half to swing open against the wall. That will give Ginger light and warmth from the fire and she won't feel alone."

Much later, as he finished the last latch, Ben examined his work.

"It is exciting to see both of Ginger's doors done. The wood that is left is more than enough to make a door for the front of the hut. Maybe I could make a real table and bench, this winter, too." He knew that the flap he now used for a front door would not be enough to stop snow and winter cold. The front door would need to be one solid door with leather hinges and a latch inside and he had to do it before the cold weather came.

After a break of jerky and tea, He measured and tried to saw but he was just, too tired. The tools were taken inside and he tidied the stack of all the remaining planks. They fit against the sidewall now and took up less room. He had deliberately taken the time and effort to cut a piece from the end of each of the longest ones for his doors.

He went down near the river to check his snares and found two nice fat rabbits. Rabbit skins aren't very big, but each one will make a front or back for a mitt he thought as he skinned them and prepared the meat for the fire. He scraped the skins and took them inside and hung them over a branch. Tomorrow, I will take them outside and work them some more.

Ben had completed two doors in one day. He was glad to take them off his mental list of things to finish before winter.

After the front door is finished, the next thing I'll need to do is get another big hide so I can make some trousers, he thought. It is getting chilly at night. I won't concern myself about a coat now, because I can wrap the bearskin around my shoulders, or I can use the quilt.

Thinking and planning for winter, Ben had brought wood back to the hut each time he had walked through the woods. Dead branches were broken or chopped to size and stacked. He had a good supply inside, and lots more under the big pine trees and the pile continued to grow with each trip he made.

The weather was beautiful. I should get busy on that front door before the weather starts to get cold, he thought. As he worked on other jobs, Ben's mind continued to work on the challenge of getting more hides.

One evening, he felt inspired to try to fashion a shirt from the deer hide. He made sure to cut the pieces, larger than his old shirt. He made holes on the edges of the leather by pounding a large nail through it. He laced the overlapped seams with carefully cut strips of the leather. This is slow going, he thought. It took him several nights, sitting by the campfire to complete it. It feels stiff and too big, he thought, when he first put it on. I like it though. It is going to be warm.

The next evening he decided to work on his winter boots.

"They should be large enough to stuff with something to keep my toes warm," he said as he stepped onto the piece of smooth horsehide that he had reserved for boot soles and drew around his feet with the blackened tip of a branch from the fire. He giggled when the stick slid near his instep.

"That tickled." Cutting on the line won't leave room for sewing the top on, so I better be sure to cut the soles larger. I'll cut two pair and glue them together so that the soles of my boots will be thick, he planned.

"The hooves and joint bones of the horse had been boiling for a long time. The liquid in the pan condensed and turned amber.

"I wonder if I am supposed to do anything else to turn this into glue." Ben used a pair of sticks, to remove the bones and set the pan away from the fire to cool.

"The tops of the boots will have to be rabbit skins with the fur turned inside. I think that should help keep me warm." As Ben fitted the skins around his foot and ankle he realized that each top would take three skins to make it calf high.

"That's disappointing. My small stack of furs will not be enough to make them as tall as I wanted. Maybe I can add to them later." Ben slathered the glue between the pairs of horsehide soles, fitting them together.

"I'll put these out to dry in the sun tomorrow. No I guess I shouldn't. Something might carry them off when I am not looking. Probably Stump would chew on them, too. I guess I don't need to worry if the glue is all right. It is sticking my fingers together." He hurried to the river to wash his hands. He ended up putting the soles on the floor with a piece of slate on top and another rock on top of that.

That night he made holes in the soles and stitched them to the tops. He worked late into the night, excited to see them finished. He draped a rabbit skin over his toes and slid his foot into the new shoe-boot. It felt a little loose, and the soles were stiff but not bad. He did the same with his other foot, slipping it in slowly. The idea to secure them by wrapping a cord up the leg and tying it, made all the difference.

"Now they feel good!" He said. He walked around the room several times before he took them off.

He coated the stitches with glue and after it dried, he covered the entire outside with grease and rubbed it in to make them water-resistant and then hung them on the tree in the middle of the hut. He felt proud of his new shirt and boots.

"They are fine to look at hanging there. Thank you, Father, for helping me, to make the warm shirt and boots." He smiled at the little cloth doll that sat on the highest branch above his shirt. I am glad that I saved it for Sarah, he thought. I wonder what she will wear this winter.

"Lord, please provide her with all that she needs."

Stump had resumed his old pattern of leaving the camp for several hours to spend with the wolf family. Ben had followed him again once in a while to see them and was surprised each time by the amount they had grown. The mother was aware of Ben, but as long as he kept his distance she didn't seem to mind his occasional visits. He always left an offering of meat. He didn't realize it but she didn't feel threatened by him because she had accepted his scent on Stump's coat.

The cubs had watched him come and go and were quite casual about his presence. One day when he placed a long piece of meat down and turned to leave, the young female cub, boldly dashed up and grabbed the meat. The other two ran out to get their share and there he stood in the midst of three young wolves tussling. His heart raced with the excitement of the moment and the joy of acceptance. He backed away and returned to camp with a big grin on his face.

Ginger shook her head up and down and blew a neigh of greeting. She had learned to eat grass and was nibbling the grass growing near the hut. She is growing fast, he thought, as he gave her scratches and talked to her. She instinctively knew to stay away from the wolf den. Ben and the hut offered security.

"My sweet, Ginger girl, you are getting bigger and more beautiful every day." He checked his snares hopefully and found a rabbit that he put over the fire to cook. The skin was scraped and stretched to dry. I need lots of these for a hat and mitts, since I used what I had for my boots and liners. What I really need is to get another deer.

As the days, passed the prairie turned a golden brown and seeds ripened, ready for picking. I need to dig a cache to hold grain for Ginger. This one will be in the corner of Ginger's room. It needs to hold all the grain that I can gather, he thought. He dug it deep and wide. "Instead of lining it with river rock, I want to plaster the inside and bottom with a mixture of mud and chopped grass to make it bug and rodent free. This stuff is messy but it should serve the purpose," he said, as he smeared it thickly on the chamber walls and floor with his hand.

That evening he rolled two very hot stones into the big pan and set it into the new clay lined cache. He used the smaller pan to transfer even more stones, until the big pan was filled. Then quickly he put the slate pieces on top of it. That would bake the clay hard and the grain would stay clean and dry.

In the morning Ben removed the pan. It left a circle in the clay on the bottom but pulled away cleanly.

"The clay is dry and hard as a rock, just as I had hoped," he said to Ginger, as she walked out her door and headed for the abundant wild grains of the prairie. He spent the next few days picking grain into the pillowcase and pouring it into the cache. Each time he would dump in the grain, he would wonder if it would be enough when the cache was full. He knew this was a food source for Stump and him as well. He liked cooked grain and a little drizzle of honey on it made it perfect.

Next, Ben gathered armloads of the sweet grasses that grew near the lake, piling them high on the old sheet and coming back to camp looking like a pretend Santa Clause. I think I should tie this into bundles before I stack it inside against the walls of Ginger's enclosure. She can use it for feed and bedding. It will provide insulation, too. The pleasant aroma of the drying grasses was wonderful and fresh. It reminds me of hay baling on the farm, he thought. I used to love to go up in the loft of the barn and lay on the hay. Sarah would run around looking for me. I wish I had Dart Away. I could go look for Sarah right now. No I couldn't. What would happen to Ginger? Something could hurt her or worse. She needs me here to protect her until she is bigger. Then she can take me.

"God, please protect Sarah and give her favor among the people she is with. I wish she were here with me. Will I ever see her again? Where did they take her? I don't even know where to begin to look."

One morning just before sunrise, he heard a fearsome sound he could not recognize. It was loud and not far away. Ben crept through the trees to the edge of the tall grass. He stood in awe, as the mighty elk lifted its chin and made a very loud bugling sound that gave Ben chills. He had never seen an elk. This male was in his prime and he proudly displayed his tremendous antlers.

"God, your creation is marvelous and powerful. All the earth is filled with creatures that are a wonder." Ben returned to camp with his entire mind focused.

"I want to hunt an elk. The meat would be enough to feed us all winter and the hide would make me a pair of trousers. I have to get another big animal before cold weather. I want an elk."

That night Ben sat sharpening the points on the ends of his spears. He had cut several small, straight trees, when he made his bow. Although these two, wouldn't bend enough, they hadn't broken, so he kept them in the hut to make spears. The tips had never been properly hardened or sharpened. I'll char the wood and then scrape it and char it again and again until the wood is as hard as stone and as sharp as it can get, he thought. I can remember that much from listening to Grandfather's stories. It didn't take him long to figure out that the spears he had made were far too heavy to throw any distance. He would have to be very near an animal in order to use them for hunting.

"I will have to be really cautious. If I throw one at that elk and he just gets angry, he could chase me. I think I would climb a tree faster than a squirrel with him after me. He laughed at the mental image of himself in the tree and the elk beneath it bellowing. I wonder just how dangerous they really are."

CHAPTER SEVEN
THE FIRE AND THE ELK

As the days passed, Ginger became more self-sufficient. It concerned Ben that she wandered alone on the prairie having her fill of the food that grew there. She enjoyed her mash for the attention, but it no longer was necessary. She was growing more beautiful and filling out. Her mane and tail were black and so were her legs from the knee down, but the rest of her remained the gingerbread brown that had inspired her name. Ben would call her back to camp several times a day and she always responded. He hoped that by encouraging her to stay closer to home, that she would be safer.

His mental list of things to do was still very long. At the top was the need for a large animal for some warm trousers for the cold months ahead and more meat for his cache. Once again he planned a trip.

"This time I will pack enough food for several days. I want an elk. I need to take the quilt to use as a tent; the nights are growing cooler." He stretched the bearskin, fur side up, between the spears, with their points up and tied it on; making sure it was high enough so that it would not drag on the ground when he pulled it. His bow and arrows would be handy for any small game. He planned to set up a temporary camp and hunt wherever he found elk sign.

"I think I will be able to recognize the feces or that strange smell he left in the air. I noticed it where that big fellow was bellowing. His prints looked like big deer prints to me. If I find a big deer, that would be fine, too. Lord you have helped with so many things this summer. Please protect us and help us on this expedition." Ben slipped on his ragged shirt and rolled up the remaining sleeve. He had grown during the summer and now it was tight when he buttoned it. I don't want to wear this if I don't have to. He pulled it off and tucked it in his bundle. That reminded him of the times he had used pieces of it. He took the precaution of taking some willow bark, and one of the infection fighting plants just in case. He folded them inside one of the soft leather pieces Jed had left for him. He wrapped the strip from the sheet around it and tied it. I hope I never need these again, he thought, slipping the package in next to his Bible.

After securing his hut and camp area, he used the raft to get his things across the river and with his arm around Ginger he took her across. Stump swam beside her and gave her a shower by shaking hard as she and Ben came out of the water. She hadn't liked it, but she had managed to swim in the middle and trusted Ben enough to do it.

They headed out on the prairie following an animal trail. Stump and Ginger traveled close.

"What a hunting party we are," he said, with a laugh. "Father, please be our guide and our protection."

As the day wore on, Ben found that he was traveling parallel to a ravine that was growing deeper as they followed it.

"I didn't know this was here," he thought. I must have walked very near it last time and didn't realize it. He set the travois down and walked to the edge. The wall dropped at least twelve feet to a rocky bottom. Only an occasional old, wind twisted tree marked the edge. There was nothing else in sight that could be used for shelter. Ginger walked up beside him and pawed the ground acknowledging the danger. She backed up and pranced away.

"Yes, little girl. Be careful, while I fasten the quilt to the tree limbs as a windbreak. I think I can hold the bottom edge in place with rocks." Thunder clapped in the distance and lightening streaked across dark clouds that quickly covered the sky overhead. The travois with his belongings was pulled close inside the quilt. Ben released the top edge from the branch and pulled it over him as the rain began to come down.

Stump ran under the shelter and cuddled close. Ginger tried to follow. The rain didn't bother her, but the thunder was frightening and she needed reassurance. She stood with the edge of the quilt over her head and reached for Ben's fingers to suck.

"Aren't you getting a little big for that, you silly girl? I need my fingers to hold this over us." The short rain had soaked through the quilt and was dripping on them.

"I am glad that the storm didn't last long." The sky cleared overhead to reveal smoke from a grass fire, moving their way pushed by the wind. Ben packed up his gear and looked around for cover from the prairie fire.

"That fire is coming our way fast! Help me; Father, to keep the animals safe. I need to do something quickly!" He picked up the handles of the travois and hurried back along the ravine as fast as he could. He knew that Stump and Ginger would have no trouble keeping up.

"Here is what I was looking for. See the area where the wall of the ravine has collapsed? That run of gravel to the bottom suggests that it is a wash for times when this area floods," he said to no one in particular. He headed down still pulling the load behind him. It snagged here and there jostling back and forth but didn't take long to reach the bottom. Stump came running down dislodging small stones that bounced ahead of him. At the top Ginger's whiney told him that she was going to need help. She could not come down by herself.

He crawled up the side, spraying small stones behind him. She pranced and skittered. She was becoming aware of the approaching fire and instinctively knew that it was danger. She was ready to run in fear. Only her trust in Ben kept her from running ahead of the flames.

"Come sweet little girl," Ben said, scratching her ears and easing her to the edge where Stump stood at the bottom barking. He felt the tension.

"God, please help me to get her down to the bottom where she will be safe. Protect her from falling on the loose gravel. Protect all of us. If she slips she could break a leg. I have to take her right now. If I wait much longer she will bolt." He held tightly to her neck with both hands and started down the slope, trying to hurry just enough so that she couldn't change her mind. They both slipped on the loose gravel and nearly fell. He held on to her mane and pulled as he gained his footing. She slid almost sideways at one point and he had all he could do to keep her upright and continue the rest of the way down. At the bottom they both stood shaking, with his arms wrapped around her neck.

"Thank you God," he repeated over and over softly as he comforted both of his companions.

"Thank you Lord, that we were near this ravine for shelter from the fire and thank you that we are all unharmed."

Stump stood leaning against Ben's leg. He was shaking, too. Ben reached down and hugged the shaggy neck, patting, stroking and talking to him to reassure him.

"Stump, you have been through a lot in your life. Haven't you? Don't be afraid. We are safe here. The fire will be gone soon and we will be just fine." Ginger was calmer now and seemed to take a cue from Stump's returning confidence. The fire was producing a loud roaring and crackling sound and the gray smoke crept like heavy fog over the ravine.

From above them, they heard a heart-wrenching cry as a large female elk leapt over the edge of the ravine and landed among the huge rocks at the bottom just a few feet away. The smoke had hidden the edge until it was too late for her. She could not stop. Her abrupt landing had startled all of them. Ginger jumped back against a large boulder pulling her ears back, squeezing herself as far from the offending strange animal as the small area would allow. Stump jumped back growling and placed himself between the elk and Ben. Ben, though startled; immediately recognized that his prayers had been answered and in a most theatrical way.

The fire snapped and popped as it passed by quickly, pushed by the wind. Soon the wind cleared the air. Stump made his way between the boulders and cautiously sniffed the elk. She had broken her neck in the fall. The elk was the answer to Ben's prayers for a large hide and winter meat, but he hadn't expected to have one delivered to him, here in the ravine.

"God, you are so good. Thank you for the elk. Thank you for always answering my prayers and keeping us safe from the fire. That elk's skin will be the leather for pants that I need, and we will have meat enough for all winter for Stump and me."

Where he stood was an area about twenty feet by thirty that was nearly clear of the huge boulders that covered the bottom of the ravine in both directions. The water that ran down must have slowly moved them back over centuries of time.

"Well friends, I think this is going to be camp for the next few days until I can get this elk skinned and the meat dried." Ginger stamped her front foot and fidgeted. "But first I'll feed you. Come here Ginger," and he offered her a little mash on his fingers as he held the pan. He knew that food was a comfort. He handed Stump a piece of dried bear meat. There is probably lots of meat waiting for us up on the prairie, he thought. He scrambled up over the edge, checking the temperature of the ground carefully. It was already cooling. It was raining in the direction of home and he hoped the fire would go out before it reached the trees near the river crossing by the hut.

Ben instructed Stump to stay and guard Ginger and the camp. As he walked away from the ravine, some spots were still sending up small curls of smoke. The fire had not touched the other side of the ravine. He would need to get fuel for a fire, by climbing up that direction.

He looked across the prairie and sadly knew that there would be animals that could not keep up the fast pace the wind had set. With that much food available I don't think I will need to worry about predators bothering us in the ravine. I would take advantage of it myself, but I can only drag so much. That elk will be heavy even after it is dried, he thought. As soon as Ben got back down, Stump went scurrying up, eager to investigate.

Ben crawled up the other side, where the fire hadn't reached. Climbing up the steep side was far more difficult. He gathered branches from the few trees and bushes nearby, hoping that it would be enough for a small fire to last the night and for drying racks. As he tossed them down he realized he would also need to gather armloads of grass and toss them down into the clearing where Ginger could reach them. Tomorrow I will have to gather more.

He worked far into the night until every bit of the meat was sliced thin and hanging from branches near his small fire. This time I will save the stomach and intestines. I want to eat the heart and liver. I'll just slice them into the pan with some fat and let it cook.

Stump returned. "I can tell that you will not need to be fed," he said. Stump's tummy was round and full. His fur was covered with black ash. He plopped down near Ginger and started licking his paws, cleaning them. Ben checked them to be sure they were just dirty and not burned.

He took the big pan with the stomach and intestines and the pouch and climbed up to the unburned side again. I

126

saw a pool of water in the bottom of the ravine a short distance away. There must be a spring there. If I can get to it, I will clean these and bring back fresh water for the camp. He found it easily but getting down to it was anything but easy. The clean stomach was filled with water and tied with tendon on one end and the leather strip from Ben's hair on the other. Getting back up the side with a pan of water and water filled stomach was impossible. With great difficulty he made his way back to camp over and around the huge boulders in the bottom of the ravine.

"Father, please help me to get this back without stepping into the home of a snake." Ginger and Stump were standing near to greet his return with a nudge and a lick. He offered the pan to the animals and they drank greedily. The meat was drying quickly and was ready to be turned. The hide had been scraped and greased but would need lots more work. It was in the shade, draped over a boulder, and fine for now. The fat in the pan was melting.

"Everything is on schedule," he said. He looked at the teeth of the elk and decided to remove the four largest to keep. Her teeth are shaped differently because she grazes. They are not as big or as pointed as the bear's, he thought. Ben carried the bear teeth in his pocket and now he added the four from the elk. "Stump guard the camp, he said, I need to get more wood for the fire."

I'll take one of my spears, he thought, as he passed them. It will make climbing up the steep side much easier. At the top the wind felt stronger. He laid his spear down and gathered grass for Ginger.

"It wasn't far from here that I found you," he said, as he pitched the grass over the side. Then he headed along the ravine gathering the scarce wood wherever he could find it.

Movement in the distance on the burned side of the ravine caught his eye. There were two men going along at a slow walk. Their horses were carrying a load and the men were leading them. He had not been seen. I'll crouch down, and stay perfectly still so they won't notice me. They have been gathering food provided by the fire. I am sure of it. I wonder if they are the same Indians I discovered in the woods earlier in the summer when I found Ginger. Waiting until they were out of sight, he then hurried to the spot he had been using to climb down. He tossed the wood over the edge, next his spear and then followed it.

Once down in the ravine, he spent time with his companions by the fire, scratching fur covered ears and eating some of the meat. He poured the water from the clean stomach into the big pan and then blew air inside and retied it. He hung it from a branch to be smoked and dried, then tied one end of an intestine casing and filled it with the melted fat. Getting the fat in it was a little difficult until he figured out that by placing three fingers in the opening, it was held open and his hand formed a funnel. Another knot secured the top end. Now it would be easy to transport and store.

Picking up a long leg bone he got out his knife and without really thinking about it, he began to scrape and carve. When the shape of a long bladed knife actually began to appear he was surprised by the work of his own hands.

"This is exciting! This is something that I really enjoy and I can make all kinds of useful things this winter!" The afternoon sped by unnoticed. Ben was totally entertained by his new craft.

Towards evening, he turned the stomach inside out and once again blew air into it. It was stiffer and felt like leather. He hung it back on the branch near the fire. They settled down for the night. The next day was spent much like the last, keeping the fire going, gathering grass and wood and carving.

At first light, the fourth day, Ben was up preparing to take the meat, hide, and his two precious companions' home.

"Getting everything to the top is not going to be an easy task," he said to Stump.

He was glad to see that the fire had swept by the old gnarled tree at the top of the gravel run without burning it. The tree had a unique and beautiful, wind twisted shape. There was sparse grass under it and the high wind had hurried the flames along. He fastened one end of his rope to the trunk, knowing that the rope would make it much easier to go up and down.

He tied the free end to Ginger's neck and with his arm around her he eased her up slowly, coaxing, talking, almost willing her to the top. Each step had to be a sure one so she wouldn't slide backwards and be injured. Her little hooves had trouble finding a solid purchase in the loose gravel. They struggled together, climbing slowly; then she was up and over the top and into a fresh breeze.

She pranced with joy at her accomplishment and after the rope was untied from her neck she reared on her hind legs and whinnied loudly, racing away. She returned at a slower pace flicking her head up and down and swishing her tail. Ben laughed at her and shared her enthusiasm. Stump ran back and forth barking. He knew that bringing Ginger up meant that they would be moving. He was excited.

"I'll wrap the dried meat in its own hide and form a bundle. The new hide is difficult to work with but once I get it tied, it will be fine. If I am careful, I can slowly pull it to the top." Next he brought up the quilt, with pans and tools.

"At last, everything is at the top," he said. He went down, one last time to look around and found the leather pouch he had left in the shade.

The travois was packed. The smoked, dried stomach was now a new water bag with clean water in it from the spring. I'll fasten this on top, along with a pan, for easy drinks along the way. The heavy load slowed their travel. Ben had to stop to rest often. It didn't help that at the last minute he could not resist tucking two long leg bones for carving into the bundle next to the half-finished knife. The fourth had become a favorite entertainment for Stump. I don't want to drag that all the way home. Stump can find a bone anytime he wants one, he thought, but at the last moment he tucked it into the top bundle anyway.

They crossed the river where he had so many times before, using the raft to take the bundles safely across. With coaxing, Ginger crossed beside him. He was grateful that they had not had a heavy rain to raise the level of the water. When the familiar shape of the hill, that was his home, came into view, Ben let out a yell of victory.

"Yeah! We are home Stump! We are home Ginger! We have only been gone four days, but it seems much longer." Stump ran to the door of the hut barking and sniffing.

Ben's palms were sore and he found they were blistered when he set down the travois in front of the hut, and looked at them. Stump was running around sniffing the ground with excited interest, and Ginger stamped the ground and laid her ears back.

"What is the matter with the two of you? The door is still secured." Then he noticed all the dog type prints in the dirt around the fire pit and near his door.

He hurried to open the door, rolling the stones away and tossing the boards aside. He wanted to see if the temporary door he had put on the side had stayed secure. The branches and brush were still in place, but a few tiny prints in the dust let him know that a small visitor had been inside. Perhaps a squirrel had come in the side door. I must make that completely secure he thought as he went back out. Stump still seemed excited.

"I think you had a visit from the wolf family, Stump. When you didn't go see them, they came to see you. She brought the young ones on an outing. She was probably checking to make sure that you are all right. Maybe you should go visit while I unpack all this stuff and put it away. Here take a piece of this dried elk meat. The pups will have fun with it." He handed a long thin piece of elk jerky to Stump and motioned the path to the lake. Stump understood and gratefully headed up the path with his gift. Ben lifted the slate from the cache and the sweet smell of the crabapples drifted up. He pinched a couple to see if they were keeping. They were firm. He adjusted the contents so that the deer meat was on the end and started to fill the middle with the dried elk. The first cache was completely full.

He removed the lid of the second cache, moving the bear meat to one side; he put the rest of the elk meat in, leaving out two large pieces for their supper. He was tired and didn't feel like preparing anything.

"Father, You brought us all back safely and you gave us the elk we needed. You protected us from the wild fire, and watched over Ginger as she struggled on the loose gravel. Thank you for all this food supply, both caches are full. This is a bounty overflowing. You are a generous provider."

After a good shake the bearskin was placed in his sleeping corner. The quilt was really dirty but he shook it and tossed it on his bed, promising that he would wash it tomorrow. The table was reconstructed against the back wall. He put the two long leg bones on the table, but when he looked back at the low table with two bones laying on it, he thought that perhaps Stump would think they were for him and chew on them. They were intended for carving and so he picked them up and pushed them into the branches of the ceiling where they would stay until he was ready to carve them. Stump's bone was beside the fire where he often lay.

The nearly finished knife was tucked into a branch in the wall near the front doorway, where he could see it. The two spears were leaning in the corner with his bow and arrows hooked on a branch beside them. Ben was an orderly person. His hut reflected that trait. He took out his knife and sliced at the bark on top of a branch in the wall. When it was scraped flat on top, he made small indentations, which he filled with the teeth from his pocket. This would keep them from being lost until he decided what he would do with them.

Ginger had gone in the side door and had gone to sleep on the pad of clean new grass that Ben had prepared there before they left. She was tired after their adventure and grateful to be safe at home.

A gentle rain had started to fall, but it didn't discourage Ben from walking into the river. The water was almost warm. He bent low and scooped water and sand into his hair and scrubbed it and then scrubbed his skin with sand until he felt very clean. He dove under the surface and ruffled his floating hair, to make sure that all the sand was out of it. He scrubbed his trousers and noticed how worn the fabric had gotten. My trousers have holes in the knees and they haven't reached my ankles since the start of summer. It is going to be nice to have some made from that elk hide, he thought. The rain continued to fall softly.

He entered his hut still dripping and shivered a bit. After hanging his clothes on the wagon wheel behind the fire pit, his mother's skirt was used as a towel.

As he hung the skirt back on the tree in the middle of the room he felt warmth enter his heart, not from the temperature of the room, but from his mother's love that he knew he would always have. There wasn't a day or an hour that he didn't miss his family, but at that moment he felt comforted just knowing that someone watched over him.

"God I know you are here with me and watching over me. I don't think I would be alive if I didn't have your guidance and grace," he said softly. "I still haven't figured out why you have me here but I guess someday I'll know."

With the clean sheet wrapped around his waist he felt comfortable and refreshed. The air coming in the doorway was growing cooler and the rain was coming down a little harder now. The elk hide was on the floor still rolled and waiting for attention. It would have to wait for tomorrow and the rain to stop.

Making a fire is the next thing I need to do, he thought. By the time he had the fire going with a large piece of wood on it; his hands hurt badly and were bleeding. Twirling the stick had broken open the blisters. After coating his palms with bear grease he made a pan of willow bark tea and added some mint to improve the flavor. The warmth of the fire felt soothing. Stump pushed open the flap of the front door and entered. He shook rainwater all over Ben. The few drops that landed in the fire, made a sizzling sound. Ben peeked out to see that a steady rain continued to fall as he wedged the branches across his front door.

Stump accepted the piece of jerky that had been set-aside for him and gladly ate it.

When he noticed his bone, he curled up beside the fire, pulled it between his paws and chewed on it for a little while. He laid his head against Ben and went to sleep.

As Ben sipped his tea with a drizzle of honey added to his cup, and chewed his jerky, he looked around at his cozy little home and family. They were animals but he thought of them as his new family.

"Thank you for Ginger and Stump," he said softly as he crawled onto his bed, pulling the sheet and quilt over his chest, he wondered what God had in store for him tomorrow.

"I hope that it will be easy. I'm really tired," he said. He slept peacefully.

Outside his door, was a puddle and water stood in the two fire pits. He tied up the flap of the door before getting dressed. His trousers were warm and dry. This is closer to a rag than a shirt, he thought, as he put on his old shirt. He couldn't tuck the shirt in because it was too short. He had removed strips from the bottom for Stump's bandages. Soon I'll need to start wearing my new shirt, he thought. The weather is changing.

The day was bright but cool and crisp. This is the kind of day that makes me think of apples and pumpkin pie, he thought.

"My mother made the best pumpkin pie in the world," he declared to the trees. As he stretched his long arms above his head, he looked up to see that many of the trees were starting to change color. The pines outnumbered the others and their dark green, needled branches framed the bright yellow of aspen and reds of the sumac bushes showing them off to their best with the contrast. The woods past the lake showed splashes of pink and deep rose mixed with bronze, gold and deep green. The beautiful, colorful change had been gradual over the past few chilled nights, but this was the first time he had noticed it. It felt like he was standing in a scene from a painting. The lake shimmered and reflected the blue sky and the colors that surrounded it.

Suddenly he thought of the holidays and felt a pang of loneliness.

"I wish I could see you, Father, I remember getting the Christmas tree with you last year. We walked back in our woods for a long way and none of the trees looked right until we both saw that one. It was perfect. It took both of us to drag it back. When we had it in place the star was almost touching the ceiling. You lifted Sarah and let her put it on. We all helped decorate it before we went to the Christmas pageant at church."

"I remember all the faces and all the laughter, at Christmas dinner. There were our neighbors the Thompson's with their boys, Mathew and Luke and Pastor Barns and Missus Barns, Uncle Joe and Aunt Jenny and my cousins, Carolina and Eddie, fifteen people in all. Mother had decorated the coffee table and it was on a rug in the dining room for the younger children. The food tasted wonderful and I could smell the pies from the front porch.

"You and Mother had decided to prepare for the first wagon train west in the spring."

"When you told us; both Grandmother and Grandfather got tears in their eyes. It seemed to me that your news took the joy out of their faces."

I remember seeing Sarah's head slowly sink onto Mother's shoulder as we sat in the living room late that night and talked excitedly for hours about the trip. Grandfather launched into telling about when he first got the farm and how hard it was in the beginning. He is a good storyteller. Grandmother left the room for a while and returned with a tray of the decorated cookies and cups of eggnog. Her eyes were puffy and red. I could tell she had been crying. She didn't want us to leave the farm. I treasure every thought of all of you. I will find Sarah. I promise you that someday she and I will be together again!"

"I just realized that I need to post a letter to them when I can. They should know what has happened here."

Enough of this melancholy mood, he thought. The palms of my hands are sore, but the rest of my body feels great. He stretched the elk hide out on top of some rocks and scraped it, leaving it there in the shade until the ground was dry.

I am going to coat my palms with bear grease again and then get going. He got his bow, arrows, knife, small pan and the sheet. I will be going up the trail to the lake, so I better take several small pieces of bear jerky for the wolf family. The pups are growing so big. It is fun to see them.

When he rounded the trees near the den they all stopped playing and turned their heads to see him. He sat down on the ground and put the jerky pieces in a row by his feet. Once again the brave little female came first, followed by her brothers. She snatched the biggest piece and moved off just a few feet to chew it. The others claimed a share, but more hesitantly.

The mother appeared at the mouth of the den, and in one smooth leap she sat on top of a large boulder. She growled a little, and then changed her mind. In two bounds she had crossed the space between the big rock and Ben's feet; she grabbed a piece, too, and returned to the top of the rock where she chewed it. Ben's heart nearly stopped! She came within 4 feet of me! When she jumped forward, just for an instant, I thought she was jumping at me! Ben's heart was racing with adrenalin. She seemed content to watch her babies from the top of the rock and chew her snack. She knew that she had the advantage.

I think it is time for me to move backwards slowly. He was grinning widely, as he stood up back on the trail. She watched him but stayed on her rock, recognizing that his movements were not threatening.

As the trail passed under the big tree, he remembered the terrible day that they had met the bear. Stump is off hunting this morning just like he had been that day.

Ginger had wandered off to the tall ripe grass and was busy having her breakfast when he left camp.

The lake came into view as the trail turned. There in the rich soil beside it lay large wilted gray-green leaves and big yellow squash. There were several vines. The frost must have caught the leaves, he thought. I can't believe how many squash there are! I never did check on them. I better take the squash back to the hut when I go. He continued into the woods on the other side of the lake and found the clearing where he had collected the honey.

Beside him rose the maple tree in beautiful red leaves.

"If I cut a hole in the bark and dig in a ways angling upwards, and insert a hollow cattail reed, the sap should drip into the pan." He fastened the small pan with a vine. Then just to be sure that it didn't fall down he braced the bottom with a branch. I wish I had a cover to keep bugs and flies out, he thought. Jed made the basket for the melted fat from grass. I wonder if I could make a workable cover. He gathered tall grass stems and set to work, with his back against a big pine. The years of fallen needles made a soft carpet beneath the branches. It smells so good. I love it here in the woods, thought Ben as he worked.

My first attempt at weaving isn't all that bad. It is good enough to do the job. I can snuggle this small mat over the spout and the top of the pan. I better fasten it in place with a vine, so that the wind doesn't take it off. I can remember my folks not liking bindweed vine on the farm, but it comes in handy here.

"There that should do it," he said out loud. The sound of his own voice startled him. It echoed through the trees. He didn't realize that he had spoken out loud. It made him chuckle.

"There are several maples in this area. If I had more containers I could collect sap from all of them."

He checked on the hickory nut trees and saw that the big thick leather coverings on the nuts had turned brown. A few had dropped to the ground. They will soon be ready to gather, he thought, but that will have to be my next project. I need to take the squash in the hut today before it gets frosted.

"I'll take as many as I can carry this time but it is going to take more than one trip," he noted. Then he chuckled again.

Ben missed having a human to talk to. He could talk to God and did, many times each day. He could talk to Stump and Ginger, but that wasn't the same as talking with another person and having a conversation.

As he circled back around the lake, he wondered where Stump was. He wasn't visiting at the wolf den or he would have seen him there.

The squash are big and heavy. They will be good this winter, he thought, as he folded the sheet around seven, lifting it over his shoulder caused pain deep inside and in the palms of his hands. It is all right. I am healing, he thought.

"This has been a good day. Thank you, Lord, for your provision." Stump was asleep in the sun when Ben got back. Ginger came up to him and blew a greeting. He hugged her neck and scratched her ears and Stump came up wanting to get in on the attention. They wrestled and rolled, playing on the ground until they were both covered in dust and leaves.

He made a bed of dried grass along the wall, opposite the fire pit. The squash will stay cool there against the stone of the bluff, he thought, as he placed the second load single file on the grass. Another trip brought a few more, along with cattail roots, a bunch of coltsfoot and a braided string of wild onions. They would supply much needed variety to his winter diet. He tied the coltsfoot with grass cording and hung it above the squash where it would dry. He sang praises to God as a happy feeling filled his heart.

"I am looking at a beautiful, bright yellow parade," he said as he looked at the row of squash.

"Fish would make a nice change for supper, don't you think Stump"? He asked. Soon the pole was put to work in the spot by the willow roots. He weighted the pole with a rock and went back in the hut to be sure that his fire was still burning. After adding a heavy chunk of wood he returned just in time to pull a huge catfish out of the water. Two more fish soon followed. Once cleaned and cooked they would make a delicious meal.

"The harvest of hickory nuts will be fun tomorrow," he told Stump. Once again the old sheet will be called into service. I better take the pillowcase too, he thought as the skin of the catfish turned golden brown. Some more of the tubers of the cattails should be gathered and dried too. Maybe I'll give myself a break tomorrow and see what else is around to gather, he mused.

He had continued to keep his calendar on the sticks and could tell with a glance that he had been there more than five months.

"Two more days and it is Sunday again. Well, I can take a break then."

He enjoyed gathering the hickory nuts. By late afternoon, he had gone to the woods three times, returning each time with as many nuts as he could carry. The nuts were bulky now but would be smaller after they dried some more and the thick leathery outer casings were peeled away. The pile at the foot of his bed was big. His spears had to be moved to the back to make room in the corner. Now I will have to be careful to close the hut tightly when I leave it for a few hours. I don't want that curious squirrel transferring my nuts to his winter stash.

After the grass dried, the elk hide had been spread out and scraped and rendered fat was rubbed into it. Ben could tell that with more work, the elk hide would be soft for his new pants.

Calluses were forming on his palms and they were no longer sore. His mental list of things to do seemed to continue to grow.

"As I finish one job, I think of several more. Food for Stump and me is no longer a concern, but I should gather lots more dry grass. There is room for more bundles by the sidewall of Ginger's room, he thought. I want to gather pine nuts too, if I can find them and more types of tea, and it is important that I gather some of the medicines that Jed showed me, just in case. I also need to make containers. I'll bring in some grass bundles for weaving. Maybe I should try to shape some containers from bark. That glue can be reheated.

I still need to make my front door to keep out the cold and cut out my trousers and stitch them when the hide is ready. I need to make a hat and hand coverings, too."

With that he jumped up and hurried off to check his snares.

Sunday morning announced itself with a drum roll of thunder in the distance. Ben put wood on the fire and opened the flap to a cold gray day. Ginger had gone out to graze a few minutes earlier and Stump didn't seem in a hurry to start his day. He had settled near the fire and was asleep.

"Thank you, Lord Jesus, for this fall day that announces that winter is soon on the way," He prayed out loud as he stepped out into the cold air. He took the big pan to the river and filled it half full and placed it next to the fire to heat.

"It seems like you have rain on the schedule again. You must like rain on Sunday," he said with a grin as he looked at the heavy gray clouds overhead.

Getting his knife and the pillowcase, he hurried out onto the prairie to find the plants that could be ruined if the rain hit hard. The wide comfrey leaves were now shriveled and brown but he gathered a supply of them into the pillowcase anyway, trying not to crumble them. Since Jed had explained their benefit, Ben appreciated the plant more.

"The plants that had the yellow flowers in summer were more difficult to locate now, with tiny seedpods on top and few leaves at all left on their stems. If I had not made a note of where they grew I would have walked past them. They are certainly more difficult to identify." He pulled several, roots and all as Jed had recommended and shook the dirt from them. All of these should have been gathered in the summer, but even now they contain their healing benefits, he thought.

Next Ben cut short pieces from the tips of raspberry branches.

"Ouch, the thorns on these don't leave much room to hold them. Jed said the bark is good for healing burns and can be put into tea to soothe a cough, and he said to strip the leaves and dry them to use for tea as a mild tonic. The thunder rumbled loudly overhead as Ben picked a large bunch of clover, and hurried back to the riverbank to wash the roots of the healing plants he had collected.

Ben rolled the elk hide and leapt inside the flap of the hut with it just as the rain began. He glanced at the pan of water and it was starting to steam. He cut up dried meat and wild onions and cattail tubers and then decided to add crabapples as he had before. He liked the flavor they added along with the greens he had gathered and some dried herbs. The starch in the cattail roots thickened the soup as it cooked. Feeling generous, he added a pinch of salt, giving himself permission to use a little.

"After all, it is Sunday." He stirred the soup with a wide stick he had collected for that purpose some weeks earlier.

"I'll carve a good spoon this winter," he told Stump. "I still have so much to do. I don't know if I will be ready when the cold weather comes." Jed had mentioned that clover leaves and blossoms mixed with bear fat made a good salve. "I will dry a bunch and mix it later. That will be easy to get. It grows everywhere."

On impulse he stripped his clothes off and with his mother's skirt in hand he dashed to the river, tossing the skirt under the willow, hoping it would stay dry there. He plunged into the river and took a quick bath. With the skirt wrapped around his waist he hurried back in the hut laughing. Stump greeted him with barks and wagging but had not been interested in swimming.

"That felt good Stump. The rain doesn't matter when you're in the water anyway. The rain is warmer than the river." He rubbed his hair and body and got back into his clothes. He was shivering as he ladled the soup into his bowl and Stumps pan.

"It is hot Stump, we will have to wait."

With his father's Bible in front of him on the little table, and the soup cooling nearby, Ben was content to read, eat and rest.

CHAPTER EIGHT

THE COUGAR

Ben worked very hard, every day and things were getting better. Some things were becoming routine.

After he ate his soup, he lit the stone candle and settled near the doorway where he could see best to read and watch the rain. At first his mind wandered, thinking of his family and about finding Sarah.

"How will I find her Lord? I don't know where to look or even what direction they took her."

He opened to the words of Christ, in the book of John, chapter eight. After reading it, he prayed.

"Lord I hope that you are pleased with me. Help me to see it, if I do anything that is not your will. Help me to keep your commandments always, so that I can live forever with you. Amen" He continued to read. He felt peaceful and sure that he was not alone.

Thinking back to the day that the Indians attacked the wagon, he wondered again where Sarah had been taken.

"I know that she is protected by You, Lord. I long for the day that I can find her and bring her back." He no longer felt content to stay inside and rest. He had to do something or he would burst! He missed Sarah and his parents so much. He didn't know how he would stand it, staying inside, all winter, without them.

He pulled the soup away from the fire and put a big chunk of the glue in a small pan to melt. He decided he would busy his mind with trying to make a container. Ignoring the gentle rain, he went outside.

Long ago, lightening had struck a tall birch tree and it hadn't burned but it had died and fallen. He decided to try to peal a wide strip of bark from it. I will cut all the way around the tree, and then two feet above that, I will do the same thing. Next I will cut straight down the side. He placed the tip of his knife in the last cut, and began gently to pry

143

away from the tree. It was working! The bark was loose for about an inch. He placed the blade in the cut again, this time sliding it up and down against the back of the bark as he pulled gently. The beautiful white bark peeled away from the tree with only one flaw, where a small branch had grown. He used the same procedure with a second piece and slowly it gave way. He held two beautiful, complete slabs of white bark.

To make the bottom was a puzzle until he figured out that he could cut a slice from the trunk of the same tree. He got the saw and began to work. The first cut was to remove all the jagged edges on the end where it had broken off. It was hard work cutting the wet wood and by the time he had cut the end off, he was covered in sweat. He started again. He seemed to be learning the rhythm of it. This slice was easier.

The glue was melted when he returned with the wooden bottom and the bark sides. I can make holes with the hand drill, on the edge of the bark so I can stitch it, and another row on the bottom edge that will fasten the bark to the bottom.

Next with the hand drill, he made a row of holes around the edge of the wooden slice. I will thread mother's darning needle with some of the horsehair I saved and a strand of the strongest thread. He stitched the bark together and fastened it to the base. With his mind and hands busy, Ben no longer thought about missing his family but the ache from their loss was with him.

"Now if I coat all the stitches with glue and put a small leather patch on the inside over the flaw, this should be strong enough to hold some of the nuts. I like the way it looks. Birch bark is beautiful."

Ginger came in through the front door, and stood beside Ben. She tried to stick her face in the pan of glue. She had eaten mash from that pan many times and expected to find some there.

"Oh Ginger, are you looking for some mash? That is glue and I don't think it would taste very good." Stump had gone out, so at least he wasn't getting in the glue. Ginger's coat was wet from the rain. She didn't mind the water, but she wanted his attention.

The new container was cautiously placed in the corner, behind the fire, while the glue on it dried. He carefully turned Ginger and headed her back to her area and closed the bottom half of the side door. I really need to make that front door, he thought. He could feel the cold air coming in and it made him shiver.

She didn't need it with lots of grain available on the prairie for the taking, but as he brushed her, he decided he would make her a pouch of mash, just because she enjoyed it.

The next morning, taking the lighter of his two spears for practicing, Ben headed for the lake area to check on the pan of sap from the maple tree. The pillowcase was tucked in his waist as he often did, just in case he found something to collect.

Peeking under the big pines he could see that the wolf den was empty when he passed. She has taken them out for a hunting lesson, he thought. Stump is probably with them. The lake was quiet, with only a few ripples from the wind. All the ducks are gone. They have flown south where it is warmer. It is so quiet here, thought Ben. He stood on the path looking for any sign of life. The rest of the world is getting ready for winter. I am not ready. I don't think I will ever be ready for a winter alone.

The beautiful maples are still decorated with red leaves, but they will start falling soon, he thought. The forest floor was sparsely dotted in many shades of yellow, brown, and red. I love the way the air smells this time of year, so fresh and clean. It's like hay and dried apples. He threw his spear, hitting a clump of grass he had aimed at. It wasn't far now to his syrup tap.

He peeked into the pan to check on the sap. It is working but not enough has collected in the pan to bother taking it apart. Maybe I did it early, he thought, as he tucked the mat back securely in place. I'll check it again in a few weeks.

He lifted his spear and threw it with all his might, back toward the edge of the woods. I need to figure out how to make one that is strong but lighter. This doesn't go as far as I would like. He picked it up and threw it again, with the same results.

His step was light. He was enjoying the day as he passed the start of the bluff. It was a perfect fall day. I wonder if the wolves are back.

A sudden movement above him, a flash of golden tan, caused him to bring his arms up to protect his head as he slammed hard to the ground with something very heavy on top of him! He could see that the weight on his chest was a cougar. She had clawed painfully into his left shoulder and upper left arm. He tried to pull free, but his spear was pinned against him by her weight.

Her head lay on his chest, eyes glazed, not moving. He pushed with his left hand and the spear in his right. The big cat rolled to the ground beside his bleeding arm. His spear had gone into the cat's chest. Its weight combined with the speed of the jump had pushed the spear into her heart. She had raked him as she landed. It was a case of being in the wrong place at the wrong time. The big cat had sat watching the trail for a long time, waiting for game. She was hungry and had a litter of half-grown cubs to feed. Now they would have to use the skills she had taught them to survive.

He hadn't planned this!

Why am I even here? How is it that I brought my spear? I wasn't even going hunting! How can this be? One minute I'm happy about maple syrup and the next I am on the ground with a mountain lion on my chest! Ben's thoughts were racing. His heart was pounding. He didn't know it but he was going into shock. He was losing a lot of blood. His body started shaking as he got up.

He felt dizzy. Next, the nausea came. He bent down breathing deeply.

I have got to stop the bleeding. Maybe this will help, he thought, as he wrapped his arm and shoulder with the pillowcase. I want that cat's skin. His adrenaline was flowing. He did not realize how badly he was injured. Ben pulled out his knife and skinned the cat where it lay. He would not eat the meat of a cat, but he did take the canine teeth and drop them in his pocket. His collection was growing. He rolled the fur and put it over his good shoulder and headed for camp leaving his spear where it was in the grass beside the cat. He was not far from the wolf den. They will not need to hunt for a few days, he thought. His arm had rivulets of blood running down it, across his hand and dripping on to the path. He was leaving a steady trail of blood. He felt dizzy again as he reached the hut, dumping the fur inside. Never once did he consider that his fresh blood could bring a predator.

With its nose to the ground, the huge black wolf had followed Ben's trail out of the woods, lifting his head to sniff the air and then lowering it again, continuing to track. Just as he was able to see his prey ahead, the mountain lion leapt.

He would wait. He would not challenge the big cat. The scent of blood in the air stirred his hunger. He crept closer. The man he followed had killed the cat. It lay beside the path, its flesh exposed. He would eat and wait.

Ben staggered to the river and laid down in the edge of the moving water, letting it wash over him, cleaning his wounds and the blood streaks from his arm and hand. The water was cold. He shivered uncontrollably.

"I can see my blood coloring the water as it passes. I must be losing a lot of blood. I have to try to stop the bleeding. God, please help me." He squeezed the water from the pillowcase and wrapped it around the wounds again. His world was spinning. He made his way back to the hut by, first holding onto one tree, and then the next.

"Help me Father," he cried out.

When he entered the hut, he found that the fire was just a small glow in his fire pit. With his shaking hand, he added a couple of small branches and one larger one.

"Please God, make it burn, please let it burn! I need to make some medicine, and a poultice." Ben dipped water from the barrel and set the pan on the stones near the flames. The fire had caught.

"Thank you Father. He submerged several large leaves in the water and a handful of willow bark scrapings he had previously collected. Now he was so glad that he had followed Jed's suggestion and these things were here and he didn't have to go gather them. The wet pillowcase wasn't slowing the bleeding at all. His arm was dripping blood onto the dirt floor of the hut.

The water in the pan was steaming now. He sat down near the fire, waiting. Soon it would boil and he would be able to sip the tea and ease the pain.

I need strips of cloth for a bandage. How can I make them with only one hand? The sheet had been washed, and dried in the sun. He pulled it from a space between branches in the wall where he had stored it.

Ben tore two strips from the old sheet by standing on the corner and pulling with his one good hand. Very gently he took the leaves out of the hot liquid with his stir stick.

They pulled apart at the slightest pressure. He blew on them so they wouldn't burn his arm and then one gash at a time was covered until he had removed every bit from the tea. He put one of the pieces of sheet in the boiling concoction and stirred it with his cooking stick, then pulled the pan away from the flame. The bleeding wasn't stopping.

After sitting a few minutes waiting for the pan to cool, Ben decided that he would put another layer of the leaves on his arm. This time I'll use the dried ones, he thought, and he patted them on. The cloth was cool enough to handle now so he squeezed it out and wrapped it around and around his wounds, and then he did the same with the dry one and tucked the end under to hold it in place. He picked the pan up and drank from it, forcing himself to swallow the bitter medicine. He crawled to his bed and collapsed into a deep sleep.

It was the middle of the night when he woke himself up thrashing. He was wet with sweat and the fire was nearly out. He knew that he had a fever. He stuffed wood at the fire and hoped it would catch. It was then that he realized that he hadn't used the plants that fight infection. He didn't know if he had the strength to start over, being a nurse for himself was his biggest challenge since the bear hurt Stump.

"Father, help me." He felt like he might pass out.

The fire caught the added wood and warmth and light radiated to surround Ben. Once again he dipped the pan in the barrel for more water and thought, what a wonderful God I have. The fire has caught and the water barrel is here with fresh water. He was shaking so badly now that he thought that it must be freezing outside. He crushed two of the plants, dried tuber and all and added them to the warming water and added more of the big comfrey leaves and more willow bark, too.

As he sat by the fire he knew that without God's help he was in real trouble.

"Help me Father, please help me," he prayed.

Stump whined from the end of the bed and came over and lay down beside him putting his paw in Ben's lap. He knew that Ben had been hurt, but he couldn't help.

While the pan heated, Ben stroked the dog's beautiful multi-colored fur.

"I know you want to help me boy. You help just by being here with me." When the liquid was cooled, Ben removed his bandage and was glad to see that only a small amount of blood seeped from the deepest wounds. He scooped up a poultice of all the plants in the pan and patted them onto his arm.

"It hurts so much," he said out loud. He was gritting his teeth, as he rewrapped it. He had put both of the bandages into the boiling liquid. This time he used both of them around the arm and shoulder to hold the poultice in place and then he covered his arm with the soft leather that Jed had left for him. Another dry strip of the sheet was needed to secure the whole thing.

"I feel so weak that I can barely tear the cloth," he told Stump. By the time he had tucked the end of the strip of dry cloth in to hold it in place, some of the pain in the arm had subsided. He was totally exhausted.

Ben was thirsty from the fever and gulped the bitter liquid down and followed that with a drink of water.

After lighting his stone, oil candle, he went back to bed and slept until the afternoon. It was the best thing for him. It gave the herbs time to work and with him lying still, the wounds were able to seal. The bleeding had stopped while he slept. He was unaware of the pounding rain that washed away the blood trail he had left.

He sat up slowly and felt the room sway. I need water, he thought. The pan used for the medicine was only a few feet away. He slid to his knees and crawled to the pan, scooping it full of water from the barrel, he took a long drink. He crawled back to his bed and set the pan near the wall where he could reach it. He slept again.

When Ben woke the next time, it was night. His hut was cold, but the tiny flicker of a flame deep within the stone candle relieved the darkness.

His head was no longer dizzy when he sat up, but for a moment he was disoriented. He was used to seeing a banked fire in the corner. He was very glad when he recognized the little flicker of light from his candle displayed on the wall, but it puzzled him. He couldn't remember lighting it.

Each movement was difficult. His arm and shoulder throbbed, as he stirred the fire pit. It held no embers.

"I can use the candle to relight it." He moved slowly.

"Thank you, God. What I need to survive is close at hand. You have guided me all summer, showing me what to do. I know I will come through this with your help and I'll be stronger for it."

Soon his hut was warm again and he sat near the fire trying to decide what he should do next.

The growl of his stomach reminded him that he had not eaten for a long time. He wasn't sure just how long.

"I don't feel hungry, but I know that eating will help me gain my strength back." My arm is aching and badly swollen. I need to start another pan of medicine, too, he thought, and with that heating, he dipped water in the big pan and dropped in several pieces of jerky. Getting the lid off and on the cache was almost more than he could do with one hand. He tossed in wild onions without cutting them up and then took a squash and laid it near the fire.

With the big pan on to heat in its usual place, he rejoiced at the usefulness of his candle.

"I would be sitting here with no fire if it weren't for that candle. I couldn't start a new fire with this arm. I need to refill it with fat and a new wick and light it again. Thank you

Father, that you showed me that rock with the indentation, that day." The bright glow on the wall was a comfort as real as the presence of his two animal friends. Ginger raised her head and blew a greeting when he looked in to see if she was safe.

Ben had not wedged the branches in the front doorway, and Stump had watched over him the entire time. Realizing Ben's vulnerability, he had positioned himself in the doorway to guard, and now, Stump was taking advantage of Ben's absence from the bed and had sprawled in the middle of it to rest.

Ben was weak, and the job of getting the fire and food started, had taken his small reserve of strength. He pulled the quilt from the bottom of the bed and sat with it wrapped around him, near the fire. The only cup he had was tin and the handle soon became hot, after he dipped up some of the medicinal liquid. He set it on a rock and lay down near the fire to wait for it to cool. He slept, unguarded.

When he opened his eyes again it was morning. The fire had died down to a soft glow. The meat in the soup was soft and hot and his pan of medicine was hot and very strong. His arm ached terribly. He poured the cup of medicine back in the pan and stirred it with his cooking stick. He dipped a new cupful and saw that it was black, and looked like strong coffee.

"Ugh," he said, and then gulped it down. It was so bitter that it made him gag. He dipped his cup in the soup and drank some of the broth. It helped take the bitter taste from his mouth, and stimulated his appetite. He hooked out a piece of the meat with his cooking stick and ate it. The bear meat was stringy but nutritious. The bear had been old.

"Your provision and the work of The Great Physician, has brought me through this ordeal to the point that I now feel that I am starting to recover. Thank you for being with me." The sound of Ben's voice woke Stump. He rolled over and looked at Ben with a sleepy yawn. I wonder if Stump and the wolf family have found the cat and eaten. Ben didn't realize that Stump had stayed there on guard, the whole time. Then he looked over at the rolled skin on the floor. I can't help but marvel that I had the presence of mind to bring home the skin. I hope that it will be all right until I am well enough to process it.

"I am getting better. Thank You, Father."

Stump nudged Ben's hand and then sniffed at his empty pan. Ben realized then that Stump had not left him to hunt or eat.

"You are a good friend, Stump." He said as he filled Stump's pan with cooked bear meat and broth.

I'll change the poultice and then rest again. By noon he was tired of his bed. After adding a piece of wood to his fire and having another cup of the soup, he sat outside his doorway in the sun with the quilt wrapped around him. The chilly breeze stirred the trees and caused a rain of colorful leaves to swirl and fall. I wonder what the real date is. I should celebrate my sixteenth birthday when I feel better. I need to mark my calendar stick with two notches when I go back in. He didn't realize that he had lost a full day.

It doesn't take long for me to get tired again, he thought, but I am definitely feeling better. He leaned his head back against the grassy exterior of the hut and fell asleep with the warm autumn sun on his face. He was unaware of his vulnerability, and the black eyes that watched him from the cover of the trees near the river.

Stump came out and snuggled close, sensing that his protection was still needed.

CHAPTER NINE
JED'S RETURN

When Ben opened his eyes, he was looking at Jed's most brilliant smile.

"Jed! Hi! Jed! Oh, I'm so glad to see you and I have so much to tell you that you aren't going to believe it all. You saved my life! If I hadn't known what plants to use I would have died but now I'm getting better and I owe my life to you!" Ben was so excited that he couldn't contain it. His words tumbled out as he struggled to stand up.

Ben's weakened condition was immediately apparent. Jed's smile faded when the quilt slipped down and he saw the big bandage on Ben's left shoulder and arm.

"Here, let me help you up," said Jed. "What happened to you anyway"? Jed held the flap of the door for Ben to enter, guiding his unsteady steps carefully to a spot near the fire. Jed noticed the lumber on the floor stacked against the sidewall. Then he saw the side door with the top half open and a beautiful young horse's head sticking through it.

"Well, it looks like you have been very busy this summer. I guess you do have a lot of stories to tell!"

Stump was bounding, barking and wagging. He remembered Jed and greeted him boisterously. Jed got down on one knee and rubbed Stump's ears and gave him a hug and scratches all over until the dog calmed down.

"He seems to have recovered completely from his fight with the bear," said Jed.

"Ben, if you would like to lie down and rest; I'll make us some coffee and a sandwich. How long has it been since you had a slice of bread?" Jed asked.

Ben's eyes lit up and a wide smile appeared.

"I haven't had a taste of bread or even a biscuit, since I've been here. My Mother baked the best bread I ever had, back home. We would put fresh churned butter and honey on it. It makes my mouth water to think of it. Sometimes we had biscuits on the trail though."

"The folks I have been helping all summer gave me a fresh loaf of bread and some meat for my trip home," said Jed. "I'll go get it." He went to the canoe and when he returned, his arms were full of things including more bandaging materials. "It seems that I do a lot of doctoring at this camp. You two should be more careful," he said with a chuckle.

True to his word, coffee was soon brewing and a thick sandwich of soft brown bread and roasted deer meat was on Ben's plate.

Stump came over and rested between the two young men, happy to listen to their conversation and enjoying their company. They each offered him morsels as they ate, but it was easy to see by his round tummy that he had eaten a meal recently and wasn't hungry. Jed was very eager to learn the story of how Ben got the young horse, and listened with a serious expression on his face, when Ben told about the mud bog.

"Don't you know enough to stay away from places like that? What could you do, if you had gotten yourself stuck in that mud?" he said sternly. Then more lightly, "But, that is a marvelous story."

"You haven't heard all of them yet," replied Ben. "While we were out hunting, we were chased by a prairie fire and had to take refuge down in a ravine. An elk fell right in our laps!"

"What?"

"Well, not exactly, but it was running in front of the grass fire and didn't see the edge of the ravine until it was too late. She fell just a few feet from where we were! That is her hide on the bed. I plan to make trousers out of it, but I can't do much until my arm heals."

"Gosh it is good to have someone to talk to! Jed, now it's your turn. Tell me what you have been doing all summer."

"I have been doing better than you by the looks of that bandage. I'll change it for you. Did you pull and dry any of the plants that I told you about?"

"Yes, but I have only a couple left now. I was so glad that they were here available, when I needed them. They are right there on that bark in the corner. When I feel better, I will get some more, before it snows. It was a good thing that I had those on hand when I needed them. I appreciate, that you taught me about them."

Jed had developed the ability to steer a conversation away from himself or his activities. He did it so smoothly that Ben didn't even notice it.

"Maybe, I will stay a few days again and help you, if that is all right," said Jed.

"It sure is," replied Ben.

As Jed put the crushed plant in the small pan with water and willow bark, and put it on to heat, he asked Ben how long ago he had been hurt. Ben really had to think about it.

"I am not sure, because I slept so much after it happened, but I think it was three days ago."

"What did you do to it?" Jed asked, as he started to gently remove the bandage.

"I was coming back from the woods by the lake, walking on a game trail where the bluff starts and a mountain lion was up in one of the trees and she jumped down on to me. I had a spear with me and she jumped right on it. She died instantly, but she clawed my arm as she landed on my chest. It bled for a long time."

"Ben, it looks pretty bad yet!" said Jed. "You should have that arm in a sling. It is better to rest it. Do you ever have a normal, uneventful day?" He asked.

"The day that I brought the wagon over went well. None of us got hurt anyway."

"Is that where you got the lumber?"

"Yes, I took that whole wagon apart, bit by bit and brought it over here. I used some of it for the two doors on Ginger's area and that on the floor is more than enough for a front door to keep the snow out." While they talked, Jed had put a new poultice on Ben's injury and bandaged it.

Jed took down the skirt that hung on the clothes tree and smirked at the mental image he had of Ben coming out of the hut wearing it after his swim.

"Do you mind if I tear this to make you a sling?" Jed asked.

"I would rather you didn't, it was my mother's. Jed managed to fashion a sling without tearing it. Once the sling was on, the muscles in Ben's arm could rest.

Jed had made the liquid from the plants he had boiled into a tea for Ben with chamomile and to improve the taste, he added a pinch of mint. They talked until it was late.

Ben had not given Ginger any attention since he was injured. He opened the bottom door and went in beside her. He scratched her ears and talked to her.

"Hello, my pretty girl. I'm glad you were able to feed yourself while I was down healing. I will clean your area as soon as I am well enough." He gave her a pat and pulled down a bundle of the sweet grass from the pile. He could tell that she had been munching at the edges of the bundles while he had slept. She appreciated having him near as much as she did the food. As long as the prairie was not buried in deep snow, there was abundant grass and wild grain for her to eat and the river was there for a fresh drink anytime she wanted one. She looked to him for companionship and security. Jed was amazed at the relationship between Ben and the young horse.

He had never been around animals much, but he liked them. Since he had traded his grandfather's horse for the canoe he had always preferred to travel on the river. He didn't like leaving tracks. There was no one that knew his whole story and that suited him just fine. He was twenty-one, but looked and felt older. His skin was dark and lined by the sun reflecting off the water. He had stories he could tell, but some didn't have endings yet. Others underlined his loneliness.

Jed carried his bedroll in and put it near the fire.

"Ben, if it is all right with you, I'm going to sleep right here. I'll bank the fire and add some fat to your candle if you want."

"Thanks that would be great, but I really don't need the candle burning. It lasts longer than the fire when I don't tend it, so it helped to not have to relight the fire the hard way. With both of us here, we will be able to keep the fire going with no problem. We should probably save the fat," replied Ben.

"It was a good idea, using the candle for a second source of flame. You are a clever kid," said Jed.

"Say, tell me. How old are you?"

"I think that it is about time for my sixteenth birthday. We always celebrated it with fresh cider and cake." That gave Jed an idea, but he didn't share it.

"I think we should turn in," said Jed and Ben agreed that it was late. Ben silently thanked God for bringing Jed back for a visit and for helping him to gain his strength back. He fell asleep as soon as he curled up with Stump on the bearskin. Jed slipped out the front door and went to his canoe. He gathered what he wanted inside and then pulled it up into the trees, behind a clump of thick bushes where it was out of sight.

At first light, Jed put wood on the fire and quietly moved about getting a new batch of medicine ready. He took the big pan out to the prairie and picked it half full of wild oats. As he was returning he spotted a grape vine climbing over a fallen tree. He rummaged through the leaves and found a few remaining wrinkled grapes. The birds and animals in the area had eaten most of them. Even a few added to the pan would give the grain a good flavor. I wonder if Ben found these, thought Jed, as he removed the seeds from the dark purple grapes and with a clean rock he crushed the grain and grapes against the bottom of the pan. He added water and put it on to cook. Ben still slept. The sun was peeking over the horizon and coming in the door so Jed dropped the flap and placed his bundle at the bottom to further block the sun's rays. I want Ben to sleep as long as he can. Rest will help him regain his strength, he thought.

Both animals were out. Jed quietly used the shovel to clean Ginger's area and with his knife he gathered dry grass and put a mound where she slept. He went back out and gathered more, piling it in several bound bundles against the back wall, copying what Ben had done on the sidewall. He noticed the slate pieces on the ground and lifted one and peeked in. He was amazed at the huge clay-lined cache, full to the top with hand-picked grain. This kid sure isn't afraid of work, he thought. He has a good place here. The location is great, too. It wouldn't take much to make an easy path to the top of the bluff for a lookout spot, to watch for animals or Indians on the prairie or anyone else that might come along.

Jed went back in the main part of the hut closing the bottom half of the door. He stirred the grain and pulled it and the medicine back from the heat. He had added another plant to use on Ben's arm. He picked out the plants so they would cool on top of a rock and added more water and some herbs to improve the flavor. Just as he finished that, Ben sat up and yawned.

"That's the best I've slept in a while," Ben said. "Thanks for letting me sleep and thanks for being here."

Before he sat down by the fire, he peeked into both pans. His first comment was "Yuk," over the medicinal tea and then "What is that purple stuff? It smells pretty good."

"That's my version of oatmeal. I added a few wild grapes that I found. I thought it would sweeten it a bit. Did you find the grape vine?"

"No, I didn't. I guess there are still surprises here for me to discover. I wish I had though." Ben went over to his little table and lifted the lid of the honey container. "Look what I found in a downed tree." Jed stuck his finger in the honey and licked it off.

"That's wonderful!" He said. "I love honey. A man could get fat if he stayed around here very long." They both laughed.

Jed went out to his canoe in the bushes. He brought in another bundle.

"I have a small birthday gift for you," he said, as he entered the hut. He rummaged in his pack and pulled out two beautiful wooden bowls. They had been handmade, by hollowing out a piece of wood and sanding it until it was silky smooth and then rubbing it with oil.

"These are beautiful!" said Ben. "We can certainly use these. Did you make them?"

"I made one and a friend made the other. He showed me how."

"Thanks, Jed. It is a happy birthday with you here. Maybe you can show me how these are made before you leave. I'd like to learn."

Jed said he would be glad to show him as he filled the bowls with the oatmeal and poured some of the medicinal tea into Ben's cup, and coffee in a wooden one he carried for his own use. They each scooped a conservative amount of honey on top of their oatmeal, before Ben said a heartfelt grace.

"Thank you Lord, for sending Jed back to visit, and thank you, for all the blessings you have given us. Thank you for my animals and this home and for this purple oatmeal." He ended with a laugh. Jed laughed too, and said "Amen."

Stump came in wagging his tail and sniffing at the bowls. Jed plopped a scoop of oatmeal in Stump's pan and Ben scraped a little of the honey out of his bowl and put it on top of Stump's food.

"You sure spoil that dog," said Jed laughing.

"He is more than a dog. He defended me and guarded me. He is a true friend," said Ben. "I love him. He is family." Jed turned his head a bit and ate without speaking. He didn't want Ben to see his face at that moment because it might reveal his thoughts. He wished that he had someone that felt that way about him.

After breakfast, Jed removed Ben's bandage and said that the arm was healing well. He put on the new poultice and wrapped it up again.

"It doesn't look as swollen and red as it did. If I had been here when it happened I would have put stitches in that deepest one, but it looks like it is going to be all right anyway."

"Maybe you can explain to me what you had in mind for that door and I can cut the wood for you, before I leave."

"That would be great," said Ben. Jed carried a couple pieces of the wood outside and Ben brought out the saw in his right hand. His left was back in the sling. Ben drew his plan in the dirt with a stick and Jed nodded agreement that it would work just fine.

"I can measure its height with this branch." He made a mark and then held it against the doorway to mark the width. He cut the pieces for the frame and was impressed when Ben provided nails that he had salvaged from the wagon. Jed installed the level frame.

"Let's lay the door out on the ground and nail it together with its cross braces," said Jed. "And I have a piece of buffalo hide in one of my packs that would be big enough to make some strong hinges."

"That's great! I haven't anything that strong."

"I knew that piece could be used for something," said Jed, as he stood the door in place. He rested it on the top of a small piece of wood and Ben helped steady it with his good hand while Jed nailed the hinges to the doorframe. "There, it has just enough clearance to swing freely. If you want to, you can glue a strip of soft leather to the bottom to keep the wind out."

"It fits well. Thanks a lot. Now all it needs is a latch. I'm sure glad to have a real door to secure this place. The door opens out so it will be easy to use one of the big bolts from the wagon, put through a short board that turns on the inside of the door." Jed drilled the hole and put the latch together. It worked fine but was a little loose. He turned the bolt and tightened the big nut on the inside, at the same time and then it worked fine. Ben opened it and closed it again to be sure. "Thanks Jed, for your hard work. This door is wonderful. It will keep out the cold weather, and I will feel much safer at night."

"Now if you're not too tired, let's go fishing." Jed chuckled.

"I'm not tired at all. You did all the work." Jed produced a pole, ready with line and hook from his canoe and Ben got his pole from the corner of the hut. His spears were also kept in that corner. That's when he remembered that he had left his other spear where the cat had jumped him. He wanted to get it as soon as he could. He also wanted to set his snares, he figured by now they probably had been tripped and were empty.

162

Jed had the shovel and was digging worms when Ben came out. They sat on the bank of the river in the late afternoon shade, enjoying the companionship.

As usual the deep area under the roots of the willow trees produced a generous supply of fish.

"That one makes six!" said Jed. "This is more than enough food for two people."

Just then, Stump showed up. He started licking Ben's face, and then Jed's, causing both of them to laugh. Stump was taking advantage of the fact that they were sitting on the bank, down at his level.

"Here," Ben said, handing Stump a fish and motioning toward the path. "Take this to your friends." Stump gripped the fish in his teeth and headed down the trail toward the lake, wagging his tail as he went.

"Where is he going with that?" asked Jed.

"I'll show you when I feel a little stronger. You won't believe your eyes." Ben replied, with a strange grin. Jed was puzzled but didn't question him.

"I'll clean these fish right here and use a fresh willow branch to string them over the fire," said Jed.

As they entered the hut, Ben looked at the shriveled squash near the fire. He couldn't remember putting it there. He picked it up and pitched it out under the trees. He chose another one.

"This time, would you split it and remove the seeds to dry and save?" They put the two halves back together and plastered the outside with a thick layer of clay before it was tucked into the hot stones near the fire, to bake.

Later, while Ben rested, Jed went up on the prairie and cut several more bundles of grass and brought them back, he tucked them under the row of squash. They were now on a bed of grass nearly two feet deep. We can use the grass for a number of things, he thought. Jed made a couple more trips and had a big pile next to Ben's bed when he woke.

"What are you doing?" Ben asked with a hearty laugh. "I'm not a horse!"

"If you will go sit by the fire and drink a cup of that new batch of medicine, I will show you." Jed pulled the hides from Ben's sleeping area. He put the grass down and adjusted it until it was an even, soft layer and then after shaking the hides, outside, he put the bed back together and took the quilt to the river, where he gently washed it over and over until it was clean. The wet quilt was very heavy, even after Jed pressed as much water from it as possible. He tossed one end up over a big branch and left it hanging there to dry.

"Tonight, you will sleep like a baby," he said.

"That bed looks so inviting, I might get back in it, and let you serve me there," Ben teased.

"Hey I don't think that's necessary!" Jed was laughing and was glad that Ben appreciated his efforts.

Just then Ginger entered her swinging door and snorted and stirred the fresh grass on her bed with her nose.

"It looks like she is saying thank you, Jed. I want to say thank you, too, for all you have done. You have been working hard ever since you got here."

"I do it because I want to. A guy has to earn his keep, doesn't he?" said Jed, with a big smile. "Tomorrow we can use my trousers for a pattern and cut a pair from that elk hide, if you want. I noticed the nice shirt and boots you made," said Jed. "You did a good job."

"Thanks." Ben was pleased with the compliment. "I really didn't know how to go about it, but just copied my old shirt and made it bigger. The boots still aren't as high on the leg as I would like. I think I will add more rabbit skins when I get everything else done and can take the time," Ben replied.

Jed nodded in agreement. Sitting by the fire sipping left over coffee, he pulled a chunk of wood from his bundle and a half-round flint knife and continued to hollow out the inside of it.

"This is a cup that I started just before I left. It will take a while to get it carved out as much as it should be," said Jed. Each time he pulled the archaic, curved stone blade up the inside of the growing hole in the middle, a small curl of wood was removed. He scraped at the inside a bit more and then said, "The fish and squash were done long ago. I think we better eat." Jed bowed his head and prayed quietly.

"Thank you Father, for giving us this food; and thank you for giving me the opportunity to be here with Ben."

That evening, Ben was especially grateful that the new front door was there to close. The weather was changing. The night air was cold, and a strong breeze moved the tree branches, causing a flurry of color to come swirling down. When Stump found the new door shut, he ran around to Ginger's area, where he easily sailed in, over the half door in the sidewall.

"Well, you made quite an entrance. It didn't take you long to figure that out. Did it boy?" Ben asked, as he scratched the dog's ears noticing how heavy Stump's under coat had grown. Then he looked up and saw that Ginger's coat was fuzzy and she had a thick winter coat. "If their coats are an indication, I think we are going to have a very cold winter."

"I think you are probably right. I noticed it too. Stump seems to have grown a layer of wool under his hair," said Jed.

In the morning they found frost on the bushes and most of the colorful leaves were down.

Jed had scraped and greased the cougar's skin and now it hung on the wall away from the fire. He took it down and scraped it again; rubbing more rendered fat into it, and then hooked it back onto the wall. It had gotten stiff lying on the floor rolled up, but with work, it would be fine.

"By getting this skin in the fall, the fur is thicker and it would make you a wonderful warm coat," suggested Jed.

"A coat is a good idea. I really wasn't thinking about it when I got it. I just brought it," said Ben.

"I am still amazed that you took the time to skin that cat, as bad as your wounds were."

Jed slipped out and walked along the river to check the snares. He was happy to do all that he could to help Ben. I love the smell of late fall, and the sound of the leaves, crunching under my step, he thought.

The snares held two rabbits. Jed reset the snares and skinned and cleaned the rabbits, returning with them so quickly that Ben hardly had time to wonder where Jed had gone.

"We still have three fish left, but I'll put the rabbits on to roast, anyway." He put one of the fish on a plate and gave it to Ben, and ate one himself.

Jed spread the elk hide on the floor and slipped his trousers off, spreading them out smoothly on top of it.

"You are nearly as tall as I am, but not as big around. I will cut them just a little bit smaller at the waist. They can turn under, and then when you get taller, you can let it drop down. Leather clothes last a long time and get softer and more comfortable with wear."

Using a blackened stick from the fire pit, Jed drew the pieces on the leather just as Ben had, for his shirt and boots. He cut the pieces out with his knife and also cut three, thin strips from the edge.

"These are to braid for a belt like mine," he explained. From his pack he took a tool with a sharp thin point. He punched holes along the sides and along the inside of the legs, and then turning the top edge down; he made holes through both layers. He did the same at the bottom of the legs, turning them under. Ben was excited about having pant legs that actually covered his legs.

166

Ben remembered the heavy quilting thread that he had in his mother's sewing kit. "Will this do?" he asked as he lifted it out for Jed to see.

"That's perfect," said Jed. "And it is strong enough to last. We can use it doubled."

Jed reached over and removed the sling from Ben's arm and then the bandage. He checked the arm and shoulder carefully.

"I think you can do a little sewing. Just don't lift at all with that arm for a few more days. I have something else I want to do."

Jed had slipped the sod cutter into Ginger's area earlier when Ben wasn't looking. Now, he went out the side door and took the sod cutter with him. He headed up the bluff above the hut, climbing carefully. He stopped when he got half way up, where there was a grass covered ledge and a baby pine tree. I think I can pry the sod loose and cut it into strips. I hope there is enough to cover the top of Ginger's room, he thought. He stacked the sod and then very carefully dug around the little pine tree, making sure that he didn't damage the roots. The hardest part of this job will be to toss the stacks of sod down so that they end up on the roof, where we need them.

When the first stack landed with a thud, Ben came running out to see what had happened. He couldn't believe his eyes as one pile of sod after another came dropping down.

Jed carefully scrubbed the surface of the ledge smooth so that from a distance it would look natural again. The next rain would finish the job. He carried the little tree down and planted it near the seam where the roof met the bluff. "Camouflage" he said with a grin, as he jumped down. Only half enough sod was available from the ledge. Jed cut more from behind the trees. He pieced it together tightly.

"The top of the addition looks like it is just part of the hill now. Thanks Jed. That was a lot of hard work."

"It will take a bit more effort but we can pile dirt against the sides and cover them if the weather holds," said Jed.

"That is great! I had planned to do that but just hadn't gotten to it. I have a pile of loose dirt in the trees, from digging the caches. That will get us started on dirt for the walls. There is still so much to do. I was able to finish one seam in my pants while you were out," added Ben.

"How is your arm?" asked Jed. "Not bad, just sore."

"I'm going for a swim," said Ben. "You could use a bath, too, after playing with all that dirt!" Ben laughed as he turned and walked to the river. He pulled his clothes off and walked into the water. The water was very cold and it didn't take long for him to begin to shiver. He scrubbed his head with his right hand and rinsed the sand off. His sore arm ached from the cold water. He walked out, to see Jed sitting beside his clothes, dripping water and glad for the sun's heat, radiating from the rocks.

As soon as Jed was dry, he pulled his clothes back on and said, "I am going to see if I can gather medicines from around the lake."

Ben thought it was a good time to show Jed the wolf family. He pulled on his shabby looking trousers and asked Jed to wait a minute, as he slipped his arm into the sling. His arm felt strangely free without its bandage. He grabbed some bear jerky pieces and stuffed them in the leather pouch.

"Come on, I'll show you where Stump goes," he said. As they followed the path, Ben instructed Jed to stop at the clump of trees and sit down quietly. Ben walked closer, peeking under the lower branches of the big pines, but no wolves were in the den. He was disappointed.

"They are not here. Let's try again on the way back." Jed was still puzzled but decided to let Ben have his fun and not ask the questions he had on the tip of his tongue.

At the edge of the lake Jed cut an arm load of cattail leaves and sat down under a tree. In just a few minutes he had woven a loose patterned collection basket with a wide handle. "This stuff is strong and makes a good basket for herbs or teas because the air can circulate through it and you can leave them in there and they will dry evenly," explained Jed.

"That's wonderful, how you can do that so fast. It's really useful. I need to learn," said Ben. "Who taught you?"

"I learned it from Gentle Fawn. She was making one, the first time I met her."

"Who is Gentle Fawn?"

"She and her husband Tom are the ones I helped this summer. We finished their house just a few days before I came here." Jed gathered some of the plants he had used for the poultice and washed off their roots in the lake before putting them in the basket. He worked fast as they walked on, plucking leaves or stems and leaves, explaining how each could be used.

Once in a while he pulled something from the mud, roots and all. Ben recognized those as wild onions. Jed snapped off seedpods and dug roots of others. Soon his large basket was full.

"I just remembered that I have a tap on a big maple tree. I should go check it."

When they got there, Ben was glad to see that the pan was nearly full of liquid. They carefully set the pan on the ground and Ben pulled the tube from the tree and plugged the hole with a small twig coated with pine pitch. "No use leaving it to drip on the ground," said Ben. Jed picked up the pan and carefully carried it.

They followed the path back around the lake. Under a big tree, Ben picked up his spear, showing Jed where the cat had jumped him. There was nothing left of the cat now.

They continued up the trail until Ben indicated they were near the den. This time he could hear the sounds of the little ones scuffling around and playing. Once again he had Jed sit down and he laid down his spear. He got as close as he dared, before he sat down, too.

Stump came over to lick him and get scratches. Ben reached in the pouch and pulled out the pieces of jerky and put them by his feet again. The wolves took this as their cue to snatch and run. All but the little female took a piece and moved away quickly. She picked one up but laid down by Stump to chew on it.

She watched Jed. As long as he stayed back where he was she felt safe. The mother kept starring at Jed, but didn't growl. She came out of the den, took a piece of dried meat and jumped up on her rock. Ben eased back slowly and stood up when he was once again on the trail. Jed followed his example. He didn't say a word until they were around the clump of big pines and away from the den. Then Jed exploded with excitement.

"That is the most amazing thing I have ever seen! How did you get to be friends with a pack of wolves?"

"Well really they are Stump's friends, but they let me visit as long as I stay back and I have never tried to touch them."

"Thanks for letting me see them," said Jed. That is probably the closest I will ever be to wild wolves. They are beautiful, but scary too. I realize what they are capable of doing, especially that mother. I could see it in her eyes. She was not afraid of us."

"I know what you mean. My heart nearly stopped the first time the mother jumped down from that big rock to get a piece of jerky. I thought she was attacking me. I wanted you to know they are special so that you wouldn't shoot them."

"I promise I won't even bother them. That was really something!" He was still excited.

"I don't know for sure but I think the pups are about five or six months old. They are getting big."

When they got back to the hut, Jed separated the things he had gathered and fastened some of them to the wall above the squash where they could hang and dry without being in the way, explaining again what they were and how they could be used. He tucked the basket between the squash on top of the dry grass. The rabbits had been pulled to the side of the fire, but were warm and ready to eat along with another squash Jed had prepared. He put his knife in the crack and the two halves separated. They scooped the steaming squash out with a spoon. It was soft and delicious.

"I'll pour this sap into the big pan and set it near the fire. That way if it boils or foams, it will stay in the pan. We don't want to lose a drop. Have you ever had a cup of chicory?" Jed asked, as he added a handful to the coffee pot.

"No, but I'll try it."

"This is something that grows wild here. If I see any I'll show it to you. It gets blue daisy like flowers in the summer.

"I don't remember seeing any blue flowers in my foraging trips but I think there are lots of things here that I haven't noticed yet." He sipped the chicory brew and found that he didn't like it.

Jed reached over and pulled the sewing to him. He was efficient, and never wasted a minute.

"Ben is your arm hurting?' he asked. He noticed that Ben was cradling his elbow in his right hand and his face looked a little flush.

"Just a little" he said. He was trying to be tough. Jed laid down the sewing and poured a strong cup of the leftover medicinal tea.

"Your arm is swollen and I think you have a little fever. After you drink this you should probably try out that soft bed. I'll go get your quilt. It should be dry by now."

"That sounds good to me. I am tired," agreed Ben.

"We did a lot today." Jed slipped out and returned with the clean quilt. Sitting down near the fire, he went back to his sewing, but was uneasy.

Ginger wasn't in her stall yet. He decided to go out and look for her. He had grown fond of the young horse in the short time he had been there. It was nearly dark and growing quite cold outside. She was still out. He quietly picked up his rifle and went out.

In some places, the tall grass hid anything that was in it. Even a small horse could be ten feet away and you wouldn't be able to see it. He heard her soft neigh of greeting and a warm feeling of affection washed over him. She nuzzled him as he put his arm around her neck and walked back to the hut beside her. Ben smiled to himself when he heard them enter her stall together. Soon, Stump made his dramatic entrance over the half door, and Ben relaxed. His unusual family was home and safe, at least for another night. I wonder what the future holds for all of us, he thought. Will I ever be able to find Sarah? Will she ever be part of my family again? Ben settled onto his soft bed.

"Good Night, Jed." He breathed a prayer, "Please Father; let Sarah have a place that is warm and dry this winter. Give her someone to love and care for her. You are all that she needs, Lord. You are her provider. Help her to remember that. Lord, is Sarah alive?" Soon after that sad thought, the medicine did its job, and Ben retreated from his grief, once again, into the relief of sleep.

CHAPTER TEN

WINTER'S ARRIVAL

Jed sat for a long time by the fire, stitching on the trousers and sipping his chicory brew. The syrup was turning thicker and a beautiful amber color. As he pulled the pan away from the fire, he had to acknowledge that he was finally getting sleepy. He banked the fire and unrolled his bedding.

Just as he was getting cozy in his bedroll, he began to hear something hitting the front door. Ginger nickered and stomped her foot. She was nervous. Jed opened the half door and went in beside her to reassure her with a pat and scratches.

"Easy girl, it's probably rain." He couldn't believe his eyes when he looked out between the leather strips of her door. The ground was covered with hail the size of small grapes. He rushed out and grabbed the two rabbit skins that he had left on the grass. Darting back in, he shook them free of hail before it could melt and tossed them on top of the dried grass bundles. Swiftly he darted out again, removing the last few things from his canoe. He turned it over, pulling it behind the pile of wood under the biggest pine where it would be protected from the hard-hitting hail. He brushed the little balls of ice from his hair and shoulders as he came in shivering, glad to be protected from the stinging pellets and again beside Ginger. He talked to her softly as he entered. She blew an acknowledgement and seemed more relaxed. Then he noticed that he couldn't hear the hail any more. He peeked out her door to see big, beautiful flakes of snow falling. Well this will surprise Ben, when he gets up, he thought as he closed the bottom half of Ginger's door and crawled into bed again, grateful for the warmth.

It was late and Jed had worked hard all day. He slept long and soundly. When he woke, it was morning and Ben had quietly built up the fire and added water to the strong chicory brew and the medicine. Both were hot. Ben had poured the syrup back into the smaller pan, wishing that he had made time for more containers. He didn't have anything to hold his syrup.

Jed raised his head and rubbed the sleep from his eyes.

"Have you been outside yet?" He asked with a grin.

"No not yet. Why?"

"Go peek out Ginger's door." Ben couldn't believe his eyes. The snow was at least ten inches deep and still falling. When he came back by the fire, Jed was up and putting on a coat, hat, mitts and boots. "I'm going to take the water barrel down and fill it with fresh water and check the snares," he said, darting out Ginger's door.

When he returned, Jed set the full water barrel inside.

"The snares are undisturbed. I'll be back in a few minutes." He headed out to the lake, where he gathered a huge bunch of reeds. He returned through Ginger's area, tossing them up on the bundled grass. Shaking the snow from his coat, he hung it on a branch near the doorway and then carried the water barrel in and set it back in place.

"I thought we should have that fresh and handy in case the river freezes over."

"Good idea," Ben answered as he borrowed Jed's hat and coat and put on his own new boots. He was excited to try them out. He headed out the front door finding that he had to use his good shoulder to muscle the door open against the snow. Ben was surprised to find that he didn't sink in as much as he thought he would, because of the added width on his boots.

His second discovery was that the soles were slippery. His feet went out from under him, and he lit on his seat! Well, I am glad that I didn't land on my sore arm, he thought, pushing himself back erect with his right arm. Ben tromped around a bit more and then was satisfied with his experience of the first snow of the season and happy to return to the warm fire inside. The bitter wind was driving the snow before it.

Ginger had been out and was back inside already, eating the grass that they had put down for her. She hadn't seen snow before and wasn't sure that she liked it.

Ben started a pan of mash for her, while the rest of them shared the last of the rabbits. After they had eaten, Jed braided the three strips of leather to form a belt for Ben's new trousers He tied the belt to a stick and threaded it through the casing he had made at the waist.

"There you are," he said. "Try them on".

Ben stepped out of his old worn pants and pulled on the new leather ones. They felt stiff just as his shirt had, when he tried it on. He pulled the belt up and made the same knot that he saw on Jed's.

"Thanks so much!" he exclaimed. "I really needed these. You did a fantastic job. They look like yours. I like them a lot!"

"I'm glad you like them. Why don't you put your new shirt on, too?"

Ben pulled it over his head carefully with Jed's assistance they protected his sore shoulder and arm. It felt warm and comfortable. He felt completely grown up until he looked down at his bare feet, then over at Jed's. Jed was wearing a nice pair of house shoes made of rabbit's skin with the fur turned inside.

"I should make a pair of those," Ben said, pointing at Jed's feet.

"They are easy to make, but let's do your coat and hat first. You can always slip on your boots if your feet feel cold," suggested Jed. It did make sense but suddenly Ben wanted to copy Jed in everything. He really liked Jed.

Stump had been out a little while and he jumped in over the half door, shaking snow all over the lion skin, they had just spread on the floor.

"No Stump, you are making my coat all wet!" said Ben. Then he realized that Stump didn't have any idea what he was talking about. He knelt beside the dog and rubbed his coat dry using dried grass. This time Jed's coat became the pattern.

"The size won't need much adjusting. All we need to do is copy the pieces. There may be enough left for a nice hat too," he said, as he continued drawing pieces with little effort. "We will use that same thread again if you have enough," said Jed, as he cut out the last piece. Then he cut a strip off the edge, the length of the leather.

"This attaches to your mitts and threads through the sleeves of your coat so you won't lose a mitt in a storm if you have to take it off," said Jed.

"You think of everything!" Ben was amazed. They made the holes for the seams on all the pieces and then both young men sat by the fire sewing all day.

Ben took a break just long enough to make toast in the frying pan, for their lunch, with the last few slices of the treasured bread. They enjoyed it with elk stew. Ginger delighted in her pan of mash, and Stump stayed in all day and was happy to chew on a piece of bear Jerky.

As they worked, Ben said," Did I tell you, that when I took apart the wagon, I found a tin box with my mother's garden seeds inside? I plan on making a garden down by the lake in the spring. I figured that if it doesn't rain enough, the lake water is right there to water it."

"That's a good idea, and we can make a fence to keep animals out of it."

Ben had noticed that Jed spoke as if he planned to be there in the spring but he didn't point it out. He felt that somehow if he did, then it wouldn't happen. Please God have him stay, Ben silently prayed.

They kept stitching. Jed was hoping that Ben would continue the conversation but he had fallen silent. Ben had nearly completed the second mitt. Jed was working on the front of the coat and Ben was surprised to see two big patch pockets on the front. "I am glad that you put pockets on it. I was planning on putting some on my shirt, too, and a sleeve for my knife on my pants and two pockets on them, too"

"That's a good idea," said Jed. "I could use pockets on my pants. I've never taken the time to put them on. Maybe we can spend a day or two making pockets after we get this together."

Ben was pleased that Jed liked his idea. Just as he finished the second mitt, Jed stretched and said, "I think we have done enough sewing for one day. I am going to make us something to eat."

Ben hung the rabbit fur mitts on the tree trunk beneath his sister's doll and rolled up the unfinished coat and hat and put them out of the way. Jed was pulling things out of one of his bundles. He put a heavy cast iron frying pan near the fire to heat. In it he put a dab of grease to melt. He measured flour and sugar and baking powder. Ben watched with interest, as Jed used a small pan, for a mixing bowl. Then he sprinkled in a bit of something else that he wouldn't show Ben. He chuckled and returned the small pack to his bundle. Jed scooped up a big handful of the hickory nuts from the birch bin and cracked them with a stone. He tossed the pieces of shells into the fire and the nuts into the mix as he freed them from their shells. The pan was smoking a little so he edged it away from the fire. He stirred a little grease into the mix and then added water slowly until it was the right consistency. He scraped the whole batter into the hot pan and quickly put on the heavy cover, pulling the pan back from the heat. They could hear it sizzling. He got their plates and brought the maple syrup.

A few minutes later, when Jed lifted the lid of the pan, a most heavenly aroma filled the room. "This is the closest thing to a birthday cake that I know how to make," Jed said, as he sliced the cake in half and plopped half on each of the plates. It was about an inch thick and a crispy golden brown on the bottom.

"Happy Birthday, Ben! Spoon some syrup on it and enjoy!" said Jed.

"First let's pray," said Ben. "Father I thank you for this cake and for Jed."

"Amen." They said together. Ben stuffed a big spoonful into his mouth.

"This is really good, Jed, I love it," he said with his mouth full.

Just then Stump came over and wagged enthusiastically. He wanted some. Jed got up and brought Stump's pan and with his spoon he took a piece from each of their plates and drizzled syrup on top before he handed it down to Stump.

"Now who is spoiling that dog?" Ben laughed.

"Remember, he is family," said Jed, laughing, "and this is a party!"

Before dark they looked outside to see that the snow had doubled and was still falling. Jed used the shovel to move the snow away from Ginger's door. The wind had started to blow the snow inside. Jed saw that if it was not removed, it would make her sleeping area wet. The next day was again spent sewing until the coat and hat were finished.

"Thank you Jed, I would have had a hard time making my clothes without your help. And, thank you, Heavenly Father, for providing everything I need." By nightfall the snow had finally stopped.

The next morning, as soon as they were suited up in all their heavy gear, both young men were out walking around in the snow. Suddenly they both realized that their tracks would be easy to notice from the river. They agreed that anytime it snowed or was muddy, they would use Ginger's door and walk into the woods on the side of camp and go to the river without disturbing the small clearing near the hut.

Ben decided to say what he was thinking.

"Jed do you think anyone would worry about you, too much, if you stayed here this winter? We would sure like to have you. The river already has ice on it and it will be dangerous and if you walk home, you might freeze to death!" He was trying to be persuasive but in his heart he felt that Jed could handle any situation that came along. Jed stopped in his tracks. Ben wanted him to stay all winter! His heart was starting to pound and he could hardly speak.

"Did you just say that you thought that I should stay all winter?" He wanted to hear him say it again.

"I did, but forgive me. I was just being selfish. You are probably worried about your family and I have already kept you so long that now getting home is going to be a terrible journey. I'll help you get ready and you can head out the first day that the river clears," said Ben.

"Wait a minute, now you are telling me to leave? I thought you just asked me to stay!"

"I do want you to stay, but your family needs you."

"Ben, I don't have a family. No one will worry about me, or miss me. I'm alone just like you. I would really like to stay, if you want me." Ben was so pleased and excited that he ran to Jed and gave him a big hug!

"You are like having a big brother. I don't want you to ever leave," said Ben.

Jed laughed and said, "Let's wait and see how you feel about me being here by spring. I'll stay until then."

Stump could feel the excitement in the air and circled around barking. Even Ginger came trotting back from the prairie with her nose covered with snow. She had discovered that it was fun to play in the snow, after all.

"See," said Ben. "We all want you to stay." They laughed and a snowball fight broke out that lasted long enough to send Ginger scurrying back to the safety of distance on the prairie and Stump down the trail to check on the wolf family.

The rest of the day seemed like a celebration. It was a day filled with joy and laughter. They made a hearty soup and enjoyed the knowledge that they had a family. By nightfall, Ben was wiggling his toes in his new house shoes. He closed his eyes enjoying the feeling of the warm soft fur.

"Thank you Father," Ben said, "for the house shoes and for providing all my winter clothes and thank you for my big brother, Jed. I love him. Thank you for sending him to me. I don't know why you have put us here or how you intend to have us serve you in such a remote place, but I am willing and I think that Jed is, too. I'm excited to know what you have planned for us."

Ben didn't see that he had already been used to help Stump, and Ginger and had offered Jed the first home he had enjoyed since he had lost his grandfather when he was thirteen.

Jed had avoided giving any additional information about his family and Ben had been careful not to question him, hoping that Jed would share his story when he was ready. The snow started melting the next day and the sun was so bright and warm that Ben and Jed were out in their boots, but with no coats on. They decided to go hunting when they checked the snares and found them empty.

Tracking game in the snow was easy. Jed spotted the buck in the trees. Their boots in the melting snow helped them approach quietly. Ben held his breath as Jed fired the shot. The big deer fell and never moved.

"That was a clean shot Jed. You are good with that rifle!" Each of them held on to an antler and dragged the heavy deer back to camp. They hung it in a tree and cooked the liver and heart with wild onions. Jed left a large chunk of meat attached to a fore leg and gave it to Stump to take to his wolf family.

"Those pups are big now and I know that in the cold, they need to eat more to stay warm and healthy." Ben smiled. He was glad that Jed liked the wolf cubs.

Jed could see that Ben was planning something by the expression on his face. Ben stood up and began to transfer the squash to the corner with the nuts.

"What are you doing?" Jed asked. "Be careful of your arm."

"You'll see," was all the answer he got. Ben moved more things, clearing the back wall completely. He gathered two huge bundles of dry grass in his arms from beneath the squash. Near the wall he spread the grass in a soft layer, and then put Jed's sleeping roll on it and unrolled it. The foot of Jed's bed touched the foot of Ben's.

"Your head will be over one cache and feet on the other, but I think you will sleep better in a permanent place out of the middle of the room, and an added bonus is that our beds will insulate the tops of the caches and help keep them cold. What do you think?"

"That's a good idea and if I need a midnight snack all I have to do is reach under my bed," he said with a hearty laugh.

They had many meals from the deer and worked the hide. The rest was dried on the wagon wheel inside, and stored. Ben saved the leg bones to carve but sent several parts to the wolves, including the head, after he removed four teeth and the antlers. It was funny to watch Stump carry that deer head down the trail. He acted like he was taking a present to a birthday party.

Much of the snow melted, and the south side of the trees and bushes were totally bare when the weather turned bitter cold. Jed and Ben had continued to build their wood supply. It was good that they had, because this time they were really going to need it. The snow grew deep and drifted high. It had to be shoveled out of the doorway to Ginger's room, again and again. She still made short trips out but they were usually to the river and someone would have to go with her to break through the ice so she could drink.

Jed set to work one day, and with his weaving skills, he made a big watertight basket for her to drink from.

"I am going to make a second one to place behind the fire pit to hold melting chunks of ice or snow, and then we can transfer the water into her basket or the barrel."

"That's a great idea, but I think we will have to take Ginger's basket away when she is done drinking, because she will think it is a fun thing to chew on," said Ben.

"Maybe she needs something to entertain her," said Jed

"I don't know about that," said Ben. "Do horses play?"

Together they made woven mats to sit on near the fire from some of the grass under the squash and Jed made a strong mat using some of the reeds he had brought from the edge of the lake. He gave it to Ginger to play with. She would chew the edge and toss it or flop it up and down.

Ben cut a circle from the deer hide, to use as a bottom and the second birch container for the rest of the nuts was finally finished. The outer casings from the hickory nuts were boiled and the resulting dark brown dye was used to darken the deer hide just for fun. The rest of the dye was saved in the waterproof stomach that they had processed from the deer.

Each day new projects were found and they kept busy. Ben had worked on his bone knife. It was sharp, smooth and beautiful. He had decorated the handle with a simple cross hatch pattern.

"This winter isn't anything like I thought it might be. I was sure that I would be lonely and depressed. Thanks for staying with me, Jed."

"Thanks for wanting me. Winters are difficult for everyone. It is hard to stay inside during the coldest months."

Ben had continued to mark his sticks and each Sunday they would sit at the fire taking turns reading from the Bible out loud. They each took time to read quietly, evenings or mornings but Sundays were special.

"We have so much to be thankful for. But more than anything else, I thank God for sending me to you, little brother," said Jed. "I love it here and I love you and the animals," he declared. I feel like God has finally given me a family."

Ben was surprised by Jed's declaration. A feeling of family love had developed between them. He was sure that it had, but he was surprised to hear Jed put it into words.

"Well big brother, we love you, and I pray right now that God will grant that we can always be together, as a family," said Ben. "I prayed that I wouldn't have to be alone all winter. I was really dreading it. He answered my prayer better than I could have hoped. He gave me a big brother."

"God always gives us what we need. Doesn't He," said Jed?

"I like what Matthew 6:33-34 NIV says. "But seek first his kingdom and his righteousness, and all these things will be given to you as well. Therefore do not worry about tomorrow, for tomorrow will worry about itself. Each day has enough trouble of its own." Ben remembered those verses.

"The verses above that, talk about not worrying about our clothes or what we will eat. It says that the flowers do not work or spin cloth, yet they are dressed finer than Solomon. I like that. I relied heavily on that promise when I found myself here alone. Jed, please read that whole chapter out loud."

Ben closed his eyes and listened as the words filled the quiet little room. He remembered his father reading out loud each evening after their meal on the trail and pictured the faces of the people that gathered near to listen. He felt that it was likely that they had all died when the raid on their wagons took place.

After thinking about it, he had realized that the curls of smoke he had seen in the distance that terrible day were more raiders, and the wagons of the train being burned. As he listened he wondered if anyone else had been taken besides Sarah.

The bitter cold kept them all inside as much as possible, but they had all they needed. Sleet covered the trees. Branches broke under the weight of the ice. The dyed deer hide was hung inside Ginger's entrance as an added insulation. They all managed to stay entertained, even Ginger. Jed would lay her mat on her back and she would reach around with her teeth and pull it off, then swing it up and down. She didn't know it, but this was the start of getting used to something on her back. In mid-December, the weather warmed a bit and for a few days they were able to go out for a walk and gather more wood.

Ginger made her way out to the prairie where she jumped through deep drifts and ran in the snow. She was still young and had to expend some of her energy. Stump thought that it looked like a fun game and joined her barking. They raced away and came back, covered with snow and happy to be free of walls for a little while. Stump returned looking like a four-legged snowman. Ben closed both doors to Ginger's room when the animals finally came in. He and Jed gave them a bit of grooming. They had gathered the stiff grass stems into two bundles and tied them tight. With the ends cut off smoothly they could use them as brushes. The clean grass they had placed down for bedding became wet and had to be replaced with a fresh dry bundle. Both animals laid down in it and went to sleep. Ben scooped out a pan of grain to cook for Ginger.

"She is probably hungry after all that exercise," he said. "I know I am." They put on a big pan of soup with lots of cut up elk meat, dried greens, roots and herbs, for the rest of them.

Ben was thinking about Christmas and he had secretly started polishing and making holes in the teeth he had collected, so he could string them as a gift for Jed. Jed had been working on a map, carved on a slab of wood. It was an accurate map of the Hickory River as far as he had traveled. He had made an X where the hut stood against the bluff and carved the word "Home." He had another surprise, too.

In one of his satchels he had pumpkin seeds and a small pouch of popcorn seeds. He would give them to Ben for planting in the spring. I have to admit that I am tempted to pop the corn for Christmas, but I know it would be better to plant it so that it can grow and multiply, he thought.

Next year if God blesses our garden, we will have lots of popcorn at Christmas time. Then he realized that he had thought, "Our garden," and it felt so good inside to belong here and to be loved and to have someone who wanted him here. I wonder if I will ever find out what happened to my parents.

Each time they went out in the woods to walk or hunt, Jed watched for the perfect Christmas tree. Without mentioning it, Ben was doing the same thing. He also was planning to use some of the meat of the fat ducks that he had in the cache for Christmas dinner. Jed and Ben had chosen a day for Christmas by using the marked sticks and counting forward.

It was the day before their Christmas, when Ben crossed the frozen river. He wasn't sure why he felt the need but before long, he stood at the foot of the oak where his parents were buried.

"Hello, Father. Hello, Mother. I just came to tell you Merry Christmas, and that I am doing fine. I have a big brother now. His name is Jed and he has helped me. The horse and dog I told you about are well and the horse Ginger has grown a lot. I miss you very much, but I wanted you to know that you don't need to worry about me. We are going to celebrate Christmas tomorrow and I know that I will really miss you and Sarah even more then. I still plan on going after her, and I will find her. I promise you, that with God's help, we will be together. So don't worry, and thank God, for me when you see Him, for all the help He has already given me. Well, that's all for this time. I love you both and I'll come back to visit from time to time. You know that I don't think that you are really right here, but I feel closer to you somehow when I come here."

He stood there for a moment and then dropped to his knees, in the snow, with a heavy heart. There in the silence, and in the snow and cold, he knelt quietly, not praying, not saying a word; listening. When he stood, he brushed the snow from his leather pants and found that he was thinking back to how his new life had evolved since early summer.

Suddenly it dawned on him "This is a new life." and it became that, when I started looking forward with anticipation instead of looking back and thinking in terms of just daily survival. How lucky I am to be here now, young, strong and alive to grow with this new land.

"Thank you Lord, for showing me that," he said. He walked back to the hut with a light heart. He could not imagine the exciting adventures yet to unfold.

CHAPTER ELEVEN

DIAMONDS FOR CHRISTMAS

"What do you think of our Christmas tree?" Jed asked with a wide smile as Ben entered the hut. I figured we should have a small one because of the space and anyway we haven't much to decorate it."

"It's great Jed! I think it is perfect. You're right, we don't have any of the traditional things that I remember from my childhood, but I know that we can figure out something." Ben brought out all the smallest metal fittings he had saved from the dismantled wagon. "Some are too large and heavy but the smaller ones will work and we can make them shiny by rubbing them with sand."

"Good idea," said Jed, reaching into one of his bundles. "I keep a little pouch of dry sand to smooth the things I carve. We can use this."

They hung the few polished pieces on the tree, but it still looked bare. Ben pulled his mother's calico skirt down over the little tree and snuggled it around the bottom, and then put on his coat and boots and went outside. In a few minutes he was back with an armload of pods and different pretty grasses that he had found peeking out of the snow. He had also picked pinecones. They tucked all those among the branches.

"It looks festive but we can make it even better," Ben said. He folded up the bottom of Jed's bedroll and opened the food cache. "We have lots of crabapples, more than we will ever use. Let's string some of them," he said.

"That's a good idea." They were having fun. "With the garland of crabapples the Christmas tree will really look beautiful, but we need a star on the top," said Jed. "You string the crabapples while I make a star." He pulled a couple of handfuls of grass from beneath his bedroll and like magic as Ben strung the crabapples and watched; Jed fashioned a star with five points.

"It is perfect!" said Ben. "We can use a long piece of grass to tie it on." Having a tree was a good idea, Jed. Thanks for going out and getting it. Carefully they wrapped the garland on the front side where they would see it. Now, I need to finish something, said Ben, so if you would make us a pot of tea or coffee, I will be out in Ginger's area for a while." Jed was glad that Ben was busy for a few minutes. He wanted to put the finishing touches on the carved wooden map he was making as a gift for Ben.

Ben was sitting in the fresh straw, leaning against Ginger's side. The beautiful young horse was always glad to have him near.

Now that the tiny cross is finished, I can put the cross in the middle of the cord and then the pairs of teeth, one on each side, in size order, first the bear, lion, elk and then his deer and last mine. Ben added a bone bead on each side, and then tied the cord in a loop big enough to slip over Jed's head. Each had created the best gift they possibly could. Jed intended to tell Ben that he wanted to take him in the canoe next summer to see the area of the river on the map and to meet his friends down river.

Ben stepped back in the main room and slyly slipped the necklace under his bedding.

That evening after they had eaten, they read the Christmas story from Luke 2:1-20 NIV and munched on hickory nuts and shared stories of their best Christmas as a child. Just before they banked the fire and went to bed, Jed shared some of his history.

"It was a baby that helped me believe in God."

"What do you mean?" asked Ben.

"I was never taught much about God or having faith when I was at home. My Grandfather didn't go to church or read from the Bible, and as I was traveling alone, I always felt that something was missing."

"One day I rounded a bend in the river and there was a camp with a young couple. The wife was very young. She was in labor with her first baby and having a really bad time. The husband wasn't much older. He was holding her hand and kneeling near her praying. When he saw me, he jumped up.

"Thank God you have finally come," he explained that he had been praying for help most of the night and that he was scared that something was wrong because she wasn't having the baby yet.

"He was sure that I had been sent by God to help them. I wasn't so sure. I didn't know any more than he did. I knew that if the baby didn't come she would die so I figured that I had to try to do something quick. I made her a strong infusion of the tea for the pain like I made for you. Then when we checked, instead of the baby's head, we saw its back side. I talked her husband through turning the baby."

"The next time she had a contraction, the baby boy was born. He was strong and healthy. That young father never stopped praying. He told me that he knew that God was there and that as long as they trusted in Him that everything was going to be all right."

"I stayed with them a few days and hunted for them. He told me more about God and His Son, in those few days than I had heard in all the rest of my life. They named their baby Jedidiah after me. Just before I left their camp they prayed with me and I accepted Jesus as my Savior. I know that something special happened to me. I don't feel alone anymore and I can't let a day go by without talking and listening to God. I love to read the Bible whenever I get a chance, but I don't have one. I hope that you don't mind me using yours."

"You can use it anytime you want," said Ben, "and thanks for telling me. That was a wonderful Christmas story."

Ben got the candle and lit it. Jed was puzzled.

"Why did you do that?"

"I just thought it was a good thing to do, being Christmas and all. Jesus is the light of the world." Ben answered, as they got into their beds.

"I'm surprised you didn't want to put out milk and cookies!" teased Jed, and they both laughed.

"Santa Claus will have to make do with some nuts and the rest of the tea," Ben replied, with a yawn. "Good night Jed, Merry Christmas."

"Good night, little brother, sleep well." Neither of them went to sleep right away. Each was lost in memories.

Ben prayed silently, thanking God for all that he had, but other thoughts intruded. His mind slipped to the day the Indians attacked and killed his parents and to the fear in his heart as he searched for his sister Sarah.

At first I was afraid that I would find her somewhere in the trees, dead, and when I didn't find her, I was even more afraid of what might happen to her.

"Lord, if you will give me one Christmas wish, it is that she is safe and cared for, by someone that has grown to love her. Lord, is she alive and with the Indians that took her? Make her strong enough to survive. She won't have a Christmas celebration with them, Lord, but let her feel your love for her." He prayed silently. "Let her know that I love her and will someday come for her." He sighed deeply, trying to relax. Finally, once again, sleep brought relief from his anguish.

*****

Christmas morning brought a glare of sun on snow. The world was beautiful, decorated with frost diamonds everywhere.

Ben took the axe, and ice basket to the river and broke through the ice so Ginger could drink. Then he filled the basket with the chunks. She pranced and frisked, snorting

190

and bunted Ben in the back, nearly causing him to fall. He turned around and scratched her ears and ran with her until she quickly outpaced him.

"You are getting so big! I can't begin to keep up with you." Stump came through the trees and ran around barking and then a snow clump hit the back of Ben's head.

"Hey," he yelled. "I thought you were never getting up!"

"I have been up and working. Ginger's area is clean and I took in some more wood for the fire."

"It sure is cold out here, but look at all the diamonds."

"It's too bad they melt," said Jed. "We would be rich."

"We are rich," said Ben. "Merry Christmas, Big Brother. Let's go see what we can fix for our Christmas meal." They hurried in through Ginger's big door, hanging their coats and boots to dry on branches near the inside door. Ben quickly brushed Ginger's coat to free it of the snow before it could melt. Jed added wood to the fire and then rubbed his hands together, blowing on them and held them out to the fire. Ben pushed the coffee pot closer to the flames so they could sip the last bit it contained. He wanted something hot.

"I saw some cans of spice tucked over by the coffee. What kinds are there?" asked Jed.

"I don't know, I just picked them up and brought them when I found them, cleaning up the wagon area. The outsides of the cans are badly rusted, but maybe you can tell by the smell when we get the lids off."

Jed tapped gently on the lids and finally they unscrewed. The first one was cinnamon and they found one of cloves. "Smell it. Yum! They smell like Christmas pie," said Ben.

"Let's try to make one," said Jed.

"We don't have any apples, just those crabapples."
"Didn't you ever have a pumpkin pie at Christmas?" asked Jed.

"Yes we did, Jed, but we don't have any pumpkin either."

"We have the next best thing. Squash can taste like pumpkin if it has the right stuff added." Jed was already cutting a squash in half, and scooping out the seeds. He headed for the river to get a small pan of mud using the hole that Ben had broken in the ice for Ginger. He coated the squash thickly with the clay and set it where it would bake. Ben smiled to himself and went to the cache to get the duck meat.

"It is dry and we will need to cook it in water, but we will have duck, for Christmas dinner," he said with a flourish.

"That sounds great! I didn't even think about it but it makes sense that you would try to get ducks with the lake there. You are a clever kid! And, we can cook some of the dried greens that we gathered. We will have a feast." The two young men worked together preparing the meal, each inwardly pleased that they had a special gift to give the other after they had eaten. Jed mixed flour, salt and grease, and added just enough water to form dough. He patted it into the heavy frying pan. As soon as the squash was soft, he scooped out the entire yellow center and mashed it in a pan, adding sugar and spice and stirred it with a spoon. It looked delicious already. The mixture was transferred into the crust and the pan set on rocks that he pulled from the fire. The slate from the top of the cache was used to stand against the rocks blocking the heat in, forming a partial oven.

The big pan was full of the duck and, onions and tubers. He added a pinch of this and that and then Ben suggested a bit of salt since it was a holiday.

They sat enjoying the wonderful aroma coming from the pans. "We can have some mint tea while we wait," said Ben, as he put the small pan near the flame to heat. He also put a pouch of mash on to cook for Ginger and added a handful of crabapples. She should have a treat today, too." Jed thought that Ben looked excited and happy as he busied himself.

Finally when the meal was prepared and cooking, Ben got down an elk bone from the ceiling branches where he had stored them and began to carve it.

"I want to make a cross for the wall and I'll date the back of it to mark our first Christmas together." He pulled a second bone from the cache where he had kept it. "This is from the deer you shot. I saved it for Stump as a special Christmas treat."

Jed got out his carving tools and started to work on a small piece of cherry wood he had kept in his bundle. "What are you working on?" Ben asked.

"I thought I would try to make an angel to hang on our tree."

"That's quite a challenge. Are you going to put a face on it?" "I'm not sure yet". They worked quietly for a while just enjoying the day and the companionship. Jed reached over and lifted the tea away from the fire and poured some for each of them.

He turned the frying pan and carefully traded the rocks under it for hot ones. "This is nearly done," he said. He worked on his angel for a little while longer, and then declared it time to eat. Their crafts were set aside and plates brought to the fire.

Sitting on the mats with Stump's pan between them, Ben said a prayer.

"Thank you, Father, for salvation through your Holy Son, Jesus. Thank you, for all the blessings that we have. Father, I ask a special blessing on Sarah today, that she is protected and cared for in a loving way. Amen." Jed looked over to see Ben quickly wipe a tear from his cheek as he picked up his plate.

They scooped out pieces of the duck and vegetables. Stump's pan was filled. He sat near Ben wagging his tail and waiting for the chance to start eating. Ginger's mash had been removed from the fire earlier and poured into her pan. She was enjoying it. When the pan was empty, she banged it around and played with it.

"She sure is having a good time," said Jed as he checked to be sure that Stump's food had no bones and was cool enough to allow him to eat. Both animals soon settled down for a nap. Stump lay on his side with his foot draped over the meaty deer bone that Ben had given him. The hut was quiet with only the crackle of the fire to break the silence.

"The duck was wonderful, but I saved room for that fantastic smelling pie," said Jed with a chuckle.

"Me too," said Ben. They ate half of it.

When Ben stepped over to the side door, intending to retrieve the pan from Ginger's area, he stopped short of the door.

"What is the matter Ben?"

Jed could see by Ben's expression that there was something unusual. A smile broke across Ben's face as he quietly spoke.

"We have a Christmas guest. Come see." In the soft light that filtered through the swinging leather strips of Ginger's door, sat a rabbit. It was all white, colored by nature to blend with the winter landscape. She had been drawn by the smell of the bundled grass, and was sitting quietly by the wall, eating her Christmas dinner.

Jed looked first at the rabbit and then back at Ben. The smile had not faded.

"She probably has a hard time finding food, with all the deep snow. She is welcome to have her fill," said Ben. "That was the best meal we have had, thanks to you! You are a good cook, Jed! And now," said Ben, "I have a small gift for you."

194

He walked over to his bed and pulled the necklace from under the bearskin and held it up for Jed to see.

"In the middle is a little cross that I carved of bone. This pair of teeth, on either side is from the bear that hurt Stump, these are from the mountain lion that jumped me and these I took from the elk that fell in the ravine with us and the next two are from the deer I shot with my bow, and then the last two are from the deer you shot with your rifle. That deer was the first big animal I ever hunted."

Jed was so surprised and affected that at first he couldn't say anything. He took the necklace and put it over his head.

"This is the nicest gift I have ever been given. It holds many interesting stories. Thank you Ben, I really like it and I'll keep it always. I have a cord in my bundle made with some horsehair that will be stronger. When this one starts to wear, I will string them on that, but shouldn't you keep this yourself? You are the one the lion jumped, and you killed the bear?"

"No, I want you to have that. Besides I have another set of teeth just like those. I took four teeth from each animal. I put one top tooth and one bottom on there. You can see the difference. When I get the rest drilled and make a cross, I'll have a necklace, too."

Jed went to his bundle and pulled out the two small packets of seeds.

"These are for you. This one is popcorn, and these are pumpkin seeds. You can add them to the garden next spring."

"That is wonderful! We will have the best garden anyone ever had!" Ben exclaimed.

"I have something else for you," said Jed. "This is a map of the Hickory, as far as I have been in either direction and the X on it is this hut. I want to take you next summer to meet my friends and see some of what I have seen. Will you go with me?"

"Oh Jed, this is fantastic! When did you find time to work on this? Sure I will go. I would love to go, but you will have to teach me how to paddle. I have never been in a canoe!" The idea, of such an adventure, had filled Ben with excitement.

"Is this where you helped build the house for your friends? I wish we could go right now!" Ben pointed to the map where two lines, representing the rivers, merged.

"Yes their house is here." Jed made a small mark on the map with the tip of his knife. "I thought we could go after we build the fence and plant the garden. If we hunt and dry meat as often as we can, we will have lots for next winter and won't be short even though we were gone."

"That's a good plan, but do you think we could make time for two trips? I want to follow the wagon train route around the bend and find out for sure what happened to it. The only time I headed that direction I found Ginger in the mud bog and didn't finish my intended route. Instead I brought her back here."

Suddenly Ben looked serious.

"What will we do with the animals if we leave in the canoe? There is no one to take care of them?" With that thought, their faces became serious.

"We can't just leave them. They count on us," said Ben.

"We will need to think about it and pray for a solution."

That night they joined hands and prayed.

"Thank you God, for a wonderful Christmas. Thank You for your Son, Jesus. It is His birth and our rebirth in Him that we celebrate. Thank you for our new life here and thank you for the Christmas visitor, too."

Then Jed closed his eyes and prayed.

"We thank you; for our animal companions, and ask that you show us how we can take the journeys we have planned and still take good care of Ginger and Stump."

Later, as they lay in their beds, their minds were busy trying to solve the problem.

The next morning the Christmas tree was placed out in the woods with the crabapples still on it, as a treat for the birds and animals to find. The metal fittings were back with the rest. The finished angel with a sweet smiling face was hooked on the wall above the front door to remind them of their wonderful day. Ben finished work on the bone cross he was making. He used two pieces of bone. The horizontal piece was glued on. He had carved a star in the center where the two pieces connected. On the back he carved the year, 1861 and the words, "First Christmas." They hung it in the corner by their beds. Next to it was hung the star made of grass.

Jed got up one morning before daybreak. I hope I can get her to understand what I want to do, he thought. Jed folded the old sheet into a square pad, and put a smooth rock in the center of the folds for a little added weight. I want to put this on Ginger's back and tie it on with that wide woven strap I have in my bundle. Ginger immediately thought that it was to play with and tried to pull it off, but Jed pushed her head back and held a bit of grain for her to chew as he scratched her ears. She tried again to dislodge the weight on her back and again he distracted her with hugs and whispers in her ear while he rubbed her coat with grass. I don't know yet, if this will work, so I won't mention it to Ben, but I think if I use patience, even though she is young, she could learn to carry a small load on her back without harm to her. Each morning he would place the padded weight on her back, tie it on and then hand feed her and scratch her.

Finally when she acted as if this was a normal morning event, he left it on and walked out her door to the prairie. She followed him out and started to eat the grass where the wind had blown the snow clear. He strolled along and she nibbled and followed. She is totally ignoring the small weight on her back. That is what I wanted to see. Jed took the pad off and patted her rump.

"Ginger, you are a smart, good girl." I wish I knew a way to keep her safe, he thought as he returned to the hut. She is so vulnerable out there alone.

Jed built up the fire and put on a pot of coffee mixed with chicory. He liked it that way. The next several weeks continued in a comfortable routine with the weather promising to warm and then swinging back into a bitter cold. It snowed again, adding to the difficulty of going outside.

Jed had carved several bowls and cups and had woven two very large baskets that were flat on one side. The faces of the baskets were rounded out and each had a flap that covered the top and tied. A loop on the back would make it easy to fasten the two together or to fasten them to a wide strap.

"What are you making?"

"I am making backpacks." Ben thought that was a good idea. What Jed didn't say was that they were for Ginger's back.

Jed had continued his early morning lesson with Ginger and she now would allow him to put several heavy stones inside the pad with no question. Any day that the weather allowed, he would quietly go out with her carrying the weight. She had learned to keep pace and walk with the weight on her back, without a rope lead. She loved the attention and thought of it as a new version of an old game she and Jed had played with the woven mat. She was strong, like all the wild mustangs, and the pad seemed very light to her.

By spring, Jed and Ben had hunted several times and the deer hides were processed and made into a small tent.

The caches were full of dried meat, when a warm spring breeze began to melt the snow. Stump was out and gone for days at a time. The men worried about him. Ginger was losing her winter coat and Ben saved the clumps of hair tucking them into a hole between branches in her area. He brushed her every evening until her coat shone.

When he was around, Stump wanted to get in on the brushing session, too. His coat was changing and he enjoyed the scratching of the brush. Ben put Stump's hair in the hole, too. The hair would add strength, when they made cord.

CHAPTER TWELVE
SPRING AND A JOURNEY

The thaw brought mud and the renewal of the grass and trees. Early wild flowers dotted the prairie. Soon it would look like a beautiful painting by a great artist. The leaves on the trees appeared in their early yellow green shades. In summer, they would darken to rich dark greens, but now they created the perfect back ground for the catkins on the willows and the gray fuzz of the pussy willows at the edge of the lake.

One morning, Ben suggested they walk to the lake area and pick the location for their garden. The trail was muddy. They automatically stopped to peek at the wolf den, but found it empty. As they approached the lake, ahead of them they could see Stump frisking with one of the young wolves. It was too far away to tell which one it was. They laughed at the antics of the two.

"This is where I stuck the squash seeds last year. They grew big. I think the ground is good here. What do you think?"

"I agree. It is a perfect place and we can easily get wood to build the fence, to keep the deer out of our vegetables. Let's stake out the corners," said Jed.

As soon as they dug down to place a post, their holes began to fill with water.

"We need to move a little farther from the lake," said Ben, as he looked up at the clearing sky. "Father, we ask your guidance and blessing for a successful garden." The branch posts went in with no further difficulty. They worked on the fence until late afternoon before heading back to the hut. It had been tough to select cross rails thick enough to stop animals from entering and to place them far enough apart to allow the sun to shine in.

"We have to remember our Christmas visitor. We don't want her whole family in our garden." They laughed but knew that the bottom of the fence had to have enough upright branches to stop the little nibblers. Branches as big around as their thumbs were pressed into the soil every two inches, all the way around the fence.

As they passed the den, they were greeted by Stump. His playmate of earlier was with him. It was the little female. She stayed back until Ben pulled a piece of bear jerky from his pocket. Crouching down, he broke it in half, giving the first to Stump and held the second piece out to her. She eyed him suspiciously. He had always put the treats that he brought, down on the ground. She looked at Stump and then the jerky. Slowly and hesitantly she drew near it until finally she took it from his hand, and then swiftly, she darted back to stand with it in her mouth near the den. Jed couldn't help laughing out loud and the sound sent her running into the den for protection.

"Hey, I think they are becoming a couple. What do you think?"

"It wouldn't surprise me. Stump has been around her from the very beginning. Stump and Bold One; they would have cute pups." Jed and Ben walked back to camp smiling. They had accomplished a lot on the fence, and had discovered the growing bond between Stump and the young female wolf. Life felt good.

After a quick wash in the river they both acknowledged how hungry they were. The snares yielded one rabbit. It didn't take long to get it sizzling over the flames. Jed put on the coffee pot of water but added several herbs instead of coffee. Ginger returned sticking her head over the half door and nickered a greeting. Both young men gave her a pat and a scratch. Ben had cleaned her area and put down a fresh bundle of dry grass. She was content to lay down in it.

"I think this horse is getting very spoiled," said Ben.

"Yes she is, but I like having her near us," Jed answered.

The next day started out cool and cloudy. They packed some jerky for themselves and a water bag. They both stuffed in extra jerky for the wolves, hoping they would see them. Ginger followed them to the garden area and munched the new grass as she watched the progress on the fence.

"She is another good reason for this fence," said Ben, as he watched her take a mouthful of grass.

"That could be our carrots," he said laughing.

They started to spade the ground, taking turns. One would turn the sod over and the other would shake the dirt off the grass clumps and toss the grass and roots out of the fence.

"This shovel is hurting my foot," said Ben. "I am going back and get my boots."

"I'll keep working but I need mine, too, please," said Jed.

The day went by quickly and by evening the garden was ready to plant. They didn't see any activity at the den, but on the way back, they left several pieces of bear jerky under the pine for them to find.

Back in camp, Stump and Bold One were resting under the trees in the shade near the river. She disappeared into the trees as they approached, but Stump came tail wagging. Ben gave him a scratch of greeting.

"You have been romping all day, Stump. It is no wonder you were finally resting."

"My back is sunburned," said Ben. "And so is yours."

"We shouldn't have taken our shirts off. I'm going down to take a swim while that rabbit roasts. Want to come?"

"Yes I do," shouted Ben, as he ran toward the river, peeling his clothes off as he ran. "I'll beat you to the farthest willow!" The race was on. Both young men laughed and screeched as they plunged into the cold water, and stroked hard pulling themselves up stream. Ben reached the spot first turning and continuing to swim hard as the current carried him back to their clothes. He jumped out and sat on the rock, just as Jed started out of the water.

"I'll get you next time!" Jed laughed. "That water made my back feel a lot better, but tomorrow, maybe we should leave our shirts on. Let's put some of the bear grease and clover mixture on when we get inside. That would probably be the smart thing to do. Ben it was good to watch you swim with that arm. You seem as strong as ever. Does it hurt anymore?"

"Once in a while I get a twinge, but nothing I can't live with. It just pulls and feels tight where the scars are. I guess they will stretch and loosen as I use it."

"I am glad that it turned out as well as it did. I was worried when I saw it the first time. I was sure that it would never be as good as it had been."

"I try not to think about it. Right now I am thinking that I am hungry. I wish that we had a big slice of that wonderful bread that you brought when you arrived," said Ben.

"That would take an oven. We could make one," said Jed. "I could get a yeast starter ball from my friends, when we visit."

"That would be great," said Ben, but his heart sank at the thought of leaving Ginger and Stump.

"We haven't really talked about going, since we realized that a trip down river would mean we had to leave the animals. I'm afraid that something will happen to one of them while we are gone. Ginger doesn't have a herd to protect her."

"Well, Little Brother, Ginger and I have been working on that. She has learned to accept and carry a pack on her back, and I have taught her to walk beside us when we walk. I was saving it for a surprise until I was sure it would work, but you looked so concerned, that I thought I should tell you now. She can show you in the morning. Of course she still needs a lot of work before we leave but I think a foot trip without a load on our backs would be fun. She doesn't seem to even feel the pack on her back." Ben was eager to see and relieved that the problem had been solved. His mouth dropped open and a smile spread across his face.

"I wish it wasn't dark out. I would have you show me right now!" He said. "It is a wonderful idea. She is too young to carry anything heavy but she won't have a problem carrying a tent, light bedrolls and the backpacks you made, with a few supplies. This is the best idea you have had yet! I am so excited that I probably won't sleep all night."

"After working on preparing the soil for the garden all day, I think you and I will be asleep as soon as we lie down, and remember, we have a garden to plant tomorrow."

"I want to look at the seeds and plan where things will go." Ben thumbed through the packs in the tin. The corn should go in the middle, because if it is on the side, the deer will reach over the fence and be able to eat it, and my mother always said, never put squash and pumpkins together or they end up tasting the same. We should put them on the opposite ends. The rest can go in rows down the length." He read the delicate writing on each packet. "We have carrots, cabbage, turnips, tomatoes, green peppers, beets, beans, sweet corn, sun flowers, poppies and marigolds, plus the pumpkins and popcorn. She always had the marigolds up by our door and some between the tomatoes. She said they helped to keep the bugs away. The poppies bloom red in the summer and the little black seeds are really good in cakes. Did you ever have a poppy seed cake?"

"Can't say that I have," yawned Jed.

"I'm going to bed. Are you?"

"Good night, Jed. I will bank the fire." Stump came in and licked Jed on his cheek and then went to the end of Ben's bed where he laid waiting for Ben.

The next morning Ben was eager to see what Ginger had learned. Jed put the padded weight on her back and fed her a bit of grain while scratching her ears. He turned and walked out her door to the prairie. She walked beside him as usual. They made a wide circle and came back where Ben stood watching.

"That's great! Will she walk with me and carry it the same way?"

"I think so, I just say let's go and she seems to fall in step. Try it."

Ben patted Ginger on the neck and said, "Let's go." He walked a little way but Ginger stayed there beside Jed.

"She thinks this is your game, I guess," he said sounding disappointed.

"Try again, and this time, say her name first." Ben stepped in front of her.

"Ginger lets go." She blew a soft knicker and fell into the rhythm of Ben's steps. She was delighted that he had decided to join the fun and displaying her sense of humor; she reached over with her muzzle and bunted the back of his head. Jed and Ben both laughed. They knew they would have to increase the load gradually until it was as bulky and heavy as the traveling gear, but she would be ready soon. She was a full year old and like all the prairie mustangs, she had grown sturdy and very strong. She had enjoyed good care and plenty of food. Ginger was a beautiful horse.

That same day, the rows of seeds were sparingly planted. They wanted to make the most of each precious seed.

"Some of these seeds are so tiny that it is difficult to handle them," said Jed. "How should we mark the rows?" Jed asked. "We will want to know what is coming up."

"We can make a mark on the paper, and a mark on the fence that matches, then if we can't remember all we will need to do is check the packs to see what it is."

"That will work. Now all we need is a nice soft rain."

They were so busy talking and planning that they walked past the den without checking it.

As soon as the last seed was planted, their minds had turned to their coming trip. They talked about the possible routes and what to take.

After that, the conversation changed to the oven they wanted to make. They decided that it should be built behind the trees against the bluff.

"A short distance from Ginger's door, there is a natural hollow in the side of the bluff. I would like to build it in there," said Ben. "The smoke will slide up over the bluff and disperse. Although someone may smell it, it will be difficult to know where it is coming from."

"You're right. That is a good place for it, but it will take a few weeks to make the bricks; and it should be hot, and dry weather to sun bake them. We should wait until we get back to start it," suggested Jed. "The spring rains will be here any day now."

"That's true," said Ben, "and I have been thinking about something else, too. After we get back we should build on a bedroom to the right with a window with shutters. What do you think of that idea?"

Jed thought for a minute and then replied. "With our beds out of the way, we would have more space in the main area. We could make some shelves in there, to put things on. I like the idea."

"That would make it more comfortable and a window would give light in the back of the main room," said Ben. "It gets pretty dark away from the fire."

"We can do that, too, when we get back."

"It looks like we are going to be really busy all summer and fall," said Jed. By dark they could hear thunder in the distance and Stump came jumping in over the half door just a few minutes before the rain started. Ginger snuffled and blew a hello as she entered.

"I think I will cook us all a huge batch of grain tonight," said Ben, "and we can put honey or syrup on it."

"That sounds good to me," said Jed.

Ben crushed some of the grain and left some of it whole. As he waited for the grain to cook, he put the coffee pot on and made coffee.

"I am not going to put in chicory."

"I wondered when you were going to admit that you didn't like it! Jed smiled teasing.

"While you are doing our meal I am going to grind some meat and mix some duck fat in it to make some travel food."

"Jed, guess what I have stashed! I forgot all about them. I have dried crushed raspberries. We could add some of them to the travel cakes. It would be delicious."

"That will be tasty. Where are they?"

"I put them in beside the crabapples. I hope they are still good." While he was getting the dried berries, Ben asked, "Do you want some of the crabapples in the grain for our supper? We had it that way before and it was good."

"Go ahead and add some," said Jed. "Ginger will really think she is being spoiled when she gets her share."

"Well, she has earned a treat. That was a good performance this morning. Jed you have got her trained well. I'm glad that you like our animals."

"The berries are a little sticky. They have picked up moisture from the crabapples. We better take the apples out of there. They could cause mold to form on the meat," said Ben, as he scooped the rest of the crabapples into a basket. Many of them had turned soft and a little mold had formed on the leaves he had put under them. The leaves were tossed out into the rain. Jed put a very hot stone in a small pan and set it down inside the cache and left the top off to dry it.

"I think we need to take the meat out of there and put it near the fire for a while. It would be a shame if all the meat in that cache spoils. Let's put a bunch of dry grass by the wall behind the fire and pile the meat on it. It is important that we know we have a good supply of meat before we leave. I doubt if we will have an elk falling in our laps this summer," said Ben with a little laugh.

They emptied the cache and were surprised at the amount of deer and elk meat it held. Ben knew that the other cache had lots of bear meat, elk, and some duck left, as well as deer meat they had recently added. It was full. He wasn't as fond of the bear meat, but he would eat it and Stump loved it. Ben usually chose it to take to the wolf pups when he went to visit them.

He nibbled a pinch of the travel cake mixture and was honest with Jed

"We should add a little honey to this. It seems a little bland. What do you think, or are the berries enough?"

"I think it needs a little maple syrup but not a lot, and also a bit of salt," suggested Jed. Ben agreed and they added a small amount of each. "We can carry it easily in the empty stomach, but I'll need your help to get it in there." Jed smiled as he stuffed the meat mixture in tightly.

"I want to make a few containers to take, with lids, one for grain, and one for dried meat. I plan to make them as waterproof as possible just in case we get some heavy rains while we are on the trail."

"That's a good idea. I still haven't learned to weave very well. While you do that, I will work on making us each a pair of walking shoes, with double soles. That should make our trip a lot more comfortable," suggested Ben.

"Maybe we should take a few things to have on hand that we can barter with, in case we meet a trader. There may be people along the way. We both have things we have made over the winter, that we can trade," said Jed.

"I haven't seen anybody, except one morning, early last summer when it was still not quite daylight. Two men were paddling up river. I never saw them go back. They never looked this direction or they probably would have seen the camp. Stump's growl woke me or I wouldn't have known."

Jed was glad that Ben had not noticed his reaction to the news. He wondered if they were the same men that had pursued him for so long.

"That reminds me. I want to put my canoe inside Ginger's area while we are gone and if we shovel more dirt against the outer wall of Ginger's area, I think it will blend the hut into the bluff even better."

"That would help insulate it, too." I'm all for it," said Ben. They worked hard the next two weeks getting everything done that they could think of, to secure their camp and prepare for their adventure.

They used the crosscut saw to bring down an oak tree and made a door for Ginger's main entrance. It was very thick and heavy and would stand open when they were there, but made a barrier against unwanted visitors when they were away. They piled dry wood inside and lots more under the nearest pine trees to replace what they had used. They checked their garden and found it had come up with tiny shoots in pale green rows. They worked very hard and everything they did was with a happy heart, because this was their home. They thought the trip would be a fun adventure, but they knew there would be gladness in their return. There was still much for Ben and Jed to discover about their area and about the changing new life they were living. They had no idea that the events of that trip would change their lives forever.

CHAPTER THIRTEEN
TRAVELING

Winter was gone and the sun warmed the earth. Ginger looked nearly grown and she easily carried anything they tied on her back.

They made an overnight trip up river as a test, to be sure they had thought of everything they would need. Ginger's back was covered with a smooth deer hide and then the bundles and packs were secured with wide braided straps. It was bulky and a little heavier than she was used to carrying but not hard for her. Both young men knew that it was better to be cautious and keep her load light. After a few steps she was happy to play their game.

"Camping on the open prairie with no fire is a lot different. I feel safer in the hut," said Ben.

"Next time we camp, we should make a fire. Ginger and Stump are staying near. They fear the presence of predators in the dark." Jed kept his rifle by his side wanting to be ready to protect his family if needed.

"If we made a fire, it would keep animals away, but I'm not so sure that would be a good idea. The fire would announce our presence to anyone that might be in the area."

"Including Indians," agreed Ben.

"If we could carry fire we would have all the comforts of home, but you are right about the fire. We would have to keep it really small and not build it in the open. Let me think about it. This is a real challenge," said Jed.

A few days later Jed told Ben that he was ready to try to carry fire. He had woven a small, tall basket with a loose fitting lid.

"I lined the basket inside with slate on the bottom and sides and top. The edges fit loosely so the fire can draw air. I want to try it out and see what we have to do to keep the coal going." He placed a coal from the fire in the center of the slate lined basket and covered it with the lid. Mid-morning when he peeked in to check the ember was out. He dumped the ashes in the fire pit and placed another coal in the basket. This time he added a few small twigs to feed it. He peeked in later to find the ashes still warm but he wasn't able to rebuild a flame. He knew that it was simply a matter of trial and error. The third time he placed the coal on a bed of hard wood twigs. When he opened it later, it held a glowing coal and he was able to start a flame very easily. They were both delighted.

"There you are, Little Brother, a portable fire. All we need to do is practice so we know how often we need to feed it."

"I think we are about as ready as we are going to be," said Ben with a broad smile. He was feeling very excited and it showed.

"I'll let you decide on which route we should take."

Jed didn't say anything for a moment. "I have been thinking about it ever since we first decided to go. If we travel in a big circle we can combine both trips into one and come home part of the way on the wagon trail. I want you to meet the folks at the settlement and you want to see what happened to the wagon train after you left it. I don't see any reason that we can't do both.

"We could cross here and head down following the river. We can stay just inside the trees when we get to the woods where you saw the small Indian camp. The less conspicuous we are the better. I know it is less than two days by river, paddling easy with the current. An overland trip walking will be longer," said Jed.

"After we stop to visit, we can leave the point where the rivers join, and follow the Silver until it meets the wagon trail. I have been up that way and we should stay on the left side until we get past the mud flat, then cross the Silver, where the wagons do and follow the trail back until we think we are parallel with the hut, cut through the prairie, cross back over the Hickory and we are home."

"Jed that sounds like a good plan to me and I want to bring the map you made so if we find things that aren't on it, we can add them," said Ben.

"Let's take a walk and check on the garden and the wolf den and when we come back we can eat and go to bed early."

"We need to make sure we keep Stump here tonight so that he doesn't hold us up in the morning," said Jed. He was eager to be under way. They walked toward the lake and saw the ducks swimming on the edge.

"When we get back, I plan on putting some more of them in the cache," said Ben. The garden was growing well and held the promise of good things to come.

As they headed back on the path, they were met by the big black wolf that had stalked Ben the day he was attacked by the cat.

"Where did he come from?" said Jed quietly. The wolf advanced a step, bearing his teeth and growling. Stump growled back and had raised the hair on his back. He was ready to take on this stranger.

"No Stump! We don't want you to fight him. It looks like mother wolf has found a new mate. Let's back up a little and see what he does."

Stump wasn't sure he wanted to back down so easily but that was what his human family wanted him to do. He could tell they did not want him to fight. Ben pulled on Stump's neck fur, inching him backwards with an arm around his neck. The wolf took another step toward them. His growl showed that he meant to defend this territory, and wasn't going to let them pass.

Jed raised his rifle and shot into the air. The wolf whirled and disappeared into the pine trees near the den.

"We better make a mental note to be careful when we come down here, said Jed. We mustn't forget he is here when we get back. With us gone he will figure he has all this area for his pack. Let's make double sure Stump stays with us tonight!" They hurried back to camp.

As soon as they had Ginger inside, they closed the outside doors.

They fed Ginger some grain and gave her a big basket of water. She was content to watch over the half door, as the travel bundle was arranged on the floor. They filled one side of a backpack with dried meat and put the travel food into the same backpack. The big bundle would have a few pieces of extra clothing, their water pouches, cooking gear, dried herbs and medicines and some light bedding, Stump's pan, a covered pouch of grain and some bear jerky were included. The big pan would be washed and added in the morning. Ginger's area would be cleaned and fresh grass put down before the shovel was added to the pack. They were taking several tools including a small hatchet. They had put the snares up until their return.

Ben was taking his Bible, bow and arrows, and his bone knife as well as a second bone knife he had carved. He had two crosses from wood, as well as a large, bone cross and three large wooden stirring spoons he had made. All these were added to the bundle to use for trade. Jed had a set of beautiful wooden bowls and two extra cups he had carved, sanded and oiled. Each was a work of art. The coffee pot and coffee were added to the bundle. They drank tea and ate the last of a rabbit stew, before going to bed early but they were too excited to fall asleep right away.

In the morning they brought Ginger around to the front door. As they settled the packs and bundles on her back, they decided that it was best to tie the fire basket on the side where it would be easy to tend and away from Ginger's back just in case it might get hot on the bottom.

Ginger's area was cleaned and the hut was made ready. The bedding that they were leaving behind was rolled and hung from the ceiling with cords. All the food they were leaving behind was sealed in the caches with heavy rocks on the lids.

As they prepared to head out, Stump ran back and forth barking. He knew this was at least another overnight stay. Ben had gathered a bundle of oak twigs and tied it near the fire basket. Everything was in order. They bowed their heads and asked God to care for their little place while they were gone and to bless them with a safe trip.

"Lead us Lord," he said as they set out on their journey.

They had the calendar stick, and saw that it was about the middle of May. They planned to continue to mark it each night when they camped.

They crossed the Hickory without incident. Ginger had made that crossing many times. The water was cold but only deep enough to wet her belly. The packs were tied high on her back so they would stay dry. They walked under the big oak and out onto the beautiful prairie. The grass was responding to its natural urge to reach for the warm sunshine. It provided a soft, colorful carpet for them.

"I am glad we were organized and did everything we could before we left. It feels good," said Ben, with a big smile.

The sun was bright and the new green grass of spring invited Ginger to nibble here and there as they started out. Ben soon commented.

"At this rate she will be a long way behind us."

"We didn't give her time to eat her breakfast," said Jed. "Let's stop right now and we will eat a piece of Jerky and give one to Stump, too, so he doesn't wander off. Let her munch a few minutes. We don't want her to get in the habit of lagging behind." Jed pulled out a braded grass rope that he had made and slipped it over her head and tied it loosely around her neck.

"That will just give her a little encouragement to keep our pace. I made a collar of leather for Stump. If it is all right with you, I think we should put it on him so that if we run into a situation like we did with the black wolf, we will be able to get a hold of it. It would be better than just grabbing his fur," said Jed.

"You always come up with these things Jed. That's great. Let's put it on him right now." Ben called Stump to him and showed him the collar and let him sniff it. He slipped it on Stump's neck and fastened the buckle.

"It fits just right," said Ben. "Using that buckle from the old harness fittings was a good idea. He is strutting around like he has been given an award." Ben bent down and hugged Stump and scratched his neck to help settle the collar comfortably in his fur.

"He is pretty special. He should have an award!" Stump was wagging happily and eager to get going again.

"I cut a piece of the harness leather off to make it. I hope you don't mind," said Jed as they started to move out.

"That's why I salvaged everything, so they could be put to a good use," said Ben. "It amazes me all the things that you do before I wake up." Jed laughed and said that he thought that they had made a good start but that they needed to keep going or they would never get anywhere. Ben spoke to Ginger and they made a second start.

With the soft rope on Ginger's neck she stayed in step. It was long enough so that she was still able to grab a mouthful of grass as she went but she didn't amble off in the wrong direction. Ben tucked the end of the rope into his belt and she walked near him as she had done ever since he had found her.

As they rounded a clump of trees and glanced back across the river, they saw the black wolf again. He was with the whole wolf family on the other side of the river in the area near the end of the bluff. They were all watching the humans leave.

"I think with him in the pack, they could become a threat to Ginger and Stump. We will need to keep them closer to us, when we get back."

"You are right," agreed Jed.

"It feels strange to be on this side and not over by the lake," said Ben. They hadn't walked next to the river on this side unless they were hunting.

"The game trails make it easy to walk here," said Jed.

At noon they stopped and filled their water bags. They all had a fresh, cool drink from the river.

"I don't feel like eating yet." Do you?" Jed asked. They moved on. As they followed the trail, they were able to identify prints of elk, deer, rabbits and bear.

When they neared the woods, Ben noticed tiny handprints in the mud.

"I think those prints are from a raccoon," he said. Stump was having fun but was staying closer now. The trail they had been following turned away from the river and so they were making their own trail, in the new grass. The trees grew thicker as they went along.

"Over in that direction, if you could see that far, you would be able to see where I got a chunk of burning wood and carried it back to camp so I could have a fire," said Ben. "I didn't know how to start a fire then and was so hungry that I ate a fish raw. I promised myself that night that I was going to learn to start a fire. I haven't had to eat raw fish since."

"Getting a fire going is hard sometimes. That is why I thought your idea of taking fire with us was such a good idea. That coal is doing fine, we just have to remember that it likes to eat as often as Ginger," said Jed. They both laughed.

216

Far in the distance they could see the start of another bluff similar to the one the hut was against.

"We should be able to find a good place along that bluff to stop for the night," said Ben. They walked quietly through the woods.

As the sun dropped below the bluff and glowed between the tops of the trees, they chose a comfortable spot to camp.

"I will check out the area while you set up camp. We won't need a fire but we should make a small one so that we have good coals in the morning for our fire box," said Jed. He climbed part way up the bluff and looked around. Bits of the river appeared here and there between the trees.

He spotted a small cave and carefully checked it out. He didn't want to camp under the home of a mountain lion or bear. The cave was empty, but it seemed to have been used recently. He found scattered nutshells, and in the back he noticed tuffs of black hair. Ben had a nice camp set up when Jed returned with an arm full of dry branches for the fire.

"There is a neat little cave up there. Nothing is using it right now. I didn't see any animals, just some nutshells and hair from a bear that must have wintered there. You can see the river from up there. It gets wider up ahead, and then comes the part where it gets narrow again and deeper for a ways. Where is your map? I'll show you." Ben pulled the map out of his bundle and then looked up toward the trees, checking on Ginger. Doing that was an automatic action. She was standing in the trees eating the grass that grew at the base of their trunks.

Ben handed the map to Jed.

"Here is where we are now," said Jed. "There is about where she gets narrow again."

"According to this map, we haven't gone very far," said Ben.

"At the rate we traveled today, it should only take us about three days to make it to the point where the rivers join," said Jed.

"Ginger makes it an easy trip," said Ben. "I was a little concerned by the size of the load, but she didn't seem to be bothered by it. A lot of it is bulky but not very heavy. It is good that we practiced with her and increased the size of it slowly so now she is used to it."

He had started a small fire against the face of the bluff and had situated the bundles, packs and tent in a half ring around it, to shield it from view.

"I like the way you have arranged the camp. Most of the fire is blocked from view," said Jed. "After we eat; let's bank it and turn in."

"That's fine with me," replied Ben. "My legs are tired. I haven't walked that much in a while. They will probably be sore tomorrow. Jed, you should have been here when I pulled the stuff off from Ginger's back. She was so funny. She rolled in the dirt over there. She was trying to scratch her back. She had all her legs wiggling in the air!" laughed Ben.

"Maybe we can make it more comfortable for her by putting the quilt on her back first, and then the deer hide." She had walked to the edge of the river and was getting a long drink.

"I will bring her close to our camp now. She will be safer if she is nearer the fire and us. She is used to being close to us at night anyway."

Stump was happy to lie at the end of Ben's bedroll. He was tired, too. He had always been free to come and go as he wanted, but he wasn't used to traveling all day either. The soft glow of the fire gave a feeling of security that hadn't been there when they had camped up river.

As they settled in their sleeping furs, Ben prayed.

"Father, we thank you for a good first day and ask your continued blessings." Soon after he said that, he fell asleep.

CHAPTER FOURTEEN
THE PREDATOR

The next morning, when Ben woke, Jed was up and had given Ginger a little grain and taken her to the river for a drink. She stood a few feet from the tent munching grass and being brushed when Ben crawled out of bed.

"Hey, where is breakfast," Ben joked.

"I am hungry," answered Jed. "It must be all that walking. We should try to spot a rabbit for supper."

They packed up the bundles and made sure they had a good coal on the twigs in the firebox. Stump came over ready for his breakfast when Jed opened the pack with the jerky, but instead he handed him a scoop of the travel cake and cut another for Ben and took some for himself. They covered their fire with dirt and stirred it and added more sand until they were sure that it was totally out.

As they started out, Ben looked up at the cave in the bluff. Making sure he had memorized where it was located. Something in the back of his mind told him that someday, it might be useful to know where there was a safe place to hide. He hoped he would never need to use it.

They easily fell back into the pace of the day before and were pleasantly surprised that they were not sore at all. Ginger seemed as pleased as they were to get started again. She even seemed restless when they lingered to be sure the fire was out. She wanted to be under way. Stump hurried along at the water's edge for a while sniffing at strange tracks in the mud. He made excursions ahead or to the side and would appear again after a few minutes. When the river ran between two rather high banks and there was no place dry for them to walk beside it, they had to circle to the right and go around the high, rock bank. They found themselves walking in grass that was already chest high and still growing. Ginger nipped the tips off as she strolled along.

As soon as Stump bounded a few feet away, he was out of sight. A little at a time the grass gave way to a dense growth of a variety of trees and brush again.

They could hear a strange sound coming toward them as Stump came up proudly bringing a turkey, held by a tight grip on the flapping and squawking bird. One look at Stump's face sent both young men into peals of laughter. Jed used his knife and prepared the bird for their evening meal. Stump was heartily praised and promised a generous share when it was cooked.

"We won't need to try to get a rabbit. I guess Stump decided he didn't want jerky tonight for his supper," said Ben.

They pushed their way through to the edge of the river and it seemed like an old companion had rejoined them. The river had spread out again.

After walking several hours, they found a place where the river had overflowed at some time and had cut into the side of the bank forming a cove. They built their fire there and put the turkey on to cook.

"If the breeze grows stronger as evening comes the bank will protect the fire and our camp," said Ben.

As soon as the meat was cooking over their small fire, Jed took his rifle and went to check the area to see that it was safe.

Ben took on the duty of setting up the rest of their camp again and seeing to Ginger's comfort. She enjoyed a good brushing after her packs were removed. He admired how beautiful her coat was becoming. All of her winter coat was gone now. She looked smooth and shiny.

Ben wandered the immediate area and found dandelion greens and young fennel fern fronds to cook. He was rinsing them in the river when Jed came back with a handful of quail eggs. "We can put all these inside the turkey. They will be wonderful!" Stump sat near the fire, eagerly watching the roasting turkey. He was hungry.

They spent the evening telling stories of youthful adventures, enjoying each other's company. Ben admitted to sneaking to his teacher's house, reaching in through her open window and stealing a hot apple pie.

"It was so hot, that it burned my hands and I almost dropped it in the dirt! I took that pie into the woods and ate the whole thing. I was so sick I moaned all night. My mother thought that I was going to die! She never did find out what made me sick. That teacher was sure pretty. Every boy and man around was in love with her."

Jed confessed that he had not liked his teacher.

"He was the meanest man I ever met! He would hit me on the back of my head with a yard stick if he caught me talking. Everyone was afraid of him. He would yell for no good reason. One time the boys made a plan and we all hid in the woods behind his house until dark. When he went out to his outhouse we gave him a minute to get settled and then we pushed it over onto the door! You should have heard him holler! I don't know how long he was in there but he didn't show up for school the next day. One of the mothers came and said the teacher was not feeling up to teaching and we could all go home. Here we were all of us in our seats like perfect angels!"

Ben started to laugh and he laughed until his sides were aching.

"What did he say when he finally came back to school?" asked Ben.

"He never mentioned it. He did seem subdued after that though and he left town when the summer break came." They started laughing again.

The turkey was finally done and they pulled meat from the breast and thigh for Stump, making sure there were no bones. They shared the greens, pealed the eggs and treated

Stump with two of the six eggs. Ben ate the liver sharing a small nibble with Stump.

"That was delicious," said Jed. "I am glad that you brought a little salt and sprinkled the skin with it while it was cooking. That made it perfect."

"Thanks for saying that. I think of you as the better cook in our family," said Ben.

When they had eaten all that they could, they still had some left for the morning. They ended the day with a prayer of thanksgiving and marked their calendar stick with two notches. They had forgotten to mark it, the first day. Ben sat on his bedroll rubbing his feet with grease he had mixed with leaves from the clover that grew near their campsite.

I am glad that we are not barefoot. The shoes help, but my feet are still a little sore in places.

They were glad for their covers, as the night grew cooler. In the middle of the night Stump started a low growl and Ginger dragged the pack she was tied to, nearer Ben. He woke with a start.

"Whatever it is, she is afraid of it," whispered Ben.

"I have my rifle in my hand," said Jed, trying to be reassuring. He slid out of his bedroll and lit a branch to use as a torch. "Build up the fire while I look around," he said.

Ben didn't hesitate. He added wood to the fire and deliberately made noise to frighten away whatever was out there in the dark. Ginger pushed her head under Ben's arm and sought his fingers to suck for security.

"You big baby," Ben said with bravado. But he understood her need to be comforted. He hugged her and scratched her ears. Stump stayed near and was standing guard, not leaving the circle of light made by the fire. He looked relieved and relaxed his stance when Jed came back.

"I couldn't tell what it was but it is gone now. Let's keep the fire going brightly until it is light. Probably the smell of the cooked meat brought something.

In the morning they discovered big tracks in the mud nearby and in the dirt on the bank right above their campsite.

"I think it is a big mountain lion," said Jed. "Those are cat tracks! God was sure watching over us last night." He turned his face to the sky and simply said, "Thank You, Father for keeping all of us safe from that cat."

They left camp rather quickly and Ginger was happy to get going.

"She is skittish this morning," said Ben as he fastened the bundles on her back. "I think she can smell that cat."

They almost forgot to save a coal for the firebox as they covered the fire to put it out. They ate cold turkey and drank water on their way. All of them were eager to put the events of the night, behind them.

About noon Jed told Ben that he was sure that the cat was following them and that as soon as they got to a big dense pine ahead he planned on climbing up into it and for Ben to continue on the trail.

"The riverbank swings in and the base of the big pine is hidden from the path, for a long distance." Jed took the opportunity to quickly leap up and hide in the branches. He had instructed Ben to go slowly and not go past a particular big rock in the distance. Ben didn't like the idea at all of being separated, with a big cat on their trail. Ginger was becoming more and more agitated, switching her tail, laying her ears back and turning her head so she could see the trail behind them.

Stump had stayed near Ben and Ginger, following closely on the trail but turned back and stood ready to defend, just as a shot rang out. Ben's heart was pounding. Jed had seen the cat first from his vantage point. It was a huge male and would have been far more than Stump could handle. Ben and Jed both came running up to the cat. Stump stood over it still growling.

"It's safe now boy," said Ben. "You are a good guard. Yes, you are boy," he said as he patted the dog's back and attempted to pull him away. Stump continued to growl at the cat staying focused. That's when they discovered that it was not dead but just stunned. It started to get up. Jed put another bullet in it, this time in its head.

"Maybe tonight we will get some sleep," said Jed. He pulled out his knife and skinned it quickly, right there on the path. Then to continue the tradition that Ben had started, he removed the four longest teeth. He dropped two of them in Ben's hand.

The rolled skin was put inside a quickly woven mat and tied on the back of the packs, away from Ginger's head.

"At least she didn't run off when I shot. She really was frightened. Let's get going. That cat meat should entertain any other predators in the area for a while."

As they started out, Ben realized that he could feel his body shake with nerves and pent up fear for himself and his companions. He had seen enough of the powerful and aggressive, fierce cats to last him a life time.

"Thank You, Father, for helping us to deal with the cat safely. Thank You, for watching over us. Thank You, for the animals that make the trip easier. I thank you, for Jed and Stump who each offered protection in their own way. Father, please bless us on the rest of our travels. Amen".

As he finished his prayer, Ben could hear a roaring sound.

"What is that sound?"

"It is a surprise for you, Ben," answered Jed. "Look at your map again." Ben studied the map for a few seconds and pointed to the area he thought they were in.

"See those little wiggly lines," said Jed, "They represent a waterfall. That's what you are hearing. When I was in my canoe I had to carry everything around it, including the canoe. The river drops down here about twelve or fourteen feet."

As they drew near, the roar grew louder. Ben stood in awe at the power and beauty of the falling water. Stump and Ginger were not eager to get close. They understood that this was a power greater than any animal. They used a game trail to get to the bottom

"Let's take Ginger's packs off and rest a little while. We can swim and have some travel cakes," said Ben.

"You could use a bath!" said Jed teasingly.

"Hey, you don't smell like roses," replied Ben, and they both laughed. Below the falls they found a nice place for their stop. Ginger was happy to roll in the grass nearby and Stump joined them in the water for a swim.

The falls had created a deep and shimmering dark blue pool beneath it. Neither of them could dive deep enough to touch the bottom. The bank of the river had wide patches of gravel and grass. Beautiful green moss covered the rocks that were constantly misted by the spray. They came out of the cold water and stretched out on their stomachs on the grass to dry off. Stump came out of the water and shook. He was happy and in a playful mood. He pushed his soggy face into their necks trying to lick their faces.

"Stump you need to dry off, too. You don't smell like roses either, when you are wet!" said Ben, and they enjoyed another laugh.

After eating some of the travel cakes, the enthusiasm for moving on had returned. The early afternoon sun told them they had plenty of light left in the day. The river boiled with rapids beside them as they made their way along continuing their journey. On their right, trails into the virgin forest suggested good hunting.

Jed began to talk about his friends and the area where the rivers join.

"Tom and Gentle Fawn had friends join them just as I left. They were planning to settle in the area, too. They brought out a lot of supplies to start a Trading Post. I think they spent the winter in the new house with Tom and Gentle Fawn. They are probably building their store by now. Others were expected to join them this spring on one of the wagon trains. We may find ourselves in a small community."

"You said your friend's wife is Gentle Fawn? How did he end up marrying an Indian?"

"As I understand it, Tom was out hunting and got hurt really bad. She and some others were out gathering, and found him and the tribe took care of him until he was well again. By that time they had fallen in love and so she went with him. She's a beauty. Wait until you see her. He told me she cost him two horses and a sack of seed corn!

"How did you meet them?"

"They were camping on the Silver River, above the mud flats. Tom had shot a buffalo and they were drying the meat. I stayed a couple days with them."

"Wish I could get a rifle so I could help more with the hunting. My dad had a good one, but it was stolen along with my sister." Jed could see that Ben was getting upset again. Every time something was mentioned that reminded him of his parents and missing sister, Ben's face would get a hard set to it. Jed changed the subject.

"It's getting close to dark. We should set up camp soon." They chose a protected spot and Jed started his usual circle of the area to check it out. He came back with an armload of dry wood and sat down beside the small fire. Ben had unrolled their bedding and gotten out some jerky. Ginger came over and nudged Ben wanting a little attention. He gave her some grain and then brushed her for a while.

"She is sure attached to you. She uses you for a substitute mother," Jed said with a smile.

"In a way I guess I am."

Ben looked at Ginger, remembering the day he had worked so hard to save her life.

"It would be great if somehow we could get a couple more horses," said Ben. Maybe next year we can build a corral and drive some into it. We could use them to look for Sarah."

"Ben I don't want to upset you, but you need to know that some of the tribes sell the white children they steal. They sell them to traders from other tribes. She may not be anywhere near here." Ben had heard that before when he was with the wagon train. He heard some men talking about it.

"I don't want to talk about that! I will find Sarah!" he shouted. He stomped off into the trees.

Jed unrolled the lion skin and scraped it and then coated it with grease. He never wasted anything and knew that the skin had good value. He was glad to have a chore to keep his hands busy while he waited for Ben to come back to camp.

It was getting very dark by the time Ben returned. Jed had sat by the fire for a long time praying that God would protect Sarah and help Ben find her. He had lain awake on his bed until he heard Ben return.

"I made some tea. Would you like some?" He asked quietly. "I found some mint growing in that clearing over there." He had also added chamomile from his pack, to help Ben relax. Ben sat down beside Jed and apologized for getting angry. He accepted the tea but didn't say anything else for a long while.

CHAPTER FIFTEEN
JED'S STORY

"Jed, please tell me how you lost your family. Were they killed, like mine?"

"No, I never had a family like yours that I can remember. My parents left me with my grandfather, when I was quite little. They were going out west to find a place and then they were going to send for us. They never wrote. I guess something happened to them and then when I was thirteen, my grandfather got pneumonia during the winter and died. The doctor came once while he was sick and gave me some syrup to give him when he coughed but it didn't help much. I did everything that I could, but I couldn't make him better. I buried him on a hill back by the woods. Since then I have been on my own. I sealed the house and headed out here to see if I could find any trace of my folks. At first I had my Grandfather's horse and saddle, but when I quickly ran out of money and food, I traded them for some food and a canoe. I have been on the water ever since."

Jed continued.

"People that lived in our area back home, thought my grandfather had a lot of stolen money stashed somewhere. When I left they thought I took it with me. I discovered that two men were following me and that's another reason that I chose to be on the water. You don't leave tracks.

After that, I got used to traveling that way and just didn't change. I've tried to pick up knowledge about medicines because if I had known more, maybe I could have saved my grandfather. I just took one river and then another and eventually ended up on the Silver where I met Tom and Gentle Fawn.

After that I went up the Hickory and on the way back down, that's when I met you. So now we are not alone anymore. We have each other and the animals."

"Wow, that's quite a story. I know you must have had some scary adventures along the way," Ben responded.

"Ben, I think we have both had our share, but I think it is time to turn in now, don't you?"

"Yes I am tired, too. That tea helped me to relax. Thanks, and thanks for telling me." Ben glanced at his bed to see Stump sprawled in the middle of it. As soon as Ben started to get in, the dog adjusted his position so that he could put his head on Ben's leg. Ben closed his eyes and fell asleep praying for Sarah.

They didn't know it then but this trip was just starting. Ben and Jed would travel life's road together as brothers and each would find very exciting adventures and someone lovely to love in **Life's many Journeys.**

AN INVITATION

If you do not know Jesus, as your savior but you would like Him to be, please pray the following prayer. Invite Him into your heart. Commit your "New Life" to Him. He will be your constant companion, councilor, comforter, and protector. The Holy Bible tells us that He will never leave you or forsake you.

"Dear Jesus, please forgive my sins. Give me grace and strength Lord, so that I will not commit them again. Come into my heart so that I can start a "New Life" with you as my companion. I want to live according to your will and commandments. Bless me Lord and lead me in a life that is pleasing to you. In Jesus' Holy name I pray. Amen"

If you prayed that prayer, you are saved. You are born again. Your soul is whiter than snow. The angels in heaven are rejoicing as they write your name in the book of life.

Get a Holy Bible and begin to read it. Find a good bible believing church and start attending, so that you can learn more about Your Heavenly Father. What a wonderful God we have.

I will pray for you. God bless you. Louise Bouck

ABOUT THE AUTHOR

Louise Bouck is a follower of Jesus Christ. She has been married to her husband for more than fifty years. Together they have raised six children.

Until an early retirement from her fulltime job in 2000, not much time was available to allocate to writing or art. With many interests, Louise enjoys painting on location. The lush greenery of Michigan, her home state and the abundant flowers in her grandmother's greenhouses and flower shop all encouraged her eye to appreciate the colors and beauty of nature.

After moving to Arizona, the rugged landscape of the mountains and desert stole her heart and took her artistic soul in a new direction.

Paintings in many media cover the walls of her studio as she has deliberately turned her creative side more to the written word. Hesitantly she withdrew from the art gallery where her work was sold and left the position of resident artist at the local historical museum. Louise has written ten books in a series of Christian; Bible based stories that she is now starting to release for the first time as she works on still another story and another painting.

Some of her art work may be included as cover art on her books or as color plates of details from her paintings. She hopes that you will enjoy them all and be blessed.

Reviews

This is amazing piece of historical fiction is from the perspective of a young man named Ben. The reader is immediately pulled into the story as this 15 year old leaves his lifelong home to travel west on a wagon train with his younger sister and parents. The story tragically unfolds as Ben loses his family in an Indian ambush. As Ben struggles against loneliness and predator attacks, the reader sees the strength in persistence, optimism and faith. The author of this book seems to have extensive knowledge of what is necessary to survive in the wild. The story includes details like building a portable fire and tracking an animal. But by the end of the story we see that simply surviving isn't enough. Having faith and persevering even in the midst of great tragedy and fear is what makes a person whole. A wonderful read for teens and adults who appreciate faith enriched historical fiction. By FloRo.

By Trib Saint on December 18, 2014

Format: Kindle Edition Verified Purchase

This book reminds me to be in constant prayer once again. I myself have been a Christian since 2004 I've seen a lot of trials and tribulations I've also been a student to prophecy since that time. In my studies I've learned a lot about this world and I do believe that one day if we are left behind this book will definitely help teach us to survive in the world to come. Thank you Louise!

John Nelson
Comment   Was this review helpful to you?

Yes

5.0 out of 5 stars

Adventure By Amazon Customer on December 28, 2014

Format: Kindle Edition

Awesome adventure / survival series keeps you on your toes can't wait to read more it's so exciting. Never would expect it to be so informative.

BOOK TITLES IN THE NEW LIFE SERIES

More than Survival

Life's Many Journeys

The Land's Heritage

The Story of Sarah

Together

The Blue Stone People

Teewahpanee the Boy, Two Feathers the Man

The People of the Lion

The Lion's Den

Just the Beginning

www.ingramcontent.com/pod-product-compliance
Lightning Source LLC
Chambersburg PA
CBHW030143180626
46812CB00002B/833